About the Author

My name is Kayleigh Richardson. I have been writing as far back as I can remember, it's always been my passion and something that drives me through every single day and keeps me going. For my entire life, nothing has ever been straightforward and it's been difficult at times, but my dad, Mark, has always been by my side and always will be! He is the one I thank for encouraging me to pursue writing and setting me an example to never give up on something keep going. Never give up on what you h

Remember Me

To Michael

I hope you enjoy this book!

Kayleigh Richardson

Kayleigh Richardson

Remember Me

Olympia Publishers
London

www.olympiapublishers.com
OLYMPIA PAPERBACK EDITION

A CIP catalogue record for this title is
available from the British Library.

ISBN: 978-1-80074-411-0

This is a work of fiction.
Names, characters, places and incidents originate from the writer's
imagination. Any resemblance to actual persons, living or dead, is
purely coincidental.

First Published in 2022

**Olympia Publishers
Tallis House
2 Tallis Street
London
EC4Y 0AB**

Printed in Great Britain

Dedication

In dedication to my dad: my best friend, my rock and my support. My everything, I love you more than words can express, Dad.

Prologue

Disease. Death. Rampantly spreading across England, everybody fearing for their lives as the king sat back enjoying each feast brought to his table, gold embellishments on all his clothes, a larger chair to fit his bigger waist. Redcoats patrolling the streets as the disease we had yet to be accustomed to never ceased to stop, people died left, right, and centre daily with no sign of ending. These troubling times have brought us all to tears with fears, crimes with the times, cruelty brought to us all not by a human hand. We all had no idea what to do, no thought on how we were to process the situation set before us, the streets of London always seemingly packed to the hilt when a hanging became announced to the public. Little did they know that people dropped to the floor, dead, during these crowded periods, more and more people infected with the maliciousness the disease gave us. In the beginning everything happened gradually, one death. Nothing too serious. Ten deaths a problem, spiralling out of control to hundreds. Over three hundred dead in one area, the government not wanting to get involved, teaching us to use the *laissez-faire* approach. Did it work? No. More and more died, including my mother, at the hands of a skilled murderer — an invisible one. How did we cope? We tried our hardest, my wife being my solid rock, our children giving us light to the dark through the hope they gave us. We wanted a way out of this situation, we wanted to get ourselves out of the present life, to live elsewhere so nobody could do anything to us, no disease could kill us. We could live with barely any fears. So many questions with no answers. So many lives lost with no compensation, poor people even more downgraded with no money, lacking the necessary means to live, food becoming harder to bring to the table. Somehow, we got by, savings that I had kept back for a rainy day proving to be helpful, our friends sticking close to us in times of need. This is our story. Your story. A story you will come to know well. Remember me.

Chapter 1
We can get away from here.

Darkness lay upon the town, a pure deep black sky weighing heavily upon anyone living under it. Redcoats marching through the inner parts of the city as many began scurrying inside of their houses, blowing out any candles. Locking their doors tightly shut. Coughs. Splutters. A woman sweeping outside of her house with a broom, humming a small tune as she went on her way to keep everything tidy. In front of her face came one of the king's men she wished to not see.

"Should you not be on your way, miss?"

"Of course... sir."

Stuttering and stammering, the officer of high station made her rather uncomfortable, still he stood in front of her so he could make sure that she did go inside. She propped her broom against the wall, picking her items up from the ground, having placed them into a neatly woven basket.

"I will just be a minute... I will go inside. Just a moment, please."

Asserting his dominance over her, his voice raising over all. "You will go inside now! Everyone knows the rules! No exception."

"Oh... yes."

She grabbed everything she could in her area, with most things stuffed under her arms, her legs carrying her into her house, shutting the door quickly so he could not disturb her any more; a small nod of approval from the officer. Walking away proudly to join the rest of his men to torment more individuals who kept wandering aimlessly.

"Hmph!"

Across the street, a small house had candles lit inside, peeking out of the curtain, a young dashing young man shutting his curtain abruptly going back to the way he was before.

Rubbing his thumb on the glass of a picture, sighing unhappily, longing for the young woman in the photograph, someone he lost. Dust from the frame had been left in certain areas that he had not touched, the thought of everything that was bothering him, tormenting every living second he had.

"I miss her. It only feels like yesterday that we lost her."

"It has been hard on us all, everyone misses her."

"The thing is, I never thought we would lose her... not like this." A fair young woman stepping out from around a post, leaning against the edge of the door frame nearby offering William a gentle smile in an attempt to comfort his mind full of thoughts so brutal.

"After all this is not how she wanted to die."

"Nobody can choose how they die, some are much more fortunate. Depending on their situation."

"Why did it ever have to be her? My mother of all people."

Thoughts continuing to overlap in his mind, emotions mixing together as one, laughing hysterically, clearly lacking sleep. Screams of those around me, the screams of those I love as each of them started to pass away to the pain facing them. For so long the sight of others dying became clear to my eyes as people closer to me fell away into my arms. A way out of this dire situation brought me to the point of breaking, being the head of my household with a family to feed, there was no time for me to ever procrastinate or form ways we could be free of the deathbed set before us. Trapped inside a void of darkness with no help or call to a stop, we fell and fell until we never felt the ground beneath us. The East India Trading Company constantly coming back and forth between our ports in a triangle delivering masses of slaves, a triangle between three different places: Europe, Africa, America. Upper classes viewing this as a moneymaking affair, whilst those poor people had been forced to give up their freedom in the name of a bargain, in the name of money, forced to do labours the buyer asked of them, ending up bound in bonds at the end of the day with no way to move freely, no choice of what they wanted to do. Living or dying was never an option, working, performing gruelling labour was. People enjoying watching them suffer. We never subjected our children to such sights or ideologies, our thoughts were focusing on the point to never let them adopt that way of thinking in their lives… it was not right. You would never say such a thing or you would be classed as an 'idiot,' a 'fool', someone who 'did not understand what true business' was. I understood perfectly well what business was, how do they think I earn money to ensure my family had enough of the basic provisions? Food became harder and harder to find the longer this disease spread through, striking families in the centre of their home, cutting into two. We had no idea what was causing the spread of such a disease, what had brought on such a terrifying fate, the blood inside your body stopping still… not enough to go around. Blood came out from all avenues, mouth, ears and the rare case of it flooding under the eyelids. Sad to say, we had seen the displeasing sight of the blood, the rarity as it came from her eyelids, drying against her pale skin. Watching her die with no idea how to save her killed me, if the disease had not already taken hold of me then guilt would, knowing that something would be brought forward in the future, a cure! With that cure I could have saved her, people would tell me that it is wrong to feel guilt over something you had no control over, possibly correct. Those who have never seen what I had seen, heard the coughs and splutters as the bed sheets became sodden with her blood, listened to her dying wishes as she fell away into my arms.

'Son, take your family away from here, save them. For me. For you. If this grabs hold of you, leave these last words of mine on your tongue for generations to come. Remember me.' Falling away into my arms, her eyelids shut, her heart rate slowed down as she passed away to the depths… sunk back into a peaceful life with no more issues. At least she no longer needed to endure such a painful, loitering illness which would never have disappeared until dead, not giving up until it got the end it wanted so badly. Now we lay in wait for figures, a cure, symptoms people we knew had started to show. Our daily lives diminished, taken away from us.

"You need to get some sleep, you haven't slept properly in so long." Shortly she sighed, seeing how diminished in health I was. "When was the last time I saw you happy?"

"It will be a long time before I ever start to be happy."

"You are going through a lot. I know. It is not me having such a weight on my shoulders. We need to think of our children, Will, they still remember how their nana died."

"We need to get away from this hell. If only we could."

Just the thought of being able to get away seemed so

hopeful, peaceful and full of life. Still, it was so far away, impossible to get hold of, there had never been any means of getting anywhere else but the town centre.

Knock! Knock!

"My love, see who is at the door would you?"

"Of course." Shuffling toward the front door, a slight creek as it widened sounding before she spoke. "Oh, Mr Peterson we were not expecting you."

"It is a good job you answered your door, Redcoats are still on patrol."

Facing me was a tall man, a small moustache, a classy dresser always in a suit jacket with freshly polished buckled shoes, never seeming to fail blending in with the upper-classes although he was nothing like them in any way.

"It is good to see you, my dear fellow, how have you been?"

Taking his hat off from his head, the door clicked, shutting light from the moon away, each of the candles lightening up his downtrodden face.

"You see... my... my wife, William."

"No, she has not... has she."

"Just this morning she passed, I dare not go back to that house."

"You should stay here for a while, with us."

"Father! Father!" My young daughter started tugging away at my sleeve, her bright blue eyes staring at me lovingly. "Is Mrs Peterson okay?"

Clearing my throat, I bent down on one knee. "Mrs Peterson, she... she has had to sail away."

"Where to, Father?" Little Edward came running towards me, throwing his arms around me. "Somewhere exciting?"

"Mr Peterson was just telling us that she needed to go away on a trip of some sort."

"Yes, you need not concern yourself in their business, remember what we told you." Just as I had spoken true words, my wife was always my rock despite arguments we may have. No marriage is ever completely perfect. Shyly they both looked to the floor, fiddling with their clothing, reciting what we had taught them.

"Never get involved in other people's business."

"Very good. Now hurry along to your room, dinner will be ready soon." I focused my attention on Lewis who needed it right now. "Would you like some warm food?"

"That would be perfect, William, you should know something."

"What would that be?" I gestured my arm towards the small dining table lit with candles, we walked over to sit down pulling out three chairs. "Good news, I hope."

"We can get away from here."

"How could we possibly do that? Some magical fairy tale!" Scoffing at the idea, Lewis' face turned completely serious, sitting down with his hands intertwining, set down on the table. "You were being serious."

"You do know the Hamiltons?"

"Yes, I do, how are they these days since they moved to the higher areas?"

"Not too bad, they have a boat, a rather large boat. A ship even. They offered me an idea, a way out of this once they heard about my wife."

"Do tell."

"In two weeks, they are set to depart, I am allowed to take two families with me."

"I take this as an invitation?"

Lucy set down three cups of tea, one in front of me, one for William and one for herself as she seated herself next to me. "It is an invitation. You have experienced what it is like to feel death, to see the one you love pass, maybe not your wife but close enough. All of us need a way out of this."

"Hmm. Have they said where they will be heading?"

"A small island in the Caribbean, uninhabited."

"How are we supposed to live there?" Spitting with laughter, I sipped some of my tea, replacing the cup. "It is hard enough trying to live as it is, there will be no food, no shelter, no physician, not even a good water supply."

"That is where they come in. Alongside us and the other family I invited, there will be a craftsman, physician, a building specialist; tools and building materials will be brought, it may take a while."

"So, they are bringing all of this, for the purpose of people. Would they not want it for themselves?"

"Would it not get awfully lonely there? Of course it would, look, are you coming or not?" Glancing towards my wife, she smiled softly nodding her head up and down begging me with her eyes to go. "We will be there."

"Good. I shall let them know, the meeting point shall be at the far-left side of the port, bring what you can. Food. Water. Clothes. Building materials. Anything that could be useful, think outside of the box."

"You are coming, are you not?"

"I am." Putting down his cup of tea, a small grin lightening his face, making him look a lot more as he used to. "What a lovely cup of tea, you have a good wife, William."

"I do not know what I would do without her." Holding her

hand in mine, I kissed the top of her hand watching her blush uncontrollably as she used to when we were first married.

"Well, it must go both ways then."

"Would you like me to help you serve up?"

"No, no. I will be fine doing it, you sit down."

With that she left for the kitchen, the clanking of utensils as she served us some food up. Our substantial amount of money allowed us to have decent food, considering we were middle-class. My heart always felt for the lower-class of the people, no money, barely any clothes with holes at the elbows from leaning against a table or brick, their labours crucial for money but painful to perform. If anyone had a scary life at this very moment in time, it would have been them, as they slept on the streets trying to make ends meet being passed by countless times a day catching the deadly virus that roamed the streets. Seeking its next victim, moans of dying men, women, children, newborn babies not knowing what to do as it kept rampaging through their bodies. Whatever was to bode ill for a family, bode ill for us all.

With a few weeks to go till we left, racing thoughts battling against each other in my mind as a whirlpool of ideas popping up and down like a bobbing bird in the sea. Questions mainly came into play one after the other. How would my children react? Was this all too good to be true? It could be! This could all be a hoax, a way to see me suffer even further than we had already. Why would they do something like that? Will we be happy there? What if we don't survive? Well, in a few weeks' time, in a few days, possibly tomorrow, answers would be given to me. The conversation with our children would be the hardest, life was already difficult, restricting them to seeing different people. Still we were never sure if this was just part of the family unit, or something else. People mainly relied on religions, they helped them to pull through believing that 'God is punishing those who have done wrong'. Others preferred other sources. As did I. We were never the religious kind, it was still a dominant part of life in England, through different lands as people taught others about God. A strong smell of fish washed past my nose alongside a pleasant smell of vegetables, my wife had always been a fine cook, she did the best she could which made us all happy.

"That food smells absolutely divine I must say!" Lewis seemed to have cheered up slightly to the smell of food. "I really could do with something nice to eat."

"When was the last time you ate?"

"I... I do not recall. It has been hard on me, you must understand, coming to terms with it all is harder than I thought it would be."

"I understand better than most, she seemed to fight for longer. Blank hope."

"You thought she would survive, but then all signs of that disappear when she passes." Something told me that his wife had been suffering for longer than he had told us, a closed-up oyster without a pearl inside.

"Yes. You... understand, I see."

"They say time heals..." Lucy lay down the dinnerware on the table with some handkerchiefs in case of any spillages, returning to the kitchen to collect the food. "...time is precious, it slips away from you. Then it disappears, no longer there. Time never healed anything to me."

"People who have never been through what you have should not have a say on the matter."

"Or an opinion."

"Everybody has to give you their opinion. You give them yours and…"

"It becomes an all-out war."

He chuckled to himself, smiling as he twiddled at one of his top buttons, his double chin wrinkling then unwrinkling as his eyes started scouring the food my wife lay onto the table in front of us.

"Absolutely delicious."

"Thank you, Lewis, you need it."

Always pleased to hear a compliment of her food, she began to hum, grabbing the rest of the plates moving back and forwards between the dining room and kitchen.

"I will be back in a moment, Edward and Lily need to come down for dinner."

Walking away to the stairs, meandering between the chairs and the walls, a strong hand gripping my shoulder forcing me to turn around. "You are going to need to speak to them."

"I know, tomorrow."

"Let me deal with it. They should hear it from me."

"Why from you?"

"Will they complain if I tell them?"

"Considering how we brought them up… no."

"Good."

Nodding complacently, I felt slight relief. hollering for them to come down the stairs. "Lily! Edward!"

"Yes, Father!"

"Come downstairs! Mr Peterson has some exciting news for us!"

"Is dinner ready?"

"Come on down! Before it goes cold!"

With that, the thundering sounds of their feet echoing throughout the house, nearly falling over each other as they jumped into their chairs eager to dig into the food. With hungry eyes they turned their attention to Lewis, awaiting the exciting news.

"Mr Peterson," Lily had a look of longing in her eyes as she spoke, her honey sweet voice bringing him around. "Father told me you have some news."

"Exciting news, Lily."

"I know that, Edward."

Snapping at each other, Lewis began hushing them to be quiet so he could speak.

"That's better. Now then. Shall I begin?" Wide grins came over my children's faces, bringing my wife and I joy as she slowly sat down next to Mr Peterson. "We are all going on an adventure!"

"Where to?"

"A Caribbean island, we will be living there."

"Is there going to be treasure?"

"Maybe, we have no idea. All I know is… there are lovely animals, it's free from this scary bug!"

"Do you mean the one that Nana died from?"

Choking inside his throat, that question made him uncomfortable as he thought of his poor wife, lying at home. Stone cold. Dead. "Yes… yes, it is."

Quietly my wife interrupted the conversation, her voice sweet as honey. "We should eat before the meal turns cold."

"Of course Lucy."

Immediately, he dug into the food with no words escaping his lips, the occasional scratch of the fork against the plate, the click of the fork against his teeth from pushing the fork in far too harshly. Before any of us had managed to lift our forks and knives, Lewis had made his way through half of the meal my wife prepared, occasionally wiping his mouth with a stray piece of fish or vegetable. Small 'hmms' escaping his lips, continually eating away. Slight relief was given to me, my children no longer needing me to give the conversation about where we were going and why. That had become one thing ticked off the list, still my mind could not help but wander away to the day we had the funeral procession. Not many people came, lots of people left, seeing it too depressing for them to witness. Lewis Peterson had become the only person to stay since the Hamiltons had been unable to attend. She was a popular, well-known person in the vicinity we lived in, her bubbly, jolly, contagious personality loved by all who knew her... true to herself, she stayed bubbly till the day she died even though we had our moments when happiness lacked in many areas. Just the thought of losing her left me feeling empty inside. When she passed, I was hollow, on a different planet to my family, my friends, myself. Part of me would always love my mother, forever and always, she would stay with me in memory no matter how much it hurts me to think about the past... the times we had together. When I first met my wife, we had only been friends for quite a few months, enjoying each other's company day in, day out. Then something changed. I looked at her in a different light, how much I loved her but I never wanted to wreck the friendship that we had considering we were so close together. Saying just three words could make or break us, she could either feel the same or feel the exact opposite... it weighed heavy on my mind for weeks until somebody recognised my discomfort... Mother noticed. Her reassuring words, her warm embrace, the consoling words of advice she gave me to build the courage to tell her how I felt... 'it is now or never'...each of those words stuck closely to me throughout when I was speaking to Lucy of my feelings. To my surprise, she felt the exact same, my mother has always... will always, help me through difficult times! I know exactly what she would do, what she would say, all she would want for me and my family. To get away from this life, live somewhere else that would make me happier, make us much safer.

"William! William!" A hand waved in front of my face, snapping me back to the world. "Finally! Where did you go?"

"Oh, lost in thought, Lewis."

"You look absolutely shattered. You need some sleep."

"I feel like it." Looking down at my plate, I soon realised the food had been barely touched. "I think I will finish up eating and head to bed."

"It might be a good idea."

Continuing to eat the food laid in front of me, I felt on edge as though someone else was lurking around in the darkness. Then something came to me as I remembered something upon my mother's neck... a small hole, similar to that of a puncture mark embedded into the skin. I had never entirely become aware of it until now, all of my senses had been activated as though someone was behind me.

"Someone is outside." Pulling out my chair, I picked it up wedging it under the front door handle, closing the blinds so nobody could come in. "Blow out all of the candles, close the upstairs blinds, make sure no one can come in."

Rustling of the rubbish bins, scraps of food sounding from beyond the walls of our house. Thwump! Our bodies jumping in unison with the sound of the thwump.

"We need to be quiet, get upstairs."

"I will stay down here with you." I simply said nothing, hoping the silence was a good enough agreement, my children and wife getting up the stairs with one small lamp to themselves, one for us. All others had been blown out by just our breath in case they could be seen from the outside world.

"Will. Something is not right here."

"I know… I have a bad feeling about this."

"Same here."

"Go into the kitchen, there are no windows at all there."

We crept along the wooden floors, on the odd carpet to the kitchen on our knees like small children, the slight sound of my wife comforting our children upstairs in one of the bedrooms to do her part. Why am I even feeling like something is wrong? How come everyone else is feeling this way? Something was about to happen, whatever it was we were not prepared for anything far too extreme… soon we could leave.

"What is going on out there?"

Lewis got up to leave the house so he could investigate, until I dragged him back down so he could stay here, safely. "You will not leave. Who knows who or what is out there!"

"Shh."

"See. Even you see the danger, so stay put."

"You are right… look, I just have no clue any more."

"Of what?"

"What life is all about? Without her."

"When my mother died, it lay hard on me for so long. You need to try and remember how they would want you to live. What they would want for you."

"She would have wanted me to be happy… escape this place."

"Exactly my point. You will feel depressed at times, I know I still do. You just have to move on as horrible as it sounds, it is going to be hard… you have us, I promise you, Lewis. You are never alone."

"I appreciate that Will, your family has be—" Knock! Knock! Harsh knocks banging against the door roughly as though someone was in a hurry, our bodies lurching forwards up onto our feet grabbing anything we could use as a weapon.

"Someone is at the door."

"I can hear that, maybe if we ignore them, they will go."

"What if it is someone we know?"

"If it is not someone we know?"

Everything I had said was true, you could be thinking it one person then you open the door to find someone you never wanted to see: a murderer, someone with this illness, a Redcoat or anyone else your mind could fabricate. Opening up my door would be on the basis that I knew who was there, if I did not know who it was then the door would never open. Putting Lewis and my family at risk of harm seemed to me the last thing I would want on my plate. Still the knocking persisted getting louder and louder each time.

"We should answer the door."

"No! Lewis, I am not to put my family at risk, no way on God's earth am I doing such a thing."

"At least see who it is."

"Fine." Walking towards one of the windows where I had drawn the curtains, my eyes peered through the thin glass hoping that whoever it was could not see me… a familiar face filled with fear looking straight at the door ready to knock. "Mr Hamilton!"

"Why is Hamilton here?"

"We will soon see." Pulling away the chair from the door, turning the door knob, he pushed the door wide open slamming it shut behind him, taking the chair away from my hands. "Um... it is nice to see you as well, stranger."

"No, we must all leave. Now!"

More and more rustling heightened outside, the noise becoming irritable instilling fear into us all, whoever was out there had an idea of what they were doing to us. Where did Hamilton want us to go anyway, in the dead of night?

"Where do you expect us to go? I have a family, children, a wife. With somebody outside it is dangerous."

"We can leave, to the island, there is somebody out there who is searching to murder me. You. Us."

"Ridiculous!"

"Look, Lewis, I have seen him with my own eyes. He has something that can just kill people, you either leave with me and everyone else... or die."

"Everyone else?"

"The voyage is setting sail tonight, will you be coming?"

"I will be alone, William, how about you?"

"I... we will meet you at the far left side of the port."

"Of course, be careful, put this chair back against the door and hurry. There will not be much time!"

Hurrying out the door, he opened the front door widely, banging it shut as we propped the chair against the handle so nobody would be able to get in unless they broke it down. My initial instinct was to decline, I had my children to think of. With not much time to spare, I legged it up the stairs, starting to pack things away into some bags and luggage carriers we had lying around. Clothes, shoes, food, cutlery, anything that would come in handy. Breaking into one of the rooms, Lucy huddled with our children in a corner looking terrified... a little less traumatised seeing me still alive.

"William, what are you doing?"

"We are leaving. Tonight."

"Tonight! This is too soon."

Out there was a killer she knew nothing of, leaving ourselves in the hands of two mass murderers would not be the best option. Without worrying my children too much, I created a small lie, a bait that they would all take. "Everything is ready to go, they all have to leave as soon as possible."

"Why do we need to leave? It is not for another two weeks that we set sail."

"Unfortunate circumstances arose, the Redcoats cottoned on to their plans to make berth elsewhere..." Sighing, still heaving with heavy breath, my lungs gasping for oxygen as I continued to rush around. "...it is the gallows for them. An appointment made with the hangman's noose."

"My goodness! That is awful!"

"Which is why we must leave! Help me pack necessities."

Getting up to help, her still youthful voice reassured and comforted our little ones who were confused by the whole affair. "Now, we need to pack some items. If you both stay here, me and your father can get some of your teddy bears to bring with us."

"Mommy, where are we going?"

"To that exciting Caribbean island!"

Edward chimed in after Lily with questions! Always so inquisitive. "Why so soon? Dad said it was not going to be for a while."

"It turns out we can leave."

"Yes!"

In unison, their excitement was contagious despite the circumstances given to us. Putting in some of our children's clothes, Lucy went away to put some of our items from drawers into sacks to take with us on our journey. Sounds of banging in our cupboard echoing from downstairs, Lewis presumably had started to put together items that we would need regarding food.

"Father… are we safe?"

Pausing from the work I had set myself, I realised how I had not bothered to acknowledge my children in a time where they needed answers. Now was a small window to let them know in my own way that they were safe. With me. As one family unit. Crouching down to their level, eyes crinkled in an honest way allowing myself to smile in hope it would catch on to them.

"Before I tell you, I need you to tell me something." Moving up and down, their head movement indicated I could move on. "Have I ever let you down?"

"No, Father, never."

"What about you Eddy?"

"Well, you did forget to make that model with me."

"Did I do it with you after you reminded me?"

"Yes."

"So then…"

"You have never let us down… apart from when you forgot that model."

Ruffling his hair up with my hand, he giggled as a beam shone from me. "You both have nothing to fear, as long as you stay with me and your mother."

"We knew that."

"Of course you did. Now be good, gather things you might

miss. Not just a teddy bear." Raising one eyebrow, Lily and Eddy exchanged glances with each other, mischievously grinning, dashing to grab their little sacks to fill with the items they treasured most. Panting, huffs, puffs came alongside the out of breath sounds Lucy made with three fully packed sacks full of items that could prove useful.

"Are we ready to go?"

In between long breaths, managing her few words, releasing the bags in her hand onto the floor that would now have to bear the load. "What about Mr Peterson?"

"He said it himself, he never wanted to go back to that house. There is no choice for him, living here there is the highest chance he will die. You have got to remember he has never been a well man."

"Hmm."

"You know that I am right."

"It has always been that way, and you know that."

Grinning on one side of my mouth, she knew how everything that came out of her mouth was completely true. Every time.

"Everyone knows that."

"You, miss, are getting worse."

"Only for the better."

"Always."

"We need to leave before they go without us."

"Come on then."

Humping two sacks over my left shoulder, I wiggled my hand for one of my children to hold onto before we went outside. Making sure they were with me was far more important than having necessities.

"Edward, grab my hand."

Edward took Lucy's hand as she threw a sack over her right shoulder to hold onto our little Eddy, Lily had tightly grasped my own, walking down the stairs to see the front door wide open. Our cupboard door flung off the hinges, complete and utter mess everywhere. Pots, pans, cutlery. Strewn across the floor, most things taken from us in an instant. How did we not hear any of this?

"What happened here?"

"I wish I knew, Lucy." What had startled me was the fact Lewis was nowhere to be seen, unless he had already taken off without us... they better not be leaving us here. "Lewis! Lewis!"

"Empty."

"We best leave, something is not right."

"If Lewis could not stay, then neither should we. Follow me, hold on tight, do not fall behind." Albeit small, lips pursed as she nodded her head, Lucy proceeded with me as I held Lily's little hand walking out of the door to watch as we went. A cold chilly wind blew, her hand gripping mine even tighter feeling the icy breeze on our ever so thin clothes. "This way." Down the road, nobody walked about, with shutters down, lights out. Quiet. For the first time in what seemed an eternity, a deadly plague of silence dawned on all of us, nobody even daring to peek through their windows to be nosey as many tended to do. Everybody knew everyone else's business, you had a secret the whole street would come to know about it unless you managed to hide it beneath your skin, letting no words escape your mouth.

Actions to help when you had issues had become few and far between, acts of kindness took off ages ago, nobody caring for you apart from you and your family. Four sets of footsteps... wait... click, click, click. Clicking of a heel against the cobblestones behind us, someone apart from us was walking behind us.

"Lily, hold Edward's hand, do not let go of any of us."

Hurrying forwards, I could see the terror in my wife's face as she did not know who we were being faced with, nor did I. A mystery to behold freezing every last bit of our bones to the centre, where it all takes place. Fear can cause so many different emotions all at once: gratitude, terror, tearful, sorrowful. You can become so glued to the spot, you forget how to walk just as a newborn has to learn when they are born, to stand on two feet, tumbling a few times before finding their feet entirely. Continuous clicks of heels pursuing us with no sign of hurrying up, our pace was their pace, our movement became theirs, each time we made a turn they did the same. Miming every last detail apart from the feeling of fear, then they stopped in their tracks no longer behind us. Thwump! Thwump! Two more shots. Two more screams. Click! Click! Click! One after the other, fast paced, moving with speed, the noise of that person getting closer to us as they approached us, not giving up.

"We need to move! Now!"

Pushing both of our children in front of us, they ran out further down the street, heeding my words, if any of us died today I would want it to be me. My wife, my two children, they are the ones I want to live on... I would give anything to them even if it cost me pain. They deserved it, all of the pain given to me has torn me down from being happier. Happiness has always been in a smaller amount, it had been the last thing we ever received. My love for my family, their love for me motivated me to just keep going, no matter how hard times had become.

Lately I had been quiet, no help in the household apart from providing the money and food to get by. My wife did most of the work with our children as I attempted to remove the body of my mother from a room upstairs to somewhere she could rest since no one else wanted to help. Everything kept flooding back to me each time I tried, it was the hardest thing to see her pass away… then everything reached another level trying to put her in a place of rest that was not our spare bedroom.

We had been running for quite some time before we reached the docking area, grand ships lay in the harbour bobbing up and down on light ocean waves, the moon making the sea appear glittery like one that you see in a fantasy. Becoming distracted by the beauty of such things could not hold me back right now, as a possible murderer followed us as if we left a trail, the sacks heavy enough to give my arm and shoulder a numbing pain. Two battles being fought in one, managing to reach the docks in time, still surviving from whoever had continually kept up behind us. Those noises emanating from this person, the thwumps I had heard previously when we hid inside the kitchen… close by came the screams of the victim. Where was Lewis? Lewis had seemingly run out of the house, where to? With so many possibilities, only a few of them being a lot less disastrous, there was nothing pointing towards where he could be. I could go back, would my family survive without me to protect them? The chances of finding Lewis had been so slim. Hope, I could only hope Lewis was aboard the ship we were to depart on. I would regret not turning back for the rest of my life since he may not be on the ship. Behind us, the footsteps of our pursuer turned a corner down a tight alley, he would be able to come out in front of us if we did not dig our heels into the ground. One by one he would kill us, whatever he was using as a weapon seemed to cause discomfort, distress. Hearing the cries of pain in my children is the one thing on my agenda never to hear. Sounds coming from my children should be happy cries. Upon the day of their birth, their small little bodies came, albeit a little bit bloody, each of their cries became a sweet harmony to my ears until I held them in my grateful arms. Uncontrollable tears seeing that this was mine and my wife's creation, we had created two beautiful children who continue to bring us such joy. A few months later, I grew distasteful every time they cried, late at night, early in the morning, not giving in until we tended to what they needed. Not once did we feel unhappy, maybe a little grumpy only from the lack of sleep we had been getting... then the second came. Little Lily. No way on this earth would I let anyone hurt them, no way would I jeopardise their lives for the sake of being fearful. I loved them with my entire heart.

"Get to the right side of me!"

Keeping the sack on my left shoulder, Edward moved closer into the pack we had created, still running as our lives depended, no matter how tired our legs had become.

"William! They are about to leave!"

Ahead of us, they started to take up the anchors that weighed in the sea taking their time in doing so. Small plumes of water burst out from the sea as one of the sailors accidentally dropped the anchor back in completely soaking himself. He eyed the bottom of the waters rather embarrassed with himself.

"We still have time, Lucy! Take the children ahead of me."

"What about you?"

"There is no time, just go!"

Hesitating slightly, she looked back at me, turning forwards to then repeat the same actions all over again. That hurt. Something was wrong altogether if I let them stay with me. Somebody was here, whether I wanted to ignore it or not, they had an intention to harm us for an unapparent reason. They could have had anybody else in this town, instead they targeted me and my family. Watching them run without me, leave without me even though I had told them to, felt like a gut-wrenching pain I never wanted anyone to feel. It was my life or theirs.

Proving my love for them had never been hard, every step of the way, loving them more than anyone else in the world, this was my time to make sure they had the best life possible.

Calling to Lucy with my voice higher so they could hear, I felt a throbbing in my heart, a lump in my throat. "I am sorry, Lucy! I love you!"

"No!" Crying at the top of her lungs, a heavy man thudded on top of me, Lucy's hand stretched out, tears upon her face; both of my children wincing, watching me, screaming at the top of my lungs.

With all my might I managed my final words my mother had told me to use. "You will use these words as you die! Just as I have! Remember me!"

"I love you!"

Clenching my teeth together in agony with the pain of the heavy person on top of me, I pushed with all my might against the cobblestones, just about managing to slide out from underneath his weight.

"Lewis!"

"You!" Growling at the top of his throat, he lunged towards me like an animal, viciously snarling with saliva dripping out of his mouth, with blood from his gums mixed in his teeth heavily pressing together drawing blood.

"Traitor!"

A blood-curdling battle cry rolling off his tongue, jumping on top of me, his teeth sinking deeper into my shoulder, drawing my blood instead of his own, my bellows wailing amid the pain, my cries being the only thing I could hear. Whimpers, I needed to escape him!

"Get of me!" His teeth continued to sink deeper and deeper, a lion's demeanour as he viciously ripped apart my skin, chucking it away to the side as he went for another gash.

Memories flashing before me of my children, realising I would never see them again. Intense sobs causing my face to contort, feeling the numbness of pain as he continued to rip into me, shrills of pain screeched from me knowing I was never going to survive... This was the end of the road for me. Panting. Lewis had brought on from his eagerness to sink into my body again, straining my head to see the wound, my blood was everywhere... a dart in the side of his neck. Jolting back to the ground, his teeth sank in one more time to my chest ripping my clothes to shreds. Hands held in as fists gripping the cobbles again, my body heaving upwards in sheer agony. That was it. No more breathing. One last puncture to my body. Sinking to an abyss of darkness.

Chapter 2
He's Gone!

Father was dead. You could make no mistake about that, he put his body on the line for us, in order that we were never hurt by Mr Peterson. Mother sat on the floor in tears, her head in her hands. Our stomachs were turned, those aboard the ship watching on still preparing the boat, not quite knowing the full truth of what had just happened to them both. Tugging on my mother's sleeve as I tended to do quite often, her sorrowful eyes looking up at me, wiping away all that she could, unable to hide the puffiness all over her face.

"We need to get on the boat, Mom."

"Wha—"

"It is what Dad would have wanted." Pulling on her arm again, I searched around the area to see where Lily was, but she was not there. "Mom, where is Lily?"

Down where we had been she had started to walk towards father, he was laying on the ground, dead, still being eaten by Mr Peterson.

"Lily!" Mother cried as she ran after her to pull her back. Lily was putting up a tantrum wanting to go and see Dad.

"I want to see Dad!" Whining louder than she ever did, her feet stomping against the ground. "Why can't I see Dad!"

"Come with me!"

"No! I want to go help Dad!"

"You can't!" Mother's temper rose as she dragged Lily by her wrist, not thinking her actions through, today had been hectic, we had been thrown in the deep end with nowhere to hold onto. Ahead we could see an island, figurative and real, all we had to do was reach it. We needed to climb aboard the ship before it left.

"We need to go Mom!" I was surprised at how I had taken Father's death, it seemed unreal that I had not been bothered as he died. It then hit me, seeing all that had happened put me in great disbelief that any of this was even real; later on, I knew that Fathers death would come back to haunt me. Mourning for us all would come, no shelter when we arrived at our destination, possibly limited food and water. By now, Mother had managed to get Lily to the boat, seeing her husband die would have been harder on her than it might have been for us. Always my father's stronghold in times of need, he in turn became her refuge whenever things became tough and hard on us, each of them became co-dependant on the other, loving each other so strongly. Being so young in age, I knew for a fact what love looks like. They were the definition of love. Strong motives, strong desires to do what they wanted to, with each other's love and support they had felt as though they could do anything. Now one of the pack was gone, how would we cope, considering each of us depended on every individual for a different thing? Mother depended on him for his support, his love. I depended on my father for his advice, his knowledge followed by guidance. Lily trusted in our father's strong arms to save her from any harm, wanting his love to keep her safe. What about now he was gone? One part of our love was missing, a part of our hearts shattered to pieces among the still beating parts remaining alive… he would always have a place there, living long in our memories. Good times. Bad times. Every time.

"Lucy! Hurry up!" Shouting from the starboard side of the ship, Christopher Hamilton kept on urging us to get aboard seeing the danger of staying with a maniac on the loose. "Come on!" Another man sped down the ramp, a man I did not know taking us all underneath the crooks of our arms to bring us aboard, allowing us to walk on our own once waking up from our lackadaisical state of mind. What they did not understand was the numbness we had started to feel, now down to three instead of four. Vast were the ships decks, our feet barely the size of a plank of wood lining the flooring, tall rigging raised above our heads with clean, white sails flapping in the gentle breeze.

"Weigh anchors! Again." Christopher started yelling at the small number of men aboard, not showing any form of experience when doing the jobs commanded to them. "Why do you look so gloomy? Hey! You are leaving this place, where is your father then? Did he get lost in the crowds?"

Laughing with mockery at the idea my father had not come, his voice annoyed me more and more as each word left his tongue, not knowing when to stop as just one insult. Already he brought distaste, continually shaking my shoulder with narrowed eyes, his teeth shining as he smiled with ridicule, not knowing of the situation that had unfolded just minutes ago.

"Father is dead!" I spat at him with total revulsion deep within the back of my voice. "Did you not already see what happened? He's gone!"

There. It hit me like a brick wall, everything hurt. Tears. Heart. Mind. Body. Entirety of me. Speaking of the fatality brought it all to life for me. On the off chance something happens, whatever it may be, becomes so surreal that you cannot understand the reasoning behind why you feel nothing towards it. In that hour you tell of the tale, it tears you down, it breaks you into a thousand pieces inside of you; each piece of the shattered glass prods, pokes, pierces any skin, any piece of flesh that it comes into contact with. Your blood flow changes, pulsing underneath your skin, through your veins, into your arteries. Throbbing in your mind, spinning every thought on its back as you figure out a way to get back on your feet, instead you go around and around in a vicious circle that never seems to stop. To get yourself back up you need to have help by someone who already stands on two feet, level headed. It is the only way to get yourself back again.

"Did I see what, little man?"

Pointing my finger aggressively straight to the area where he lay dead, my young voice choked up. "My father, being impaled, eaten alive by a man we considered a friend. Bitten, chewed up until dead."

"Oh… well…" Forcing a hacking cough, his voice became clearer in his attempt to console. "This is what your father would have wanted for you, may he live long in our memories."

Proclaiming to the crew of our new situation, they raised their voices in agreement all in one vocal call. "Ay!"

With no other fatherly figure to hide my tears in, to hide my shyness as they each commented on my dad individually with a memory in the murmurs between them; thudding my head into Christopher's stomach, I embedded my tears into his clothes as he gently put an arm around my back, the other ruffling my hair, burying his head inside the strands, understanding how I was feeling. Dripping on my skin, small drips of cold water on top of my head, wetting pieces of my hair with the salty smell. My own tears drenched his top straight through, overwhelming me with uncontrollable emotion charging through my mind, no indication that these feelings would ever leave me.

"Come on, Edward, you should leave Mr Hamilton be. He must have things to do."

Holding the cuff of my dirtied white shirt, Mother pried me away from Chris letting him go once and for all. Falling away to the valuable consoling arms that my mother offered to me, her hand cupping the edge of my head to her chest with Lucy wrapping her body around the arm given to her. Sinking low. We sank. To the bottom of a pit with no ladder. Escape was now futile to us all. Laying low aboard the ship, we huddled together as a pack with streams pouring from us, knowing full well that we needed to stick together. Wafts of air came past us as many walked around the ship to complete jobs of all sorts, those gusts of wind chilled my arms which happened to be bare skinned with my rolled up sleeves. Using my teeth, I bit the fabric pulling each sleeve down to keep warm within the dark night manoeuvring into the sunrise. Each of us knew full well that sleep was vital to continue with our lives, our love forever the emotion to pull us through, giving us a rope to climb out of the abyssal state, engulfing a new life to live inside. Could we cope? Bit by bit, my eyelids let themselves flutter closed, still fighting to stay open. Instead of staying awake, my mind wore itself out from pressures incurred on thought processes going through my mind. Sleeping was exactly what we needed for now. Father had fallen to the hands of death, with a final, few words he wanted to say if anything ever happened to any of us… 'Remember me'. If we were to die, then those words would slip from our tongues. Told to our future family, our future friends, for each and every next generation to come would have those last words upon their mind so our story would not die with us, but be carried on for years to come. Small strokes across my hair, a light kiss planted on my hairline, the warm embrace as I was drawn in. "Your father loved you, Edward."

Halfway to being asleep, my lips mumbled words that came from my father before he died. "Remember me."

Tightly hugging me even more, the soft arms of someone else came closer to me, none other than my little sister Lily. "Mom, why can I not see Dad?"

"Your dad needed to leave us, Mrs Peterson wanted to take him with her."

"I thought she had already gone."

"She came back for him sweety, just sleep for now… your father loved you both… so much." Sniffles, embedded into her sleeve trying to cover up her emotions that were far more visible than she realised, not wanting to burden us with anything more than our shoulders could bear. Tightening was Lily's grip as it held on to Mother with all her might, appearing as though she would never release. "Sleep is what we all need right now."

Letting us go into a slumber, some of the crew picked up our doll-like bodies, relaxed with our arms draped by our sides, becoming limp under the arms of someone else as we were carried away to a room so we could rest.

"You will be okay." Even though my mind was asleep, my senses were not. Shaky, unsteady, cupping my face letting it glide away as I was brought away from her.

"I love you."

Chapter 3
What bodes ill for her, bodes ill for us all.

Watching one of the last people you expect to die, without a last word, last kiss, last anything is enough for you to just tell the world you want to give up living; I know that people would tell me I needed to give it up, let it go. What has happened has happened. That may be, that is the case... how are you supposed to ignore the fact someone you love just died before you? With your own eyes you watched the horrors unfold in a manner so rancorous, corrupt, cruel. Piece by piece, the man you will always love torn to pieces by the last person you expected to be that way. Lewis Peterson. Being brought aboard the boat, I was received warmly, barely any condolences after what had happened. At no point did I want condolences, words of comfort, wanting nothing more than to not cry with my children with me, so that they were unable to see the effects of his death had upon me through moments of turmoil pulling me through burning sensations. Falling away into my arms, the eyelids of both Lily and Edward flickering to a close, listening intently to words I rolled to them. Something surprised me entirely through this graft, the maturity of my young boy, seeming to take on his father's role as a leader, not only wanting to help me and his sister... wanting to stay strong to help everyone else. Thundering his head into Christopher's stomach as he would have done if it had been his father, seeking out help, wanting a hideout to be sheltered against the storm going on outside of life. Being carried away to a little room so they could sleep, my children's arms dangling down by their sides exactly the same as their little legs. Offering me a hand, one of the men aboard helping me up off of my feet, giving me a small minute to wipe away the remaining tears lingering about my skin.

"Are you all right there?"

"I would like to say I am, that would just be lying."

Nervously, a fake laugh came out to hide how I was truly feeling. "I am Jonathan, by the way, Jonathan Huntington."

"Oh, it is lovely to meet you, Jonathan. Lucy." Holding out his hand for me to shake, I held it in mine giving a little squeeze. "I suppose Lewis invited you?"

"He did. With that being said, where is that man?" A heavy exhale releasing itself from his solemn mouth, eyes drifting to the floor. What could I say, he just killed my husband. Still killing my husband. "You know where he is, why is it you cannot tell me? Eh?" Pushing me on the edge of my shoulder, I did not know how to respond since no one had ever chosen to be violent towards me. Instead of responding, lowering a glance down at my feet being in a rather awkward position. Men had always been known for their vigour, their strength, dominating women.

"I have nothing to tell you."

"Why will you not tell me where he is? What are you scared of?" Shoving my shoulders, left to right, he pushed me to the limit. "Come on!"

"Just leave me alone!"

Snapping back at him, his eyes spoke volumes of how it was not pleasing to him that my mouth had made an opening in our argument, a woman being able to fight back at him. Emotions ran high, I could not care less what they were since pain controlled me.

"What makes you think that you can talk to me like that? You should know full well, woman, that you should not disrespect a man."

Pushing me back further toward the railings, his breath lingering on my forehead since he was far taller than I was, pointing his fingers on my skin.

"How was I disrespecting you, when you are the one disrespecting me!"

Prodding my finger straight into his chest, he took my finger, twisting it around giving me a shooting pain up my arm. "Remember your place, woman."

"I know my place. It should be just the same as yours, without the ridiculous nature that follows with a man, so insecure that he seeks the need to battle a woman over what is deemed to be pretty much nothing."

Invading my space with an intrusive nature, my back hurt as it began pressing against the hard oak wood of the railings looming high over the sea. A large drop into a deep ocean. "You have a very smart mouth for someone like you. It could get you into some trouble, you ought to watch it." Stroking the edge of my jawline with his other hand, still keeping my arm twisted around, ensuring I had pain going through me as he spoke knowing I was listening intently. "Is it not a shame, your husband decided to stay behind, how are you going to cope with two children and no husband? A pretty, young woman like you, alone. With a ridiculously uncontrollable mouth."

Oh, he was pushing all the buttons he should not press, he knew exactly what he was doing to me, encroaching on my air space around me, leaving me no space to move. Apart from one arm, my legs, my knee, my head.

"Do you not know what personal space is?" Hurling my foot into his lower stomach, he released my arms which had become red raw with the tight grip he enforced onto me. Stumbling backwards, it had seemed as though he was to fall, managing to catch his balance at the last second. "Ugh!"

"What did I tell you about opening your mouth!"

Shaking, quivering, his tone changing went straight from undermining me to a passionate rage filling up his entire words and the empty air surrounding us. Why did I open my mouth?

Truthfully, I never had to open my mouth, since I was a young child finding my way in society, singled out as a bad difference. Standing out in crowds of children my age, laughing at me cruelly, seeing how dumbfounded I was with others I did not know, boys taunting me left right and centre. Why they mocked me is a story that kills me when I talk about the tales hidden behind my persona, always avoiding blending into everyone else since there was no point hiding the truth about you. You are you at the end of the day, it does not matter if your family appears odd or you appear unusual for that matter. Self-criticism hurts even more when you hear it slide straight off the tongues of others, I have been there.

"Speak up then! You are the one with the big mouth."

"Jonathan, you should just leave me alone."

"I always knew you would stay the same as you were when you were a child. Ph! Start growing up a bit." Chuckling at the pitiful state he saw me in seeming enough to condemn the way I acted, the way of being. "How was it being motherless? Still hurts you, does it not, she more than likely left because of you."

He was in my past. Memory. When they return to you, striking you so hard that it leaves bruising. "Leave her out of this! You know nothing of all I have been through, Jonathan, not all families are as perfect as they seem, yours certainly was not."

"Always blaming someone else... honestly. Start being a real woman."

Everything was building on top of me all at once, the death of William, always protecting me from toxic people seeking to pull me down into their ditch, to their standards so lax in a moral centre. Reliving my past seeing the one person who I feared I would never see again, hoping with a strong-willed heart, mind, body, soul it would all be a thing of the past instead of a future. Remembering the fact my mother left our family unit for her own purpose, so she could have a better life in a place where freedom could be found in abundance. No need to search, it was right at the doorstep for her. Breeze. Icy. Tears. Feet carrying me across the ship. Hair afloat in the wind, climbing the stairs to take some time away from all that had burdened me, more than I felt was bearable.

"Away from here..."

Clutching the railing overlooking the sea upon the stern which was highly vociferate, if seen in the distance by another passing ship, flowing in the waves the wind brought on me, my hair lapping over itself continuously, whipping my face harshly.

"She wanted a better life... for me."

Full well I knew the truth, the reasons she had for leaving us when I was so young. Sounding so valid in my younger years, now so ridiculous and heartless in her way. At the age of ten years old, Father knocked on my bedroom door carefully so his hand would not come straight through the thin, worn wooden door, pulling me away from my nefarious fate. Handing me a letter, pale, frail, not so calm and oh so frigid feeling his skin against my fingers, I brushed them away from his hold. Reading it stung as a thousand deaths to punish me, taunt me over and over repeatedly like a lonesome prayer filled with wicked truths so full of loathing none could compare. Since that day, I kept the letter in my front pocket on my dress to remind me constantly why I needed to never give up, to prove all these people wrong.

Showing I could rise above family indents, imperfections, bitterness. Gently, my feeble fingers took hold of the parchment paper, unfolding the envelope flap to unveil the little note left behind from the day she went away, leaving me to the hands of immoral men, besides from my husband who I was far too grateful to find. Scanning my eyes over its contents, the dog-eared corners, worn edges due to heavy use allowed me to reread its contents in full.

My dearest Lucy,

Whenever your father decides he would like to give you this, you may be a little older than I imagined you would be. My words are only small in comparison to what they may sound like in real life. Truth be told, I had a ticket to a better life, an escape from this world. An outside source helped me to escape this fate so many are doomed in facing; left, right, centre, people died in front of me, Lucy, I could not stand the sight of another person dying.

In this world people will not be as kind as you hope that they will be, they are going to want to tear you down as they did with me. Rely on your conscience your father promised he

would instill in you, there is a better life beyond here. Find it!
You can rise above these people. Being your mother, I should
know, I gave birth to you.

How short this is, was not how I planned or imagined for
that matter. My words only little to what would be indulged in
if we see each other in the future, remember I am always
watching over you young one. Find that better life I did! I
never left because of you, I left for you, so you could receive a
better life...

Beginning to read the last little piece out loud so I could hear
it to myself for another time, I continued in my endeavour to
finish the letter without feeling empty.

It was always my intention to save you and your father, yet I
found myself leaving you behind. I wanted a better life, you
will understand when you get older. I love you. I am so so sorry
I had to leave. Just get away from here.

There it was once more, folding the letter back up to its
original state, replacing it to its envelope where it sat inside
my apron pocket. Emptiness found me, I thought I had escaped
its clutch yet it still existed as it always had done, never would
it feel any different to now. When she spoke of a better life, I
never caught the drift, the reasoning behind why she had to
move away from seeing people die... well they were not her
family. Well, now came the time that I understood her
reasoning. Seeing people die, no matter who they are or what
they mean to you, is so different, you finally understand pain.
I just need to get away from here.

Leaning over the edge, anyone might have thought that I

was about to jump over the edge to end it all, leave my children behind to grow up in a world so devilish just as my mother had done to me. From the day I had read the letter, written so carelessly in words without any emotion of heart poured into each word created from her hand, ink, fingertips upon pen. Lonesome with a resounding pain inside, nothing would ever resolve the issue of emptiness embedded deep into me. A piece of shrapnel wedging in between somewhere, so desperate to remove with no way of being able to take out such a thing because of the place it took rest.

"William, why did he have to take you?"

"Who took him?"

"Lewis Peterson."

"Sad, that."

To the left of me, a woman with long flowing blonde locks, tanned skin, dark black eyes penetrating my gaze out to sea, removing my thoughts as our conversation proceeded. Her appearance seeming somewhat familiar to me, the uncanny resemblance biting my tongue knowing who she appeared like.

"I have never seen you before, you seem oddly familiar."

"Oh, did I not introduce myself? Eleanor Huntington, daughter of Jonathan and Dorothy Huntington."

"That is why you seem so familiar." Wanting to change the subject from the memories of Jonathan, many short minutes ago. "You seem quite young, should you not be married?"

"Father wishes for me to marry a man of high stature, having money, wealthy home. Everything else you can imagine."

"You seem unhappy about it?" I began quizzing her. Simply put, her heart did not lie where Jonathan wanted it to.

"Why should I be happy? They are all the same." Scoffing in her undertone, her actual tone hid it almost perfectly. "Where do they expect my heart to lie? With a man who never loves me apart from when he wants me to bear his children."

"Most of them are like that."

"You seem to know quite a lot about this."

"Your deductions are very accurate. Men are dangerous creatures unless you find the needle in the haystack, I did."

"How?"

"There is no special technique, but a waiting game is always an option."

"Wait!" Expressing her surprise unlike any other, her hand slapped down on the banister, laughing randomly at her actions, her head turning towards me with a smile across her face. "You are telling me, I have to wait. Father will not be pleased."

"Look at me." She carefully obeyed what I had asked her facing me, my hand holding hers. "If there is one thing you must do in this world, for yourself, follow your heart. Your heart is the most powerful thing you own, use it wisely because once you give your hand away, your heart will not go. They should both go together because one will become lonely if not given to the hands of a man you love."

"I wish it was as easy as that."

Quickly realising that I had forgot to give her my name when she was wishing to use it, my voice speeding up. A red tint coming upon my cheeks, flushing with embarrassment. "Oh! It's Lucy. I am sorry, I forgot to tell you earlier on. I always seem to forget."

Truth be told, my body was sent in a spiral, no sense of direction, no sense of anything, she must have read my heart in an unordinary way.

"I may be overstepping my line here, but you look as though something is troubling you. My mother always looks the way you do when we hear of someone passing away." Silence. I left her in silence, not knowing how to even begin telling her that the man I loved slipped through my fingers hours ago. "Look, I should be going. I am sorry for prying—"

"No! No. It is okay, it only happened a few hours ago, I still have to replay those events in my mind, each time I do it hurts more and more. There just does not seem to be a balance between feeling hurt, feeling sadness to ever feeling like life is worth living again. He had my hand, he had my heart, now he took them both with him." Gifting me her arms held out wide to hug me tightly into a wrap, a lock I was required to be encased inside, knowing someone felt for me. Warmth. Tight. Imagining that I was well kept inside William's arms, elsewhere, preferably back home by the fire trying to keep warm as I relate the day that I have been put through, end to end. Recalling that information, cracking me into little pieces, as a chisel chips away rock, wood, stone, any material with the ability to be chipped off, many pieces had been clipped off me, bit by bit, chunk by chunk, sizes varying to the size of a chipped nail.

"I want what you had."

Tears weeping from my eyes, trickling at a fast pace down washed-out, discoloured cheeks of mine from seeing cruel actions, being treated impishly by a foolish man, recalling past disturbances occurring mostly in childhood, ensuring the unexpectant visit from a person in my past who stood by, watching everything happen to me continuously, as a record relapses on the same notes unless stopped by the hand of another. Liberating myself free from her narrow envelopment, that tiny amount of normality having someone to care for, released me to a level up after falling from a massive flight of stairs, many bruises on my skin. Black eyes, battle scars, rallying cries from afar, thoughts that never will subside, knowing the rivers I cried for him, knowing the desire to have him back in my life never able to fade.

"You must wait for the opportune moment."

"Will that ever come? We are going to the island, I know near enough everyone. I might as well just admit that it is never going to happen."

"Never say never, believe in yourself, trust me."

Holding the back of the skin on her top arm, she sensed my little action, understanding me further than she had done, brushing down her skirt to smile at the ground. "You are possibly right."

"Eleanor!"

Tiny clicks against wood bouncing off the strong, firmness accompanying the sound of a woman aged older than me, seeing the slightly aged face, fair skinned, dark hair. This woman soon changed Eleanor, fear in her eyes, only wanting to please her mother. Standing upright in a formal position, calling me miss, as this woman would want her to.

"Miss, I must be going, mother is calling for me. It has been nice speaking to you. Good day."

Off she went to her mother with great haste, no time to waste. Pace quickening as the click of heels became louder atop of her own small-heeled shoes, weighing heavy on dainty feet. That was the last I saw of Eleanor, turning a corner with a miniature glance at me, a nod of approval. Gone. Along the horizon, pale pink mixing with orange skies drifted above us, the clouds painted light purple beginning to change with the heat of a rising sun drifting to sea level... halfway, three-quarters, fully high in the sky. Sending heat rays down upon me.

Wincing one eye with the brightness, lifting the left hand over my forehead to block off the blinding lights beaming straight at me. Certainly, the warmth upon my bare-skinned arms felt wonderful, a medicine I was in dire need for from the cold darkness which had been enveloping us all in its clutch. Still sound asleep, Edward and Lily resting peacefully in the hammocks they had been taken to from my arms, giving me a slight few hours on my mind, gathering the broken pieces from the shattering glass heart of mine on the ground. Still, there was not enough time to put them back together considering it would be next to impossible without the right means. Behind me, heavy footsteps pounding onto the decks.

Pants. Cries. Exasperation. Something had happened, I forbade that to be the case, not with my children aboard. Initial instincts had to be ridden out of the picture, curiosity killing the Cat. I was not about to be killed. Suppressing my desire to go over, to ask, I stood listening intently to the commotion between our 'Captain', Christopher.

"Captain! Captain!" In between heavy panting noises, he got his words out, putting his teeth back in. "Something has happened below decks! Come quickly, we have managed to detain him."

"Detain who? There should be no need to detain him."

"He is trying to ravage some of the crew, he speaks of death, we found this in his neck. Jonathan managed to pull it out."

Peeking my head around to see what he was about to produce,

they were unaware of my presence giving me time to move closer for a clearer view and hearing of the plight developing. Trench crawling to the edge of the quarter deck, I hid my body behind the edge of the right-hand side stairs getting a clear view of the situation going on down upon the upper deck below me. A young man removed a dart from his pocket, a feather sat at the end of it, a yellow colour hinting with a blood red. The tip so sharp it appeared smaller than a needle for patching up clothing.

"This was found wedged in his neck."

Holding it out for Christopher to take, he took it showing an odd complacent nature with care to not affect himself with whatever poison had infected the tip. "I am guessing he has a puncture mark?"

"Quite deep, sir."

"Hmm." Deep in thought, twisting the metal in between his fingers, taking a closer look at the piece he had at hand. "Something is on this that must have poisoned him. Who is he?"

"She, sir."

"A woman!" Surprise taking over his facial expression, a light gasp escaping my lips, praying it was not Lily. Nor did I wish it upon young Edward. Shooting their heads in my direction, squirming up into a ball in hope that my body was not as noticeable. "I will rephrase my question. Who is she?"

Their eyes redirected to each other, now I could breathe peacefully to not disclose my hiding place. "Bethany Hamilton."

"Whoever did this will return, very soon. Show me to her."

Leading him away from my eyesight, cramps had only

just crept into my calves, forcing me to stand suddenly blowing my cover altogether if they returned soon after leaving.

Shouts. Screams of terror began to amplify, deriving out of the berth deck down below; a woman filling to the brim with acrimony, displeasure being held captive against her will. Declining the small set of the first stairs, then the second, turning a corner to make my way down another staircase seeing the gun deck for the first time. Damp smell of the sea, barnacle growth on the occasional wall, lined with guns, cannonballs, unused torches and weaponry along the corridors my fingers trailing against it. Half-soaked wood on the floors, on the walls, on the cannons. Pieces of stored fabric in barrels, in crates, moist with the clammy air sailing out at sea.

"Grr!" Growling barked further down, this told me I was certainly on the wrong deck. Proceeding onwards in my venture, the next staircase came into full view. Holding the banister that led down, each of the noises emitted by a woman I had never met. Gingerly, I twisted my head around the edge of a post, one hand above the other, hugging the wood tightly watching on in fear.

"Calm down! Everyone!" Christopher chose the vociferating method so he himself would be audible above everyone else, the heaviness in his voice outweighing all in the room. Continually writhing, in the bonds Bethany had been detained in for everyone else's safety. "We need to do something from here, if left she will kill anyone in sight."

"Yes!"

Everyone concurring in agreement with Christopher, so did I, my voice remaining silent still hugging the post next to me. Watching on in despair, only wishing to help this girl with no idea what could be done. She was infected with poison, coding every movement, every thought, coding her next pounce, her next kill. Nobody aboard this ship wishes to kill another, despite hard feelings that may be lingering still after hardships and experiences in the past. Brushes of air wafting across the open skin on my neck, someone breathing, exhaling onto me, soft, careless drapings of someone's clothing against my lengthy dress.

Ghostly gasps. Looking behind me, a fully black-cloaked man towering overhead. You could not see in, he could see out with the hood completely taking over his head. Inside gaped a pure black abyss. No words came out, hollow, sluggish, arduous breaths having limited amounts of oxygen to inhale. Unsteady was the hand pointing a finger onto my bare skin, quivering, fragile as glass, thin in size appearing as a small twig from a tree.

"You…"

Prolonging, outstretched vocals talking to me, sticking thoroughly into my mind. Macabre atmosphere, disturbing words ingraining into me from a man owning a voice so empty, well-aged, well-crafted to disturb any living soul. Freezing on the spot, stuck down, unable to move, he had me tranced, my lips staying sealed shut. As much as my body yelled run, my mouth chose to seize up, begging me to just alert someone of his presence… just scream! Still standing in front of this man, every muscle in my body tingling, anxious to move once and for all… just scream! Fastening my clasp to the wooden post, the skin around my fingernails went between white and red, completely pale underneath. Just scream! Scream! "Christopher…" Unsteady, not enough to alert, barely a whisper. A little louder! "Christopher!"

"Lucy! I am trying to assess the situation."

Retreating backwards away from the thickly covered man, each of my feet rhythmically starting to go one behind the other, then the other, in a pattern. A heavy, round circular shape trod underfoot, sending me flying backwards; whacking my head harshly on the wood, the manly figure drifting toward me, casual with each step. Not a single person taking note of my situation, not a single one could care less... he walked, he drifted, he swayed.

Knowing exactly how he was affecting me, for the terror should have been clear in my eyes, waltzing over to me. I caught not a single glimpse of his face, my heavy drawn-out breaths through anxiety heaving harsher with each second passing. Do you ever have those moments when you can see your entire life flashing before you? Well... they had flown past me. If I opened my voice, it was a possibility of my death, a possibility of my survival. Edward and Lily had already lost their father, my husband, could they cope with losing me? They would be able to survive, survive with helplessness... in a way I was hoping it would be the case, I was praying it would not. Now was not the time to debate that scenario within my thought processes, especially at this point in time. Contracting the span of my hand to a fist, slamming it into the ground pushing my aching back against the wooden walls that happened to encase us. Over to my left, Christopher consulted with a few people below in the berth deck between the fabric hammocks wrapping around the wooden posts with thin, worn ropes. Within my heart, embellishing into my mind, I knew to get somebody's attention, becoming an annoyance needed to take place. 'Keep on knocking, and it will be opened to you'. Knock away at Christopher, he would eventually crack, opening the door to life. "Christopher…"

This time was different, he heard me… his response would determine my next move. "Not now, Lucy. Can you not see I am busy?"

Displeasure surfacing, irritation, displeasure of my interruptions. Sadly for him, this would occur more than just one time, two could play this game.

"Christopher!"

Sending me a cruel, discontented look, I gulped profoundly harshly. "Get up off the floor will you. Do yourself a favour."

"Stowaway!" Eyes lighting up as a midnight sky, everything clicking into the puzzle, the missing piece found so soon that he never expected my constant pressure to result in figuring out the confusion.

"Stowaway…" Speeding up as he walked, his head cocking to one side enabling him to see around the corner. "Oh…"

Helping me to my feet, one of the men I least expected to help me offering a hand, holding my back upon seeing where I was hurt. Jonathan carefully aiding me in angling my stance, after injuring my lower coccyx, encountered the heavy thudding. Shooting pains firing up my spine, Christopher immensely pressured with so many decisions to make already, not long at sea. Groans slithering off my tongue, the pains thoroughly having a dig in my nerves. "Let's make a go at mending what was lost years ago, and this. What have you done?"

"Of course. We need to get him." Wincing in agony, continuing to hold my lower back, careful to not touch any indecent areas. His care and compassion frightening me…

especially after the way I was treated hours ago. "Where are Lucy and Edward?"

"They should be on another deck lower down, that is where everyone else is being held in the meantime."

"Right, okay, I think we should go out onto the main decks."

"You will not be going anywhere, *miss.*"

Appearing from out of the lurking shadows. A man so gorgeous with blond hair, tanned skin, dark brown eyes, keeping the pieces of dirtied blonde in a neat ponytail behind his head, each of the hairs neatly kept in place, eyebrows carefully plucked to perfection.

Cleanly shaven, not a single hair out of place, easily a few years younger than me, if not the same age. In his voice, he used a tone to undermine me. Unless you were looking for someone undermining you, then could notice the way in which they speak to belittle your standing, I wanted to help figure out who did this to us, who this man was finding it so amusing to creep up behind me and breathes on the back of my neck.

"And you would be?"

"Have you not heard of me?"

"If I had heard of you, then would I be asking?"

Thumping the new person on the scene with a look so devious, telling him *you asked for that.* He did. The way he continued to hold himself spoke of self-importance, self-love, self-centred.

"I like you, you are much like me."

"Sweetheart, I am far from being like you in any way, shape or form. Have some self-respect, for me and yourself, you are quite idiotic."

"We are human." Rolling my eyes into the back of my

head, the wailing cries of Bethany penetrating the skin inside my ears, shaking up the thinking strategy, not being able to think at all. Laughing with a posh snarl, placing his foot upon a wooden crate, letting down his hair to gaze at me with those beautiful thick, dark brown eyes, hiding away under the lengthy black lashes to seal in those precious irises.

"For someone who speaks about self-respect, you do not cover yourself in it. That eye rolling is very rude you know, not to mention inconsiderate."

"Will someone just *attend* to that poor girl!"

Jonathan hollered for one of the men to come near the girl, Bethany, who was not having any form of help or treatment from the men. Thrashing around in fits of animalistic anger with more lacerations slicing through her wrists and ankles with every twist, turn, scream.

"You sort her." Tossing the medical equipment he brought with him to attend, throwing them on the crate before the man's foot, annoying me with every look he took to the equipment and up into my eyes. "I think he means you, *woman*."

Cocking my head to the side, a slight smirk widening across the forefront of my face, feeling my hand reaching for a *gun* at the back of my skirt. Why? I have never held one in my entire life, why was I thinking of grabbing one.

"What are you reaching for, little one?"

"None of your business, *shortie*."

"Excuse me? I think you are standing up to someone a lot braver than you are."

"Am I really? What are you looking at, blondie?"

"You guys, it is hilarious that he is intimidated by you." Appreciating his taking sides with me, acknowledging that I know more than what the eyes speak of.

"I am Theodore, by the way."

"Nice to meet you Theod—"

Knocking me to the ground with a fist to my head, his hot breath loitering around my body, feeding on the feelings proudly emanating from me. Something was being dragged up from my past, something from before here, before this place. Maybe I had a life where my mother went to? Another blast to the face, again, again, again. A wife beater, I know all of them, I did not know shortie. Each time striking my face in fits of anger, I smiled pretending to enjoy the pain he was causing me.

"Stop smiling beautiful, it does not work as well now that you are bruised."

"Well, *shortie boy*, deal with it."

Kneeing him straight up into the stomach, kicking back his squirming body to the wall, standing to face up to him, going up the gears of anger to make him realise that this was not who I allowed myself to be. A coward. Someone who allows others to affect me, hurt me, bruise me, torture me, punish me for being female.

"I am not short."

Coughing from the winding I had given him, walking towards his hunching body with pain. "Stand up straight. Go on." Trying to straighten himself up, unable to manage even a little bit, pinning him by his collar to the cabin walls, the stunned silence of both Theodore and Jonathan allowing me to carry on, especially knowing the history. "There. Now I can look you in the eye."

"What if I do not want to?"

"Well, you will if it means ripping them out and holding

them at a distance so I can see them."

"Oh, really?"

"Oh, yes."

A heaving came from down the stairs. Christopher, cuts and bruising all over his head, looking towards me and running back up the stairs again. Everything here has been odd, confusing, hard to understand, the mourning I should be doing for my husband was not coming. Letting go of the short man in my grip, he went running after Christopher, hobbling a little as he went, whining in pain.

"It looks like you won."

Holding his hand out for me to shake, I ignored the fact it was there, swatting away the offer with a solemn look on my face, stretching my mouth, cracking each side of my jaw.

"He was not a prize, I may have won, do not think that it is a nice way to be winning, Theodore."

A hollow unknown voice appearing behind Jonathan, a voice I did not know, speaking quietly even though no one was there. I must have taken too many blows to the head, as I was hearing people.

"You need to knock her out and head her up to bed, she needs her memories resetting."

"Of course."

Turning all my attention to Jonathan, his eyes wavering, readying his hand by his side, colliding it with my head intentionally forcing me to be hit hard on the floor. Cold. Flopping to the ground, I was in a ridiculous state, Theodore would remind me of this day… for now who was I kidding? It has been over one day, not one single sleep, a continuous loop over and over.

"Help me put her in my arms."

"Someone needs to bandage Bethany's arm."

"I will do it." Even though I was completely out of it, I still cared for this girl. I knew the voice of Jonathan, volunteering to do the job that I had purposely laid out for myself to do. Now I just could not move an inch, not even a finger, the life was draining right out of me. Underneath, the hands of someone rolling me over into Theodore's arms… so I presumed, they gave safety, warmth, shielding me from the cold draft through the gaps of the walls.

"I can walk…" Mumbling under my breath, not even my ears could understand the words I was speaking. How anyone else could would be a miracle. "Just not right now."

"I cannot understand a word you're saying."

"Mmm."

Snuggling my head into his chest, my arms wound around his neck, reassuring me of a safety line if ever there was an accidental drop. "Getting comfortable, I see."

Small murmurs of sarcasm escaped out, not that they were the slightest bit understandable. Theodore would know that it would be something along the lines of… 'you wished', 'yes, you keep dreaming'.

"Why do you wear a wedding ring, with no husband in sight?"

One of his fingers stroked my wedding ring. No. He was not about to take it, just having a look at it. Still, I uttered under my breath words he might be able to hear, not that I was completely certain of such.

"He—" Eek! A large door heavily opening, evidently to an expansive room, plentiful space. Walking in, he closed the door behind, delicately meandering around the room, laying me down somewhere comfortable, a blanket covering me from my feet to my waist. "He is dead…"

Sluggishly the words came off, lingering in the air until my head finally lay to rest on the makeshift pillow created for me. Sleep dawning, overshadowing my awareness, collapsing into the hands' weariness and fatigue. Darkness covering over my eyes, eyelids faltering slightly, eventually drawing to a close. Nothing mattered now. Sleeping, the only thing I knew how to do.

Chapter 4
How do you expect me to live?

Dry mouth. Body needing to be stretched for the muscles had been relaxing for far too long. Stretching my arms into the air, moving myself up, feeling quite calm against the gentle rocking of the ship on the high seas, hard movements of feet banging against the wood down below me, orders shouting from far away. Left, right and centre men called to their stations, given directions.

"Ay!" Many men responding quite clearly to the captain's orders, their whole souls dedicated to the ship. We may be escaping a deadly disease… Yet, one thing does mess with my head. How do we know that someone has not brought the disease on board? Who was that man I saw, cloaked in black? Was he caught? Why is he here? So many questions with no answers, next to nothing regarding my movement, the answers would not come to me just by sitting around. Brushing my hand through my hair, the soft but knotting hair waves falling on my collarbone. Over across the other side of the room, a water basin had been filled to the brim with fresh water, fresh face cloths and towels along with half a bar of soap to wash all that needed to be washed. Dampening my hair, a medium-sized brush with horse hair as the bristles, taken into my hand, brushing my locks through and through to detangle the large amounts of knotted tangles of dark brown locks.

"Ow!" In my hand, a thick clump of hair had been pulled off. No bin in sight. Nowhere to put this disgusting thing. "Just my luck."

Finding somewhere to hide it behind, my fingers rubbing together, releasing it behind the back of the basin with all the other moss growth, floating down. I made my way back to how I had been to avoid suspicion if I was caught doing something so gross.

Knock! Knock! A resounding banging of a fist against the door, a weighty fist hitting against the wood. "Lucy! Are you all right, I heard you talking to someone."

Oh… what an embarrassment, I had been caught in my casual talkings to myself. What a thing to explain.

"Yes! I am quite all right, come in."

Swiftly, I continued to brush through my hair, dampening it in the water to clean it, dashing a small plummet of water onto my face, widening gently. Theodore peered through looking rather… could I be wrong in thinking he looked rather concerned.

"There is no need to be concerned about me."

"After yesterday's affairs, I would say, there is."

Shutting the light out, a click bouncing off the walls. Taking a clean beige towel from the pile, dabbing my face dry, not even bothering to do anything to my hair, it would dry soon enough.

"Yesterday's… Ah! Yes, maybe."

"You took a very quick turn, one minute you were expressing your hatred toward me—"

"Then I was on the floor."

Rolling my eyes into the back of my head, I had already gotten the gist of the day's events. "You really hate me, huh?"

"Hmm." At first, he was a cocky, rude, arrogant man full of himself. Then you see inside of him, not all that bad, his outside appearance is to cover up for an event from his past. We all have them, somewhere, burying so far down that we begin to forget why, or what caused us to become dislikeable. "Maybe."

Whichever way, I was never admitting to not hating him. If he wanted the answer, begging would be his best option. Chuckling to himself, I joined in not wanting to appear to give him the wrong impression and the correct impression at the same time.

"At least those washing items came in good use."

"They did. I am guessing someone prompted you to bring them."

"No. How heartless can I be?"

"It depends, upon first glance, you are one who you would never want to meet, or come across *ever* again."

"Ah! Yet, you meet me again, I see no complaint."

"No, you don't."

"Why?"

Upon meeting him, I will admit his attitude, his demeanour, displeased me without reason. Theodore's attitude appearing overconfident, presumptuous about me. Now, I was digging myself a deep hole, his company might just be enjoyable. It was much like my own, strong, forward, to the point, not failing to voice a personal opinion when others decide it for you. "Admit it, Lucy, you are much like me."

"In some ways we differ." Running my fingers through the dry pieces of hair from my head, I replaced the hairbrush down onto the basin watching it accidentally slide into the bowl. "For goodness' sake!"

"Leave it!"

Our heads shot towards the door, a huge bustle of people's voices piling over each other, pure commotion in confusion. Something was happening outside that we knew nothing of. "Theodore?"

"Stay here." Walking away with him to leave the room, his hand outstretched towards me keeping me at bay. "Stay here."

"Why?"

Putting each of his hands on my shoulders, cautiously removing them in hope enough emotion had been conveyed. "Just stay here, it may be safer, lock the door."

"With what?"

Hastily speeding off out of the door, he cast a glance backwards, giving me further instruction. "Bar the door with that chair!" Pointing his finger across the room, his head nodding along. "That one over there."

"Okay."

"Do not move."

Shutting the door across, my hand held the back of the wooden chair pulling it underneath the door knob so nobody could enter. Everything had been happening quicker than I had ever known, events man had not known till this day. Tides can change with strong winds that gush over them to then pull away, leaving desolate sands once inhabited with dense waters atop its shimmering, soaked surface.

Barely any furniture decorated the room, for the most part it contained: a small writing desk, no drawer space, a small candle resting its flame, single bed, off-white sheets and a flat pillow I had once rested on. Just along the opposing wall, a tall wardrobe holding two large, oak doors on its golden hinges, four oak drawers embellished with particular floral, handcrafted patterns. Overall, it was quite basic, quite lovely to have as a room in a house. Where we... I had lived, with William, gave us peace, the quaint miniature town never giving us hassle or trouble. We knew of families that lived here prior to our moving into that area, everyone felt satisfied compared to others who had fallen into the trap of dealing with personal information around. It spread like wildfire, you cannot say something without others being told by large chains of human ears. "What is happening out there?"

Bawling screams of men came straight through my walls, Jonathan's voice starting to speak... another man's voice who I knew was unclear... Theodore! Pressing my ear roughly to the door, I began to hear their words clearly, the muffled voices no longer faint in the thick distance.

"What is it you want from us?"

Gruff, hollow, emotionless. Hatred, full of loathing, needing something. Could it be... "You know exactly who I want!"

Thudding each foot forwards, consecutive feet movements adjacent to the door in between us, his words distinct.

"You step one foot in there—"

Cut off, Theodore had tried his best, now it was my turn. Swiftly removing the chair from the door, he had no reason to suspect anyone of being inside here, having a struggle opening up. Around me, there had not been a lot of places to hide, where to go? In the wardrobe?

Too obvious. Behind the basin? Too tight. Inside the desk... he would see me immediately. Biting my teeth down on my soft-skinned lips, my eyes caught sight of a bed sheet trapped under an opening. Lifting what appeared to be the lid of a storage box, the contents remaining empty but big enough to fit me inside.

"I can go as I please, if I do not find her... there *will be* a price to pay."

"Why her?"

"A life for a life, and all that. *Captain.*"

How foolish was he, Theodore was not the captain of the vessel, Christopher was. Creaking. In the little slit of light through the top of the box, managing to slip my body through a slim gap keeping air in and out to breathe far easier than if it were shut. Whoever remained under the hood, waltzing into the room pretending to own the place giving a strong presence, it told all to back away or there would be consequences.

"You see, there is no one in here!" Exasperated, even Theodore was wondering where I had gone to. "You never answered me. Why her?"

Eyeing Theodore up and down, he let a 'pfft' of air escape out of his mouth, disgusted just seeing him.

"I never answer those... like... you."

Viciously cackling, pushing Theodore away to search the room, those long, weak fingers quivering with cold. This man had no fear. Did he? Sitting atop the bed, the lid covering me shut, closing with a thud blocking light coming through for me to see to the events outside. Voices. The only thing I could gather.

"Well, she is not in here."

"Oh, you are mistaken."

"Excuse me?"

"Excuse you. For lying. You can either tell me where she is or... we will do it the hard way."

"Tell me what it is you want? A good bargain, deal, strike something up."

"It all depends… what are you prepared to offer me?"

"That! Goes both ways."

"Hmm. How about this. You tell me where you last saw her, then we can deal."

"She—" Theodore chose to silence himself abruptly. "What do I get in return?"

"You know the information I require, you just refrain from giving it to me." Pausing, not saying any words for a while, until finding his moment. "You give me the information, or one of her children will get it in the neck."

Presumably his mouth lay, hanging open wide from shock, his shrieking gasp of utter repulsion.

"You!" Growling at the top of his voice, his rage flaring. They were not his children to care about, someone must have told him the tale of how I lost my husband, his care becoming vividly readable from just his speech. "How sick can you be?"

"As sick as I like, I think you will find it. Do you have a problem with that?"

"I—" Please. Repeatedly praying that he would not make this situation any more difficult by mouthing uncontrollable dialect. "No."

"Good. Then, you shall not mind giving me all I require." Gulping deeply, I could have sworn my thudding, thumping, pulsating heartbeat shook the surfaces of the ship, its pounding against my chest heard by him. "What are we… No. You, waiting for?"

"Nothing at all." Sensing his casual, hapless smile coming about. He had been put in a situation not so wretched, forcing him to give information to save rather than sacrifice the lives of my precious children. "She was in this room, ask any of my sailors. Yesterday, as I am sure you know, after seeing you she collapsed quite heavily on her head. The tiredness wore her down alongside her minor head bang. I am sure that is why you can smell her. Strangely, she slept exactly where you sit."

"Ah. Really? What a lovely story, where is she now?"

"I… I wish I knew."

"Are you sure about that?"

"You are a smart man. You would know if I was lying. Am I?"

"Remarkably, you have not struck me as a liar. How lucky is that for you? Very well. For all I know, you are bluffing me, just this once I will let it slide."

"Hmm." Theodore had not been entirely convinced what he was getting at. Would he leave us all alone entirely, or just this one time? Preferably, not the latter.

"When I say just *this* once, I entirely mean this occasion." Pressure releasing off the bed, allowing me to peer up. This man had got up, preparing to leave us… for now. "Do not think I will not return."

"I was expecting that much." Both of them sauntering out of the room towards the main decks, sailors continuing with their work, avoiding any accidental eye contact with that man. "I shall escort you out."

"Yes."

That one single 's' prolonging into the sound of a sly snake, wanting to trick, to mislead, to bear false in all things. He was not who he appeared to be. Something struck me quite roughly about him, I knew who he was yet my finger could not point, my tongue would not allow me to speak of his name… it was on the tip, right on the edge. Who was he? Their voices growing distant, watching him leave, how would he get away? I presumed there had been no ship with him, or we would have been alerted that it was coming about. There have been so many times whereby I had a question that was unanswered. Still, I remained covered by the box, safe from any harm. Thundering footsteps hurriedly came into the room, head slightly bowing lifting it in full dignity, hands behind the back, high with importance. Theodore. What had changed? Had that mysterious man put him in his place? I could pray he had not been brought back down to the way he was, when originally meeting me. Clearing his throat to clear the dense air, he knew full well that I was in this room but not where.

"Lucy! You might as well come out, he has gone."

Starting off harsh and demanding, he noticed the tone in his voice, dropping it to a softer voicing. Emerging from the box, making the gap wider freeing me to take my legs out one by one leaving the blankets and coverings to drop down the side. Shutting the box, a stern, hard look capturing his face.

"At least I found a good hiding place."

"It could have cost you your child's life!"

"Hang on. Hold up. What are you trying to say?"

"You risked your child's life for your own."

"I——" Dropping my normal voice, I sent it shrilling in a high-pitched noise. "How can you say that! You know full well I would not risk my child's life for my own."

"You should have gotten out of the box."

"Hardly, not when he's sat with his big backside on its surface."

"Excuses!" Grabbing some of the bedding to fold into neat squares, slamming shut the lid in anger, fuelling up by his inaccurate thinking. "Why don't you just admit it, you are only in this for yourself?"

"In this for myself, everyone except me has been in it for myself."

Lifting my head high, lips parted in a pout, eyes narrowing, struck with rage. My dark eyelashes narrowing down my green eyes shining in the glint of irritation, feeding on passionate indignation.

"Pfft. Selfish enough to make me appear a fool."

"Selfish enough to care about my own life. After watching someone I love die before my eyes."

"Just throw in the towel already." Scrunching up the blankets, a smug smile crept onto my lips, biting my bottom lip down to listen to the rest of his ridicule. "The only thing you have lost is pride, you have no husband because you never did."

Pushing the blankets into his chest, thundering past him pressing my forefinger under my eyelid to catch a stray tear, switching up how he would see me. No longer riled up, most definitely cut to shreds, shattering in a million pieces of glass. All that had been, all that had once become a lifestyle, robbed from me in a matter of hours, everything seemingly on the up. Standing atop the brow of a hill, watching over everyone, to be pushed down into a ditch, sinking below levels. Putting pressure under my nose to stop my sniffles, eyes tightly squeezing together, holding back most of the waters, a few escaping over my cheeks. Blurry visions of Theodore coming through my pupils, tears welling in large amounts inside my puffy eyelids, preparing to make me weaker.

"He is dead! Paradise was supposed to be on the other side, instead I have been thrown into obtrusive obstacles, nobody even bothering to notice how I truly feel."

"You are a very good actress, Lucy, maybe you will provide us entertainment."

"The entertainment will be me beating *you* into an oblivion."

Bitter in resentment, I took myself from his company, only deepening desires to respond in a wry style, never wanting his feet treading all over the corpse I would become. It had been far too long to be away from my children, I knew nothing of where they were, not a single soul indicating to me where their beating hearts pounded. How many chances would I get to stand, in the breeze, alone? Next to none. Rarity, priceless, full of worth. Intensely inhaling air through my nose, reluctantly releasing it from my lungs out of my mouth second upon second. A single destination in mind. The bow of this ship. Aiming around to the right, checking the area in which this mysteriously voiced man had made his exit... how did he get off the boat? Peculiarities hovering around this cloaked person, getting away on my own was certainly the best way out. Holding the barriers stopping me from falling over the edge, stopping me from all kinds of ideas floating around. Do you ever hear something, someone's voice, you know who it is... it plagues you in your mind, over and over like a prayer repeating itself in one's mind until the torture? Yes. Not a single memory coming into my thought process, the name buzzing on my skin as though I could almost taste it! Sinking my hand back inside my dress pocket, one of my hands falling upon the letter my mother had written, imagining how she would sound in real life. Father had given me photos to remember her by, each of them individually different through each stage of her growing up, every feature captured within these small frames of mind. Taking the letter's envelope back out of its hiding, an icy wind blew from the skies, each brush taking a strand of hair out from behind my ears, forcing me to tuck it behind again. Reopening the flap, a small collection of photos remaining behind the neatly tidied away letter. Randomly, I had chosen the photo with a different shade of white to the other… rather pristine for our time. Hmm. Such shiny, glossy paper, clear… unreal. Lightly touching the surface, my fingers barely held it, just as you would with a sacred artefact from ancient history.

"Interesting…"

Closely, my eyes scrutinized the surroundings of Mother, in a wood. Dark. Darker than any night I have ever seen. There was one thing I could see. Make no mistake. Tear. Cracking out in the corner of my eyes, utter trepidation. Captured clearly by the artist, my mother standing happily in the wood surrounded by other men and women, smiling as gleefully as I had ever seen through photos, always having company. From all I had been able to see, people loving her so dearly, a woman having a high reputation about town, liked by most… if not all the people surrounding her. I had only ever seen my father be the second man in any of the photos. No other woman, man, child had been seen in any of the others… each of them disappearing you might say as the years and decades passed on from her life. Why? Proud expressions they wore, a completion of a task, a goal set by the group. Mother stood strong, her legs shoulder width apart… a heavily cloaked face with wide eyes glaring straight through to the artist, a barely visible smirk he caught far too easily for me. Where was Father? Without any more hesitation, I put the photo back into its place, flicking through the other… one after the other, scanning for signs of a man.

"Father, Father, Father, Father, Father, Father." Taking the other photo, shaking my living soul, here it was in my hand once again! Why was I doing this to myself? "No, Father…"

Out of all of the photos, Father was not in this one, his disappearance was uncanny, unsettling to me quite obviously as it would to anyone else. Hang on. I might have forgotten to mention…

"Lucy!"

"Yes… who is it?"

Heaving out a large breath, I wished to speak with nobody but the thoughts competing in my mind, leaving nothing to anyone else. Burdening nobody with my conspicuous findings.

"It's me, Jonathan."

"Oh…"

Going back around, I held my back against the chilly railings, my hands holding the barriers still… just differently. Jonathan's eyes were running wild, wide, something he had seen. Why he had come to me? Would he tell me? Not unless I pried.

"Wide eyed. That cannot be good."

"You see straight through."

"If I did not, then I would be informed a lot less."

"Have you seen Theodore?"

"Pfft! Him!" Squealing with a high-pitched voice, the mention of his voice making my blood boil.

"I saw him a few moments ago, he should be in the room where I slept."

"No. We have checked the *entire* ship, he is nowhere to be seen."

"Well… maybe he has gone for a swim… the waters look

pretty nice."

"Not the time for sarcasm!"

"Now you are shouting."

"State the obvious."

Rolling his eyes into the back of his head, I saw the opportunity to make a little comment of my own. "If you do that any more, they will be stuck in the back of your head."

"Yes! Precisely, why you should stop."

"I know…"

"Back to focusing! You are not helping matters, you are going to help me find him."

"I see I have no choice."

"Good! Then you can tell me all you are keeping from me."

"I am keeping nothing—"

"Tell me later, save it all for after. Over a nice glass of wine, I brought a stock."

"Of course you would." Snickering under my words, he did not appreciate my being derisive.

"Let us find him… Captain."

"Shh! You know I am not the captain, it's Christopher."

"It was only a joke!" Belting those words out of my mouth, his eyes speaking volumes… 'shut up'. Stifling a laugh, covering up how many more bitter comments I had been aligning to our conversation… such as his hair.

"Now what!"

"Your hair…" Cut short, he never had it long, it was neat and tidy in a ruffled-up style… a little more ruffled than I had ever seen. Sweeping aside Theodore's actions, Jonathan brought out another side of me, a side I had never been willing to visit after being married. The idea I developed, creating me into a woman that needed nothing more than love, my mouth zipping up to avoid arguments with William.

"What is wrong with my hair?" Huffing, sighing, enraged with me. "Lucy!"

"It's a little messy, shaggy, untidy—"

"Yes, yes, I get the picture." Putting his fingers through his locks, straightening it back, pulling some out of the way of his face. "Happy?"

"Much better! You look a lot less like a wet dog."

Heartily laughing, I made my way past him towards the room where I had been hiding, making small eye casts to the sea, checking to see if anyone was watching. No way, on this earth, would I be casual with my life, giving it up to somebody ready to take away the last seconds of my life. Harsh, had I been towards Jonathan, at first his actions deflecting on me deeming deplorable, irresponsible pushing me against the rough railings, one inch further and the sea would have swallowed me whole, giving no mercy despite any amount of begging on my part. Stories have been told after incidents on the sea, those who have heard them are left with haunting memories, terrorising their nights, sleeping in their arms. Each memory begs a different return, depending on the tale, you revisit that time differently in comparison to anyone else. More often than not, comments are made about there being 'no survivors', how can they possibly know, without being a survivor themselves? Honestly, people really do make me question their intelligence. So gullible. Over the last few years, I have seen changes slowly developing into a modernised day, I have heard of new prospects for the future, plans ahead. Still, there has not been any mention as to dealing with this illness spreading across the entirety of Britain. With regards to other respectable countries, continents, islands in the world, barely entire stories have been given just to keep us from general wonderment. Having nobody who tends to go abroad, away from here to deliver goods between ports, not much has been fed into our imaginations. That is one of the reasons others have fed us with their personal opinions instead of pure facts. Classic.

"Always finding things wrong with other people."

Exhaling deeply, his arms slung down his sides, draining the life he once had in him, the energy he had to hold me up. Now it was my turn. A favour.

"Will it make you feel better, if I apologise?"

Pursing my lips into a straight line, folding in slightly becoming wet on my tongue. "Maybe." A smile. Simple, but effective. "It might make me feel a little better." Jonathan's tone sounded a lot like a whimpering child, giving their sweetest voice to accomplish all that they were wishing their very own parents to do.

"Okay, okay, I am *so* sorry Jonathan."

"So you should be."

Silence fell between us, listening intently to a voice in the distance, it gradually made itself known.

"Help!"

Violent screams, screams of a man I was wishing this upon embedding within the thought process inside my body after hearing all he said to me, accusing me of certain things that he was incorrect in accusing me of. Theodore. Not that I wish someone to be tortured, nor brutal inflictions on their skin, scarring them for the rest of their lives... truly a wrong conclusion to make of me. Theodore may have told me some things my ears would never want to hear, my heart to feel, my head to process, my body to act. When you act, you may or may not regret the certain things you were wishing to happen to that person. If you ever feel that way, take a leaf out of my book, now regretting the way I feel towards Theodore only ever wanting him to know how awful I feel. Maybe he would feel the exact same as well, after each of the things he chose to offend me with — his weaponry.

"Lucy, is that what I think I heard?"

"If it is, stop standing here talking to me."

"Ah… yes!"

Putting his finger into the air, pausing for a moment considering his next move, turning his heels to the direction of the cry, the stern where a British flag protruded, where the shrills emanated from. Expecting our lives to at least become slightly less stressful, without all these issues taking place. Clearly not anticipated. Certainly not correct in beliefs. Our eyes scattering to the floors, to any cracks and crevices where he might be trapped, any holes in the flooring where he could either be hiding or forced down after protecting me. Jumping our eyes to each other, our attentions drawing straight to the real edge of the stern, a much sharper edge. Oh… not what I was expecting.

"Theodore!" My cries, my hand slapping onto my mouth gaping wide with jittery breaths juddering out. "How did you get there!"

"How else do you think, Lucy? Help me out!"

"Who did it, should be the most important question."

Remembering that he could not see me, my stance, my posture was wasteful. Why did I keep needing such a sassy attitude towards him, his back was being poked and prodded by sharp edges of wood, engraving his body with a mark.

Theodore's chest heaving out in a failing attempt of relieving pressure, the sharpness wedging itself into his skin which kept refusing to be pierced or bleed for anyone or anything. Two ropes had been tied around him, one around his waist and chest, the other binding his legs and ankles together. My mind made itself over, having an opposition with Theodore seeming to be the failing option in our moment right now. In the long term it would be ill fitting having only a limited amount of people to associate with, enemies would not end up in a good place... side taking, death making, heart breaking, life changing. William... Thedore has started to remind me of him, when he was being brutally tortured there was no choice at all, his death was nigh, Theodore's death might have been on the cards, especially if the murderer held the aces of the deck. Boom! Everything would be over in one shot, one stab, seconds of strangulation. If none of those things happened and we had never found him, starvation, thirst, weariness would have killed him before anyone else. After all had been said, all had been done, I saw no reasons to remain in opposition with one another, our lives depending on us remaining civil, at least for now. The foreseeable future was nothing but a blur in my mind, surviving on an uninhabited island, stuck to slim pickings. Needing to keep as one.

"Lucy! Help me, would you?"

"Oh, yes!"

Holding Theodore underneath his armpits, using just the strength of my arms, the little resting crevice on the opposite side to my elbow keeping him upright while Jonathan made his way to untie him from captivity.

"Who did this Theodore? You never answered our question."

"I owe you no knowledge of my own."

"Deep blue sea… swimming with the little fish, appealing? Right?"

"Okay, okay. You have gotten your point across."

"Answer me then. Who did this to you?"

"Take one guess."

"There is no time for guessing when he could be back any—" Heaving out, a weight dropping onto my arms, half of his bonds being untied, my arms shaking violently, not being able to hold him. Do not drop. Do not drop!

"Hurry!"

"Surely, I am not that heavy?"

"Well, it certainly feels like I am carrying a horse in my arms."

"Charming. You know exactly how to make a man feel worthy."

"You certainly know how to blame other people." He didn't speak after that, no little comments here and there to deny his doing so.

"Why did you feel the need to speak to me the way that you did? You knew full well what was happening, how could I?"

"I—"

"The man who always has answers, has none. What a surprise?"

"Lucy. Are you listening?"

"Yes."

His voice became unsteady, suddenly overwhelmed with emotion, there was something surprisingly sincere inside each word.

"Do you realise that I was never intending to hurt you?"

"Well, it hurt me, how else do you think I would feel?"

"Wait... let me rephrase." I gave him the silence he wanted, I deserved to know his reasoning. "Do you realise I never wanted to hurt you? It came out that way, at that point in time. Things always sound a lot different inside my head."

"Yes." Deeply feeling the truth behind the tale, understanding what he was feeling inside. I had been in his position before, just different circumstances. A reassuring nod from Jonathan told me he was able to remember my past, refusing to bring it up, knowing the ruin it would bring me.

"It never works, does it?"

"No."

"This time it will."

"All done!" Jonathan gave notice to the fact he had finished his job to save Theodore, helping me heave his body above decks.

"I have got it from here."

We let Theodore get himself back up after managing a grip on the railing, careful to not puncture any more areas of skin with the long pieces of wood predominantly sticking out. "This time it will work..." As fast as a click of the fingers, completely changing my approach, especially with the experiences I had been subjected to. "What is the point in holding a grudge? They only make those who are enslaved to them far more depressed than those dead in the grave."

Giving me a laugh, I took it for granted that he was happy by deciding to forgive him... was I happy that I forgave him? Was I lucky forsaking his laugh as a good sign? Each of his hands placed on the side of my shoulders, giving them a reassuring squeeze.

"You have a good heart."

"Ah. Now… you owe me."

"With what shall I repay, your highness?"

"Bowing before me as though I was a queen." Tapping his shin with my foot as a blush colour lifting to my cheeks, shyly grinning to the floor. "Stop it."

Incandescent was the smile, lifting my cheekbones higher with ease. Forgiving a person whether or not you want to, it's your choice, sending this adrenaline rush of goodness well into you. A magical spell, transforming your movements to a hop, skip, jump in the air, rigid on fluffy clouds. If only that was real.

"Okay, okay. Well, Lucy, how do I repay you?"

"Where are my children? It has been over a day and I have not seen, nor heard them."

"About that…"

"Stop joking! It is no joke to me, where are they?" Narrowing my eyes, squinting in the direction of Jonathan. "Where are they Jonathan? Come on, speak up, you need to start giving me information. I helped you *both*. Help. Me."

"I know nothing, Lucy." Awkwardly laughing knowing how I could see straight through his pretence. "Seriously, I have no information."

"What is that in between your fingers?"

Tightly between his fingers, a piece of fabric had been torn from a piece of clothing, an odd beige that I had seen before on the clothes that my children had been wearing as we arrived. Just last year, we figured that enough money had been saved up to get her son a special garment to wear for outings and occasions, he always wore it for less important events, wearing it down to a rag, appearing as it did at this point in time. Muddied, dirtied, holes in the elbows where he had been leaning on the dinner table, out on the rocks by the sea looking over the world as though he had the trident of Poseidon — he wanted to be Poseidon. Ruler of the sea, master of all those continually sailing on its desirable surface.

"This?" A puzzling look towards me, giving his intentions entirely, not even bothering to examine. Brushing onto the floor, I knew it was futile picking it up off the ground, the wind taking it away far too soon for me to be able to examine its properties. "How did that get there?"

"You know exactly how, Jonathan."

"Come on, it's probably from the sacks in the storage compartment, we had a right job trying to sort it out."

"You try to fool me. You cannot fool a fool such as me, I am a fool for ever believing you because you know exactly where Edward is, you refuse to admit it? How lonely must it be? Knowing what has happened."

"Nothing has happened, Lucy, that piece of fabric could have been any old person's rag."

"Yet you just told me it was from the sacks down below. A liar. That is what you are."

"Wrong. Wrong. Wrong."

"That piece of fabric in the centre from in between your fingers came from a garment that my son wears, I know so. That had been a gift to him, we had saved up to buy him such a fine linen and now you have torn it. So I ask you again. Where is my son?"

"Your son…"

"I didn't say daughter, did I?"

"No… let me finish."

"Okay then. I am all ears."

"After you collapsed, Christopher came back to us, with

news. As you can imagine it did not look good, especially with a large, bloodied gash across his forehead, bruises on his arm... chest. Everywhere." Pausing, this story had no good ending, who was I to rush for answers? To him, just telling me was a pain. "For some reason, he recalls more than needs be, he remembers things from other people's past... unexplained. Each time we speak of you, a memory from someone else's life of you returns."

"Why were you speaking of me anyway?"

"Well, Theodore had to explain to him what happened before you collapsed. He cut us off before we continue. When we fail to mention your name, he asks who, and he starts."

"That hasn't answered my question."

What else could I feel right now other than fear? A common saying that many use consists of something similar to these words my father told me. 'Do the thing you fear to do and keep doing it... that is the quickest and surest way ever yet discovered to conquer fear.' Unintentionally, I mumbled the words underneath my breath, barely audible to anyone else. "Which question?"

"There is no point beating around the bush, Jonathan."

A warm arm wrapping around my shoulders, pulling me closer, Theodore's strong muscular arm was pulling me closer, he held me tightly to his chest. I understood by both of their quiet, subtle movements and actions I needed to brace myself for the apparent predicament I was to be placed in. Jonathan shifted on his feet, Theodore's grip tightening with each passing second.

"Once..." Clearing his throat a few times, giving himself the sickening push to tell me. "Once Jonathan had finished with his rants, his memories, others memories. We led him away to his quarters so he was able to wash the cut on his forehead, it seems that after we returned, we had not been alone. Everyone aboard the boat turned in when Jonathan returned, dusk had fallen on us all."

"Do you want me to tell the rest?"

A slight nod, my head changing position to look straight into Theodore's deep eyes… if it had never been for my husband having just died, I could have fallen straight into Theodore. You can easily see inside him, if you are fortunate enough to see through the walls he builds, I had been let in through the high gates building around him. All that was left was to map and explore his thoughts, feelings, emotions, past.

"As we returned, it soon became apparent something was not correct. We saw Lily asleep, no sign of Edward." Brushing some of the strands of my hair, his heavy, warm breath on my forehead. "On the front decks he held your son over the edge, your son refused to scream, so it seemed. If we came any closer he would have dropped him over the edge, I am sure you would rather know that there is a possibility of him being alive rather than knowing he was definitely gone from your life."

"Where… where is he now?"

Tears, uncontrollably, burning like acid rain. Harsh realities, 'fear is pain arising from the anticipation of evil'. Whoever lies behind that cloak deserves to be shot, for all he is putting me through. Of all people on this boat, I was the one being tormented. Being anticipated under the influence of others' evil, truthfully, he must know me very well to seek me time and time again. He had failed, why? All in all, the only reason in reality for me to carry on fighting would be to see a reunion with my son. Before, in my younger years, I had been put under the heavy weight of others' words that burnt, tore, took me apart. Causing me to become a person not even able to make the smallest of decisions, fearing the consequences. It is one thing not wanting the consequences, but, I never even decided to imagine what they would be. Looking back over everything, I realised that imagining the worst helps, in some cases more than others. To find my son across these vast seas would be impossible, near enough impossible. He is my son, he is my boy, I will miss him for as long as I do not have him by my side… he has a strong will, in comparison to any witnessed in my lifetime, making testimony. That heart he possesses will live on in my heart, he will live on in this world, I might be able to find him.

"We do not know Lucy…"

For a moment, they let me stand in an unbearable silence, necessary, intolerable.

"Make way!" Christopher patrolled by the wheel, hands in the air, clearly making known to us all. "Paradise!"

"This is not paradise." Faintly trailing away, both full lips parted slightly looking out to the sea, wind rushing to my eyes. Unmistakable tears had formed to the sizes of raindrops. "How do you expect me to live?"

"You will… I will make sure that you do."

Pulling my head into his chest, I cried until there was nothing left. There was a point. Someone skilled at murdering others, harming others without any knowledge had to be coming for me… so, I had spoken something valid mumbled under my breath, followed by hard sobs.

"How do you expect me to live?"

Chapter 5
They are both gone, now I must.

A heartbroken soul, with only a daughter left in her life, a whole bunch of situations to deal with, no one to turn to. Here she was, coming to me. Yes, what I had decided to tell her was entirely wrong on another level. Can you blame me? Everything going on in her life will tear her down, all she needed was her last child to leave her, one was enough. With every second she was taking, her right hand, fiddling with the ring on her left, plain and simple holding far too many memories to cling onto. Island, an island, one island, one chance. With only a three-year difference, understanding her ever so slightly, just not enough as I would have liked to. Behind her strength, with her weaknesses drifting around, times when her life shaped who she is into a woman having greater power than she realises. Not ordinary, not typical, desirable. Nestling into my chin, comforting her, her tears soaking my shirt in patches. Others would have minded, I did not, she needed a shoulder to cry on. At some point in life we have all needed somebody, now she needed me.

"How do you expect me to live?"

"Shh." Gently swaying her in my arms from side to side, her head embedding under the crook of my neck a lot tighter so she would feel safe. "I told you. No. I promise you, I am going to protect you, trust me."

An insignificant, ever so slight unnoticeable nod, giving me all I required, an acceptance that she trusted me with her life. Realistically I was a young boy, an adult nonetheless, these responsibilities I was giving myself might end in me falling to rock bottom as she stays on the shore. I would not mind dying, knowing I did what I could to help her.

"Theodore! Theodore!"

Pulling her behind me, her hand clung onto my right sleeve peeking around the corner to see who was calling, her silent retreat. Braveness. How bold she can be, how in all truthfulness she will tell you exactly what she thinks of you, what she feels. Shyness, watching her back away from another person that she had never met striking me as surprising. In light of her circumstances a lot less prying, far less noses sticking in, people involving themselves in affairs not of their own, making this ordeal far greater than need be. I was caring for her.

"Mother."

"Son! Where have you been?"

Darting from the staircase, her icy hand brushing the gash across my brow, seeing the dried-up blood along my eyeline, I would never tell her the happenings around here. With so many people, this news, this new story to tell would float around so, where was the point in causing so much anxiety amid us all?

"Nowhere. Where else could I go?"

"You have obviously been somewhere! Clean yourself up a little... have I not brought you up any better than this?"

"I will clean it up in a moment."

"Now!"

"You have got to stop telling me what to do! I am a grown adult."

"One day you will come to me for relationship advice, especially with the girl hiding behind you."

Lucy tore her hands into my skin, unable to know what to do, gripping tighter to my sleeve, pinching my skin a little, a lot, without realising it. "Ah. Lucy, this is my mother, Beatrice." Wiping away her drying tears from her eyes, Lucy came out from hiding to greet Mother with open arms. After all the crying that she had done, it was surprising how easily she could hide her feelings from others.

"Mrs Chamberlain, it is lovely to meet you."

"What is your name, my dear?"

"Lucy, Lucy Berrel. Well, no longer a Berrel, my maiden name will return."

"Oh, why ever so, divorce? That is never permitted."

Drifting away from Beatrice's glare, her supposed 'smile' stopping when she looked when entering my arms for refuge against the storm.

"Mother, do you really have to ask such a question."

"I only ask, you know how girls can be. One must check."

"One must check in less abrupt ways. Her husband just *died.*"

"How terrible! Did your physician tell you how he died?"

Fire burning embers within her, an inferno of flames crackling, heat rising to her face. Blazing embers highly creating inside of her heart. I knew how he died. Lucy knew far much more than I knew, having seen the destruction of his skin.

"One must check on his body, should they not. Torn apart, brutally ripped him to shreds by a man we knew well enough to not have a ravaging animal inside of him. So, why don't you tell me now. Is it divorce?"

"Well—"

"No! No. Before presuming people's circumstances, realise that they may have witnessed certain events they wished never to see. I wished to never have to think of anything that I have seen."

"If you want me to apologise, there is nothing that can make me."

"Did I ask you to apologise? No. I spoke nothing of the sort."

"Well then what do you want me to do, remember your respect girl."

"Do you call your son a boy?"

"No, he is a man."

"Then you should call me a woman. I gave birth to two lovely children, I have been married, I am also three years older than your son. Think about that."

Wow! Facing up to a woman with such class as my mother has… never have I seen someone confident enough to take her on as an opponent in word play, let alone managing to interrupt her at points to make her own quite clear. Applaud the woman. Jonathan stood still taking it all in. After a little while, he left, seeking no information from the heightening argument between them both. Why leave now, all of a sudden, it was just getting interesting. Hmm. Storming off, a sense of remorse continuing to linger in the air as Lucy left us in stunning silence. In some ways she had the ability to create an atmosphere, leaving in abrupt ways without appearing stupid, in a sulk or mood. Dominance. Being a man, I was to assert dominance over women as society decided to have it. For me, I could never see me ever being allowed, given the opportunity to assert this kind of dominance I owned over her, unlike other women. Differences, stark differences, mad enough to suggest I would never be competent enough. Without taking the wrong impression, men are leading into a world of patriarchy, always being the head of the household in any marriage, taking the headship, the *crown* as it could be likened to. Lucy had the crown in any relationship, with it she was a queen of her own destiny. Barging her shoulder heavily into my mother's, her balance taking a knocking, pushing her into a stumble, precipitously requiring not a single eye backward.

Each of my hands coming together applauding the show put on I had not paid a penny for. Although, the truth of it all had been the wrong sort, still so right in all truth, honesty.

Beatrice, my mother, has been put in her place for the first time in her life, the vulgar inquisitiveness in other people's lives appalling me, making me ashamed to be living under father's name that she proudly bears. His wife, I her son.

"How rude is that girl! You do not even think that was the slightest bit intriguing, do you?"

"By now, Mother, with all due respect, it is time you realised it is wrong to stick your nose where it does not belong."

"Now you! Know your place, young man."

"I know my place, Mother, do you know yours?"

Walking away from her, Lucy claiming somebody to be with her, there was nothing more she was depriving herself of other than comfort, care from another human being to allow her understanding, patience, a listening ear. Where was she? The vision of mine becoming blurry, focussing on that of finding Lucy, bumping shoulders with a man quite evidently.

"Oh, excuse me."

"Theodore!" Father. Shouting at me, not the right voice

either. Quite frequently using the power of his voice to show me a different passion in his heart, shaking the bones in my body, as if I was lacking in something, weakening bones.

"What has happened with your mother?"

"Off, again." Blushing with rose tints from the cold, heat of rushing mixing, gathering on my cheeks. "Pried her nose into someone else's business, *presuming* incorrectly. The poor girl lost her husband to a terrible death…"

"…thought she had a divorce."

"Exactly!"

"Well then, where are you going in such a hurry?"

"To find her, she is not too good recently."

"Why ever so?"

"Lost her husband, to death, and now her child has been taken. Did Jonathan or Christopher fill you in?"

"That was her child! Poor woman, I will warn Beatrice to stay away from her."

"No, I would leave it, Lucy is a strong woman."

"She must be terribly devastated. Just having lost her husband, lost her child, lost in an argument with Beatrice… what a life."

"Lucy did not lose, surprisingly."

Clearing my throat, Father has not seen anyone in his lifetime manage to wind their way out of argument with my mother, 'dragon lady', as she was most commonly known in the town. Talk to her, your head will be burnt by her 'dragon rage', I was her baby dragon, always *listening* to her beckon and command. Everything she asked for she got without even needing to tell us.

"We have a new 'dragon lady' I will want to meet her—"

"She is not a 'dragon lady'." Rolling my eyes with

reasonable control, feeling just like Lucy. Picking up on her little habits. "Absolutely nothing like a 'dragon lady'."

"Defending her." Raising his eyebrows to me, he saw right through me as if I was transparent. "I reckon you like her. You need not try to defend that, you like me telling you so."

"No!"

Objecting his point, I was not about to throw my unnecessary feelings on her. "What I was trying to say is that you *need* to be there for her. Do not do anything stupid to the new 'dragon lady'."

"She is not a dragon lady!" Thumping my arm with his fist, I had to realise he was kidding with me, reciprocating the thud on him, slightly awkwardly. "I knew that."

"Bet you did, Theodore. Go on then."

Smirking to myself, I went on my way to find her. Wiping away the smile as I descended with ease, holding onto the barrier with the stinging pain still in my back after having a sharp, wooden, spear-like length immersed into me.

"Lucy! Where are you?"

Despite not a single answer from her, hushed voices partly emerged from the deafening cries in the undertone of peace. Here, where we were right now, peace had never become something capable to live with. Just around the corner, a lamp hanging on the wall on a long protruding lampstand to direct the light. Whoever had put it there was not me, it was not Lucy, nor Jonathan for I sighted him on deck before making my way below. So. Who remained? Christopher!

"Listen, Lucy, I hate having to keep up this fake appearance, it is the only way."

"You have other options, do you not?"

"I am only allowed to tell you the truth, once and for all.

Then we both have to act in a way that gives way to no suspicion at all."

"You go back to revealing facts about my life before marriage, everything that has happened to me."

"The big curtains reveal, some might say."

"*His!* Big curtain reveal."

"Yes."

"Give me the truth, once and for all. Tell me I deserve it."

"So, he thinks just that."

"Fair enough. In return?"

"When we get to the island, every night it is your duty to sneak away, for a purpose I have no heads nor tails what it will land on. It just becomes a must, each night you forget, say goodbye to one of us."

"You do know."

"Hmm."

"Since you do, why not give me a taster."

"You're in, do you want me to tell you?"

"What else would it be."

Rolling her eyes towards him, her typical trait… wait, thinking of this in a different light. Was she truly upset, resting her head on my shoulders? Right now, this nonetheless looking envious, scheming, planning, plotting. Back and forth, back and forth. My mind racing forwards and back, second by second wondering if this was truly right, to eavesdrop on everything he was about to tell Lucy. Considering how discreet, yet indiscreet the arrangement was, their wits had not been very wise, for they had not been able, nor taken any notice of my head peering around to get a better viewing of the next proceedings. Foolish. Maybe, after all this effort, I should stay and listen. It would most certainly be their fault to not be so indiscreet, to not be so stupid.

"Sit down."

Christopher gestured for her to sit on the crate just opposite where he was sitting, she obliged his offer, crossing her legs over neatly, ready to listen with an unexplainable ease.

"He told you, did he, what he was planning to do with my son?"

"Everything will become clear as I tell you, I ask that there be questions after. There is limited time to tell you everything, someone may hear us… a hunch I could call it, gives me reason to fear that there is one among us."

"Search them!"

"No, there is no time. It could be that they have gone to alert the crew of this."

Putting her finger in the air, they each looked up to the tip. "No one is talking at all, just the mother and father of Theodore. Calm talking."

"Here we have it."

"Now you are time wasting."

"After you had your fall backwards, I chased him to the deck because I thought I knew who he was. Sorry to say, it was never for your or anyone else's benefit."

"And, you discovered something?"

"To you, he is more than an enemy, a relative. As it happens to be."

"I knew I recognised that voice."

Standing up suddenly, jolting my head backward, to avoid detection, I did not want them to know I was here. Still.

"He is your father, Lucy."

"Father…"

"Yes, your father. Your mother escaped, when you were

young… what is it she told you?"

"I had a ticket to a better life, away from this world."

"That was entirely true."

"What was it she found? Where is my son!"

"Edward is safe, Lucy. Your father took him in such a manner because he wanted to take you as well, there is no way he could save us all. Just you and your daughter."

"To where?"

"Beyond this world we appear to be living in, there is a place, beyond these fake lies."

"Fake…"

"Yes! He would not reveal to me the reason as to why we still have to be in here, why we had to suffer. Things happen for a reason. If there is one way, one time that you can save us all with an effort, I pray you do."

"How am I supposed to do that then?"

"Meet him. Every night after we are all sleeping, I am to remain awake. As a promise to me, I am to remain awake. You return safe and sound, all is good. You do not return, he will be forced to take us with him."

"If I choose to go with him?"

"Without your daughter, or with?"

"In either situation."

"There will be no harm done, it is your decision, Lucy. Stay with us, prove your loyalty. Leave us, prove your inner evil."

"Manipulating me to stay. Why?"

"He said—"

"What does it matter what he says!"

"Shh. They will hear us!" Christopher clearly wanted no one to hear their conversation. I took this as my signal, carefully listening to the remnants of what I allowed myself to hear. "I see the way you look at him, I see the way he looks at you. Do not deny to me that you are forcing yourself to move on. From William."

"What else do you expect of me? To stay lonely forever, to mourn, cry day in, day out, like a woman subjecting herself to the pitiful state *he* wants me to be in! Would you rather my head resting on your shoulder begging for comfort? For sympathy?"

"Remember, he is your father, not the enemy."

"How do you know if I even like him at all? People can never read me."

"Yet, your father has seen only glimpses, and he knows how much you have started to feel for Theodore."

Gravely, my feet stopped in their tracks, no longer wishing to walk away as these affairs started escalating, my name thrown into their topics of conversation.

"Pft! Theodore, Father, what do either of them know?"

"Thedore knows nothing, yet."

"You mean what, by that, exactly?"

"In your mind, you have scripted what you are to tell him. Whatever it is you have planned, I know something else. He came down here earlier, looking for you, he is gone now, aren't you, Theodore?"

Calling out for me to respond, he must have had a sixth sense that I was among them both.

"I knew someone was here!" Directly projecting her feelings outwardly, feeling her triumphant display of her correct notion. "Theodore... did you hear everything?"

"No!" Immediately rejecting the proposition, despite the full truth of it. Surely, she would trust me. Fire my shot. If it misses. Then I shall admit. "I just came down to check on your whereabouts."

"Why?"

"You *were* very much upset, before everything."

"I was most certainly not."

Even though we had been talking, I remained hidden behind the wooden wall of the corner they had been chatting in, just in case my face would give me away in any kind of way. "You were, Lucy, why do you pretend?"

"If Lucy was upset, then she would have told me so!" Christopher took control of our conversation, wanting nothing more than to get a word in edgeways after being ignored for what must have been a while in his eyes, short in mine.

"Just show yourself, Theodore, you have never struck me as a quiet man."

"Then you would be correct." Striding forwards, turning myself back around to get closer to where they sat, my head emerging around the corner. Initially, it was only my head they could see, until my entire body came around, sitting down on a crate near them with the heat of the lamp on my face. "How lovely and cosy, it seems you are no longer revealing inner truths about Lucy, you are both in front of each other, what changed?"

"Since you heard our conversation, there would be no need to repeat it, others may hear."

"Hmm. I get your point."

"How long have you been here, listening to us?"

"Pretty close on your heels, soon after Lucy left me, *very upset.*"

"You did not have to follow me. I can cope on my own."

"Considering I was coming to *comfort* you, after crying

behind me and on my shoulder. That would give me reason enough to think you needed someone there."

"Quite clearly not now."

"Shut up! Both of you." Christopher's eyes widening with concern at the heavy footsteps of people's feet coming down the main stairway to the lower decks. "Nobody knows anything."

"Lips sealed."

"Same here." Chiming in my comment after Lucy who eyed me gratefully, a minute crack of a smile forming in the corner of her mouth. She must not have been too mad, surely?

"Captain! Captain!"

"What is it, sailor?" Standing in an upright posture, his hands cupping together behind his back, swaying forwards and back raising himself on his tiptoes a few times.

"Tell us."

"Lucy. Get down"

"Lucy! Lucy!" Shouting as though he was trying to make an attempt to find her, spinning around on his heels to see if he could spot her. Each time, to no avail, ducking swiftly below to not be seen behind the crate. A smart move to fool the young sailor. "I *see* not a single woman looking like that of Lucy, nor holding the name of her. So. You were saying."

"We are here, Captain. We have made it to the island."

"Isla de Diseath, what a name, does it mean anything to you, sailor?"

"Not at all, Captain."

"How about you, Theodore?"

Smiling through pursed lips, it was then I realised who he was speaking to, catching me by surprise. "Oh. Do the words not strike you as being rather odd?"

"Rather odd? What do you mean, exactly."

"Island of the dead and deceit. Those two words must have been placed together for a reason, surely."

"Maybe, maybe not, it is hard to know exactly."

There have been tales of this place. A few knew, others oblivious to the dark memories of this island, each of the stories darker than the other as they develop. Do you know?

Possibly not, let me explain since it is not widely known. Around ten years ago, a mission was deployed with around one and a half thousand men across three gargantuan vessels, grand in the king's navy, pride and joy. Within this moment in time, I had only been around thirteen years old, fourteen just coming around the corner. Gentle breezes blowing mid-air, the summer heat causing quite a fuss with the locals stuffing themselves in long dresses which they often wore to cover up. Masses of heat building up around us all, becoming rather stuffy. When hangings came around considering they always seem to pack too tight for anyone's liking... apart from the locals who found joy in this occasion. Being an only child, I wedged myself in between my mother and father who watched me like a hawk, day in, day out. It was never usually my father who suppressed my intrigue in the world, it was my mother who decided to not approve on my aspirations, longings, wanting to belong to the Redcoats, have an admiral's jacket, be a hero. In time, she had given up since my father's insistence on training me in his free time, doing all he could to make a man out of me. That he did. Each of my aspirations coming from him, he did all he could for the king on his side of matters. What it was, he never kindly disclosed.

"Father! Father! There, look, there is a man crawling up the shore line!"

"Where?" His quick responses depending on the next events. *"Driver! Stop the cart, help me with the injured."*

Immediately, the driver caught wind of his words, stopping the carriage, leaving me and my mother in heightening suspense. Well, more me since she had been pondering on being late to the event I could not recall to mind. Creating a hole in his top shoulder, the wounded looking as though he had been shot, with an awful lot of blood coming from behind him to say the least. Why? That is exactly what I wanted to find out, with my inquisitive thirteen-year-old mind, I did not hesitate before leaving the horse-drawn carriage.

"Where do you think you're going. Leave your father to sort it out."

"No! He is hurt, they may need some assistance. When will you stop mollycoddling me, I am not going to be a child for much longer, you know I will do what I want to do!"

Gripping my shoulder tightly with her icy cold hand, despite the sweltering weather, I shook it off glaring deep into her eyes. *"You will end up just like him, you know that, son."*

"Like who?"

"The wounded, a bullet straight through your shoulder... if you are lucky, that is not a pirate's doing."

"Then who?"

"An assassin, have you not heard of him? He preys on the downhearted, blows the weak, murders the innocent, tortures the strong till they become downhearted, weak, innocent."

"No such person, even exists."

"Oh, why do you think I protect you, for the fun of it? Because it is known to the people they prey on..." My lips remaining sealed, no longer needing to discuss the matter with her, her eyes simply showing me she cared despite the

appearance displayed in front of others. *"Go on then, find out for yourself, speak to that man… if you think I am lying to you son."*

Placing my hand on the door handle to pull in a downwards motion, I found myself explaining the action I was about to take.

"Mother, this is not because I think you are a liar. It is for me to figure out the facts from the fiction, he will tell."

"I am certain he corroborates my story."

"That I am certain of."

Across from me, I noticed the smile on her lips, seeing that I truly believed all she was teaching me, no longer oblivious to how each second my heart began beating had not been to undermine her mothership, but to see for myself, the world. Not a story I could be told, my mind always telling me to confirm it in real life, in real time which certainly helped in my bond with my mother since it had never gotten off to the best start in life.

"Be safe!"

Nodding up and down, acknowledging what she had said, proceeding with my actions I was about to take. As soon as I stepped out, each immediate movement hesitated, turning down the pace to being so gradual it was similar to an animal observer, studying, scrutinizing, and playing the watching game. Here, in this world, right now, movements became the only think to focus on despite the anxiety squeezing inside when seeing deathly sights of attempted murder, torture and terror. Blood. Crimson, scarlet, covering beige floors, seeping into the calming blue waves, hesitating to spread into the dried-up brown coming from the injured man's shoulder, irrefutable stopping in its stream.

"Haul! Heave him out man!"

"Father!"

Samuel continued hauling him out, obviously attentive to my thoughts on this sight, especially since he wished for me to become desensitised to wounded men. Unlike the protectiveness my mother held, he wanted me to experience injury, understand the way in which a man has to fight his way through life, feel the agony people see. Would I be used to seeing injury after this? Had it been all too much? Yes. Father could never be told so, the disappointment would cover his face as blood covered this poor man's leg... his leg...

"His leg!"

"What about—"

Half of this wounded soldier's leg had been blown off, the remnants continually bleeding, covered in sand which had stuck to the sticky iron-rich bleeding around his skin having been cleansed by the sea.

"I bargain he hasn't much life left in him sir."

"Same here, Theodore, toss me your scarf."

Untying the beige scarf around my neck that mother gifted to me awhile back, hoping that it would not end up being wound around a dying man's leg, like this. Scrunching it up, I tossed it toward Father, catching it simplistically as though it was no bother, tightly winding it around the missing piece of his leg.

"Child!" Child!" Eyes vigorously opening wide, bulging out of his head, I saw the increasing concern developing within allowing myself to be drawn towards his outstretched hand soaked in blood, taking it tightly. *"Become like me, a hero, then end up in a state like me. End your life like this, it will be the most terrible mistake you can make."*

"Why?"

"There is a man out there, an assassin, have you not heard

of him? He preys on the downhearted, blows the weak, murders the innocent, tortures the strong till they become downhearted, weak, innocent. Ensure I am not forgotten in the world, for all I have done for this place... Theodore! Look at me!" Yanking me downwards, both eyes met each of his, wandering around his face where bruises stained his face alongside dirt and scars. *"Remember me!"*

Now, here I was, standing before a mast on top of the stunning beauty of a ship, eyeing the island far off, which had gorgeous golden sands, and an old church in the background with the masses of greenery surrounding it. Across a few miles of expanse, near to the old church, lay ruins of old houses on the hilltops, which we never knew existed. Everything that had happened in that one day reminding me of the position I was in now, was I to be as my mother wished, not to fight? Or to be a warrior, maybe not to the extent of a true warrior, just a hero in the navy having left... start on my own. Could that be possible? I have no idea. A dainty hand tugging at my sleeve, with a soft voice, seated next to the gentle touch of cold skin once or twice.

"Theodore. You have been standing there for ages." Stuck in a trance I could not shake off, her persistence did not waver. "Earth to Theodore! The ship has landed, made berth, however you wish to call it. Just wake up!"

Still tugging away, not so softly at my sleeve now, her impatience after what must have been at least half an hour of trying, I was still entrapped in my own thoughts without the ability to hear the surroundings vividly.

"We need to go!" Pulling me along with her, my feet staggering along. "Come... on!" Suddenly, without warning, I felt the wet wood beneath my body, waking me up promptly.

"Hey!"

"You're awake. Good."

"Good! I was wide awake, and now I am on the floor."

"I can see that." Her little snickers creating a widening smile on my face. Carefully rising back up, I brushed off the little bits of gravel, dirt, mud and any form of any other substance on my clothing.

"You will wipe that smirk of your face soon."

"Will I?"

Just a slight smirk grew on my own, comparing to how obviously she had created hers. "Yes."

"Look!"

Spinning me around, one of her icy hands on my back from the sea air, the not so vast expanse of sea lay in front of us, obviously closer to the land than I could have ever imagined it to be. Yes, I had seen it prior, my daydreaming causing me to have jumbled up memories in my mind.

"Isn't it beautiful."

Slightly dropping to the ground, her eyes darting, her smirk wiping away. Memories. Resurfacing as she contemplated everything down within, all that had become of two people she loved. William, her husband, having died in a manner nobody should have to witness or experience. Edward, her son, missing from her life, having been taken away under her nose while she slept so peaceful. The last time she would be able to. Why her?

"I wish I could say it was beautiful, Theodore. There just has to be a way out of this." Roaming to one of the bannisters, it had been a surprise that she managed to walk through a pathway not bumping into anyone.

"Lucy, we will always find a way." Meeting her by her side, I snaked my arm around her shoulder. Lucy rested her head against my shoulder, brushing her hair behind her head as it blew against the back of my neck. "You will always have me."

"What if I lose you? They are both gone, now I must."

"No! No. No. You can never leave me, as long as we have each other right now, we can pull through. Your daughter is the most important thing in your life."

Wrapping both her arms around my waist, her head snuggling to my chest where my heart pounded heavily with the worry of telling her something was wrong, upsetting her even further. No. Thankfully not. Carefully chosen words never harming her.

"Never leave me…"

"I promise, as long as I am alive."

Chapter 6
There are dead people everywhere.

Warmth. Something you can take for granted, being in a warm bed at night, serene songbirds when you rise, the echoing twit-twoos of owls outside of your bedroom window before your head rests on the pillow. Having your husband by your side to care for you, instead of rotting on the pavement... all that Lewis had left of him anyway. A traitor nonetheless, still, wonderment betrayed my ever longing to not ponder over a million different scenarios progressively becoming far darker than any thoughts I had ever known. That ease you feel, strongly sensing your child was sleeping soundly, tucked underneath his bed covers, not needing to have your mind toss and turn wanting to know exactly where he was. Just a few moments earlier, I had been informed of the precise place where my daughter was being taken care of, with Christopher's wife and children. Thankfully, she was okay. As for my son, his whereabouts were definitely unknown to me. Each second I worried myself sick, the stomach aches never ceasing to amaze me by gradually getting far more painful than any other stomach cramps I have endured. So, in an overall statement, I would say that it was not the best idea to have conjured. Theodore kept shooting me mixed signals. Some occasions he had most definitely been overly cruel, having no certain reason to be that way, throwing accusations around.

Most of the time, his kindness, good deeds and actions, comforting embrace giving me energising power to keep fighting for all the right reasons.

The world was always taken off my shoulders when his arms wrapped around them, nothing stopping me from figuring my life out. Somewhere beyond this place… as if that would all be possible. Was it truly? Here we were, sailing ever closer to Isla de Diseath with a history of terror, pain, death. Was it still the same? Tonight, it would be the first time for me to see my father again. I had been told by my grandma that he had passed away in his sleep, not allowing me to see his body. Truthfully, I now know that he left me after finding a way out of this disease-ridden world. Why did he not take me with him?

"Ugh!"

"Lucy. Lucy, are you okay?"

"Yes, I am fine, I suppose."

"Always full of questions in your mind."

"With no answers."

Grinning with no pearly whites, the grin decreasing, the sands before us so daunting. In the corner of my eye, the pupils dilating, with a tear welling in the corner. Boiling hot, rather large, blurring my vision until I was no longer able to see anything but the horror-filled look on my own face and Theodore's. Wiped. Happiness, disappeared. Joy, faded. Death, on the horizon.

"Theodore…" Gasping horrendously, everything seeming so little in comparison to my problems prior to this. "There are dead people everywhere."

"What is this sick joke!"

"I think it is not a sick joke, this is reality, a warning.

Why?"

'H. E. L. P. U. S.' spelling out the words that the littered bodies made on the ground, they had hoped that someone could help them survive. 'Help us.'

Within the centre of every letter, either side of the words and smack bang in between the two, people hung, flying in the wind with a note pinned onto their clothing. After all this time they had still remained here, everything must have gone wrong in an instant. How? All these questions swam around in my head, over and over, repeating repetitively as a fervent prayer rehearsed, practiced, made perfect till every line became so apparent that little thought was required as you felt the words dance on your tongue. Why did this happen? Why so many lives lost? Whether they had been innocent or not, they had the most precious thing taken away from them for whatever reason that may be. I am one who condemns the death of people. Especially when people revel in the murders, the cracking of necks, the decapitating of one's head. Tell me that it is correct? For the majority, many cheered, jeered, pushed the judge to execution without a fair trial, bludgeoned prisoners. In some cases, people felt the pain of someone no longer having the ability to breathe since the neck was severed, no longer having the ability to talk, no longer having a voice because they never did originally. Women know this pain unless you have been of a high stature: lady of a lord, a governor's wife, having an extreme wage or billing in your bank account. People knew. You are either respected, slightly respected, not respected at all... I had never been respected until William became my husband. William was kind, gentle, not commanding and cruel, he allowed me to have my say in the household, which in this time I was living in, seemed rather odd to many. I had often questioned if he was sweetening me up for me to do something for him in return in the future. How wrong could I have been? All he wanted for me was happiness. For us, he sacrificed his life back home.

"Help us…" This was our first night on an island unknown to us, littered with dead bodies. "Why would somebody, or a group of people, murder each other?"

"Driven mad till they turned crazy."

"What if this is going to be us, Theodore, do you really think we will turn out this way? Maybe we were better off back home, waiting for the disease to just kill us."

"Hey! Do not think like that, everything will be okay, it has to be."

"Since you heard the conversation, you will know exactly what I mean when I say that there is a supposed way out of here."

"You could be correct. We need to hold tight, for now you have me." Wrapping his arm gently around my shoulders rubbing his thumb up and down the small surface area of the back of my arm. "If you decide to seek out your father tonight, take an opportunity to look around, no one will even notice."

"Hmm. Will you stay awake until I return?"

"Of course. Why did you ask me to stay up for you, Christopher could have since he knows?"

"If you do not want to then I can always ask him." Christopher had already highlighted the fact that I had taken a liking towards Theodore, I never truly realised how anxious I was with him knowing, let alone the embarrassment it would bring. "It's okay, you need some rest." Gently smiling, I noticed no sign that he would speak. No words, nothing. Truth be told, the reasoning behind asking Theodore had been personal, feelings I never wanted to resurface. Love at first sight they say. A myth. Never happens in real life, fairy tales are just a dream, yet a nightmare when you stop reading as they stick in your mind, paved in until you want to rip out any memory of the tale. Why? It begins to influence you, requiring the love that the princess experiences, the sudden burst of song and dance, the sweet innocent jokes amid the confusion whether he likes her or she likes him. Obvious. Clear. Straightforward. They are in love with each other, the author wanting you to read on to seek the end of the fairy tale. Closing the book cover of the pages, you breathe quietly, softly, before reality strikes, a lead weight tearing you down till you scream for air. You will never be her, Prince Charming will never come. All along, since I was a young child, love was everything I dreamed of when I met William he was a rarity. After he died, I could never see me loving again, nor want to even move on so suddenly. Even with this feeling embedding into the script of my heart, its pages certainly tore into less important shreds since no one would piece them back together again. Theodore. Theodore Chamberlain. Every woman's dream, ideal man, perfect suitor. Well dressed, well spoken, rather self-important with self-respect for himself... never for me until now. I forced respect from him. Demanding it. William creating a new me, a stronger woman who fought for her rights, subtly making her way into the books of others under the title of 'one to be respected'. Theodore just accepted that he needed to make a change. So he did. For once...

"Look, forget about it, I have no idea what I am saying to people just lately."

"There is no need to care about what you say to me."

"Huh? I mean... Excuse you?"

"You need not care about what you say to me."

"Why do I not, of course I do. Respect."

"Mutual." Lightly, a smile maturing upon the pink lips in between the rosy cheeks, ever defining themselves against the pale skin everywhere else across my face. He cared. He understands. "Sometimes, Lucy, I really believe you think I am cruel."

"I have never said nor thought that."

"Is that so?"

"Maybe at one time I thought you were cruel…"

"Just once…"

Messing around with me, he knew every time he made any statement it would have to be triple checked over in my mind, everything he did I had to recheck over and over again. I was in love again, there was never any need to sit down for a minute and check because he was in my mind twenty-four hours a day, more than likely for the rest of my life. Even if he decided to not choose me, I know for a certainty he would always be in my memory, good and bad.

"Hey!" Tenuously pushing his arm away, he smiled again, what a smile that was forcing my cheeks to blush even harder. "You need to stop doing that."

"Doing what?"

"You know exactly what."

"Do I?"

"All these questions will get you no enjoyment."

"How can I get any more enjoyment when your cheeks are far brighter than any tomato I have ever seen."

"You're comparing my cheeks to a tomato!"

"No! Of course not."

"Good."

"I am comparing them to *tomatoes.*" Rolling my eyes to hide my feelings, faintly pushing my shoulder back with care not wanting to hurt me with a rough touch. "Your eyes will get stuck in the back of your head one day."

"Just the other day I had told Jonathan not to do that."

"Really?"

"Yes."

"Maybe you should take a leaf out of your own book."

"You should take a leaf out of my book as well."

"Knowing you, I must take a handful out of your book to make a sequel."

"For one. I am nothing like that. Secondly. There has already been a sequel, I shall allow you to make the third."

"Good."

"Good?"

"Yes."

"One word — basis."

"Not any more." Theodore began laughing to himself uncontrollably, realising just what I was considering. "No more eye rolling!"

"How did you know!"

"Your Lu—"

Our conversation soon came to a halt as Christopher made an announcement to everyone. Seeing the land just metres away from us, each of the bodies becoming clearer. How could we forget. Treacherous heart. Cruel human beings. If that is what killed them.

"Land!" Rousing the ship's men, women and children from their lethargic state, all coming upon the decks with their children, gasping at the bigger picture in front of us. The Isla de Diseath.

"Everyone gather your items together, be prepared, anything left behind shall not be collected! Gather everything you own!"

Just as Theodore was about to leave, I grabbed his sleeve pulling him back towards me, no longer knowing if he could hear me over the booming hustle of people running across the ship's decks, gathering anything that they could find, trying to ensure their children, including themselves, had adequate supplies.

"Where are my bags that we brought?"

"Jonathan is bringing them for you, I have just got to fetch mine."

"Oh. Let me help you then."

"No." Pointing across the ship, I saw my daughter standing there, wide-eyed looking at me longingly.

"Get your daughter, I can handle this. I can stop up for you tonight, do not worry."

"Thank you."

Miming the words upon my lips, the sudden thud of my daughter impacting on my side, her wet tears soaking up the side of my dress.

"I missed you, Mom!"

"Hey." Picking her up under the armpits, her legs wrapping around my waist, resting her little arms around my neck with her head on my shoulder. "I missed you too beautiful."

"Where is Edward?"

"Well, Edward has had to go on a little adventure, he should be back soon."

"When?" Pushing herself away from me, it seemed as though she wanted to hold me at a distance. "Is it to do with our new dad?"

Longingly, her eyes wandering, staring into my green depths with her sea blue, wanting an answer. "That man is not your new dad, you know nobody can replace him."

"In time he will."

"No of course he will not, you are too young to understand, Lily."

"Well, you read me those bedtime stories Edward does not like, with the princesses and fairies."

"About love." Nodding her head in agreement, her head headbutting my shoulder again, clutching me tighter.

"What about love? Something is bothering you."

Brushing her hair that someone had neatly braided up for her, a stray piece of hair wandering until I tucked it behind her cold ear.

"You are the princess, he is your prince, you love him."

"Oh, Lily, that is ridiculous."

Pushing herself away from me again, her eyes looking into mine with a stern look until she couldn't hold her gaze any longer, breaking out into giggles joyfully. "If you are looking for my permission, then you should."

"I should do what, exactly?"

"Marry him."

"What about your father?"

"Well, what would he want for you?"

"Lily, where has all of this come from, you being rather grown up."

"Well, Dad would want you to be happy. Right? It is all he has ever wanted for you."

"You could be right."

Squeezing me tighter into a hug, gazing out to sea with

118

my arms wrapping around her, enjoying the whipping breeze in my face protecting my daughter entirely now she was with me. After being away from her for a lot longer than I had intended, the least I wanted to do was enjoy the moments I had. If there had been one thing to take from this trip so far, it would be based on the pure and simple truth, events can happen so suddenly you never have time to appreciate what you have lost. Lily speaking the way she had done, watching her appear so grown up proving to me how William and I had brought her up correctly. She deserved the world. I would give it all to her. Still, there was a striking difference about her, a much older woman must have spoken to her, these words could not be hers. What would happen on this island? Would my daughter disappear just as my son had? Under my watch, under my gaze, nothing would happen to her. She was my last child and this could not be my last hope surely, there had to be more. However long my mind had been drifting, it must have been weighing far too long as my collar was grabbed, then moving easily to the top of my arms dragging me away from the side of the ship with my daughter running beside me. When did I drop her? Something was certainly not okay with me, every moment I was living seemed to pass by in a blur, fatigue was gaining rapidly, time slowing down to a pace which was unbearable.

"Come on! Move it!"

"I am coming... Lily?" No longer did I feel her hand in mine as she ran away from my grasp. I had told her so many times to stop running away from me, it could be dangerous upon wet decks, anything that had a slippery surface could cause her to easily fall down. Crack her head open. No decent medics or doctors around. Perfect. "Stop running!"

Thankfully, as I watched her every step, a fall never happened, with an awful amount of luck considering how clumsy she could be it was already unpredictable. "Teehee."

"Where are you going to…" Pausing my steps slightly, somebody pushing my back forwards with a large spanned out hand, my eyes unable to take off who she had run up to. "Beatrice!"

"Mrs Chamberlain if you please."

"Hmm."

"Short for words, are you?"

"Quite."

Taking a seat opposite her, my little Lily tugging on Beatrice's sleeve with vigour, her eyes longing for something she must have given to her. My young one's speech already spoke of the reality, she had been taken care of by someone much, much, older than I was. On estimate around twenty to twenty-five years older would be my guess. Tucking the edges of my dress underneath my thighs, brushing little pieces of my hair behind my ear with the apron repositioned by my hand to the front instead of on my side. Two boats on either side of the ship had been set for deployment. Upon one, all of our bags that had been brought sat tight along with two sailors. Across the other three, people piled on aboard trying their best to fit easily.

"Your daughter tells me that you were married, and she has a brother called Edward."

"Yes! Yes, that is true, was true. I really do not know any more." Waiting for her to pry any more, she stayed quiet examining me closely, my speech, my actions. "I thought you might have started questioning me by now."

"Good grief! How cynical do you think I am?"

"Never had I believed you to be cynical, that is not what I was implying to you."

"After our *last* encounter I wondered how I was being viewed, I always have to ensure my persona is maintained."

"Of course, well, I am not that kind of person. Advice on this subject would be lacking considering it is not my cup of tea."

"Argumentative with me. Still."

"Let me tell you one thing, I never appreciate nosey people."

"I could like you one day. Temper. High spirit. You move on easily, just like me."

"Far from it."

"Mom!" Lily sternly locked her eyes onto me, her childish frown forcing me to downplay my smile before a tantrum erupted. "This is Beatrice you are talking to, not a bully."

From then onwards, my mouth kept tightly shut for the sake of my daughter. Lily certainly had taken a shine to Theodore's mother, whether she knew that he was her son or not... changing my daughter's view of me had to be the last intention of mine. Despite my willingness to say nothing at all, there was certainly no escaping the fact I had not noticed where Theodore had disappeared to. Logically, he would be on this boat, with his mother.

Where was his father?

"Beatrice." Coming out a lot more-high pitched than intended, a slight clearing of the throat cleared me of such a childish voice. "Where is your son?"

"And husband for that matter."

"They should be here soon."

"You are right."

Even more daunting reticence, questions I had been meaning to ask, the obvious sort. Why could we not bring the ship to shore? How come there had been a particular drop in numbers? Since when did dead people lay on the golden beaches known for their splendid beauty now littered with blood, murdered specimens, secrets? For the most part, it appeared the next few days would be boring. Coming and going as I pleased, hard work, jobs being performed by men which was demeaning women's capability to deal with it themselves. Night time would dawn, sneaking out while others mourn the loss of money and possessions, succumbing to the dreadful state of life.

"This boat. Beatrice. What do they plan to do with it?"

"Burn it."

"Burn it! What if we need it to return? They cannot put us through this hell and not at least give us a hope of going away somewhere else."

"Oh. My mistake, it is not being burnt. Blown up is the better term to use."

"How can you be so calm in this, my mind is everywhere, not knowing which direction to turn. Who to turn to?"

"Lower down!"

Creaking mechanisms began to turn as sailors instigating the chains and ropes, lowering us down to the sea, where people would row us to the shoreline. Something was deeply unsettling me. Shaking me. Waking me. A voice. Towering over all the mumbles coming from the boats around us, not one of them being Theodore's. Why would it be? Why was he not here? My answer, never to be found unless I searched.

"Samuel! The shade of your skin is ghostly, get in!"

"It's Theodore!" Heavy breath from bodily exertion began

to show as the beads of sweat trickled from his brow to the nose bridge carefully to the neck where red blotches incriminated the fact something had happened. "We cannot find him, he is on none of the boats, nowhere below the decks, he has disappeared."

"Find him then!"

Motherly instinct kicking in, yet her body remaining grounded to her seat, not even making an attempt to move. The boat was getting further and further away from the railings.

"He is nowhere!"

"Get in!"

"Everyone, just stop shouting!" Screaming high above everyone, my voice went slightly pitchy after breaking note boundaries. "I will go!"

"No! Stay there, young miss. We do not want a woman getting hurt."

"Light her up!"

Christopher held up a torch lit ablaze with fire, preparing to light her up on the lengthy strip leading to barrels of gunpowder filled up high.

"Do not light her!"

Stumbling out of the rowing boat, Beatrice attempting to pull me back until I tightly wound my arms to the railings. "Get down! You will hurt yourself Lucy."

"Beatrice is right, get to safety!"

"This woman does not care if she gets hurt, I care about Theodore getting hurt!" Heaving my body up to the decks, stumbling upon the wooden floor in hope that Christopher had noticed and halted the flame from reaching its desired purpose. "Stop Christopher! You search the top decks. I will do the bottom decks."

"Okay."

Surprisingly he had taken orders from a woman, despite seeming to be a strong male wanting to be over a woman. He had agreed that was all that mattered — finding Theodore before this ship was ablaze, was most definitely my priority.

Chapter 7
Do not leave me!

If you care about someone, you let them go. True in some cases, when they wish to leave and you have the power to make them stay, make them change their plans to spend the remaining time with you. When you let them go, for a short while, you feel powerless, wishing you had made them stay; when you let them stay, you become racked with guilt for wrecking their hopes. Either way, you are plagued with a disease of upset, distress and guilt. Right now, I would be torn apart from facing those feelings if finding Theodore was not a success, far worse if I had just stayed inside the row boat to safety while he suffered and bore the flames. Tearing down the stairs to the first gunning deck, heart pounding, head throbbing, stomach back flipping violently tossing and turning me to hell.

"Theodore! If you can hear me answer!"

Raised voices arguing up above me, presumably Christopher and Samuel arguing over whether or not to 'Light her up!'. Evidently, it seemed quite clear to me, Theodore meant something to me. I never believed that he did, closer than a friend, best friend, always wanting more. Despite how everyone surrounding me saw this before I did, it was similar to a jigsaw, filling in the edges to shape my emotions. What now? The inside needed to be pieced together one by one until everything fitted cleanly, careful consideration and heartfelt understanding of each other. Unless I managed to help us both escape this ship, we would go down to the bottom of the sea, missing limbs, whichever way the explosion wanted us — injured, to be left for dead. Dead. Death. Those words, striking me, certainly something never washing through my body. A fear of dying.

"I'm wasting time." Gritting my teeth, I began massaging my temples until I heard a crash down below on the third deck where the supplies used to be. Rushing to the top deck without much thought, my voice squeaked in a high race to win over all the noise. "Samuel! Down here!"

"Coming! Do not blow her up!" Turning his heel towards me, Samuel jolting his head back towards Christopher again, his hand gripping his shoulder. "What is it now?"

"You have five minutes to find him, then I will set this ship ablaze. Be quick."

A simple nod sufficed as my feet continued propelling me further ahead of Samuel, realising the danger he could be, if it was him, or it was somebody else. Screams bouncing off the walls into our ears. For me, goosebumps lining the skin on my arms and legs, visibly sending shivers through my body. Some people say that it is *someone walking over your grave,* such stupidity. Many scenarios playing out inside my mind, gradually growing far more disastrous as the seconds ticked away

"Theodore!" Samuel called below the decks, entertaining more groans from below. "Theodore! We are coming, hang on!"

Plundering down the last case of stairs, Samuel pulled me behind him, gesturing to hide behind his back, the reason being someone might spot me as well as him, seeking to hurt us both. Personally, I could see where Theodore gained his protective spirit for people, not wanting them to get hurt, self-sacrificing.

"Stay behind me, the last thing Theodore would want is you getting hurt."

"Okay."

Lightly following behind him, tenderly dropping my feet onto the ground with every step I had taken, conscious not to creak any of the wooden floorboards. Down below, a cold breeze came from underfoot giving me shivers, time and time again.

"Shh." Holding his finger up to his lips, his eyes nudging towards the wall where two shadows cast. "Stay back here, if I need you I will call you."

"Will do."

For a while he went away, the things he witnessed nothing I could imagine unless I was with him personally. How Theodore was, only he knew unless I had been called up to give witness. All I wanted was to know, to understand, to feel his pain if he was in any. Giving up my life in order to save his life, younger than me by a small amount, he had already grown on me massively, unlike anyone I have ever known... apart from my husband. How the tides change. Sometimes, just sometimes, you get a feeling, an emotion inside of you that is hard to describe but it is there, inside of you. Try as you might, you are unable to shake it off, shield yourself from the shaking it causes inside of you. Pulling my hand to the left of my chest, I felt a strong pain shooting around a surface area of my chest in a circular motion, stabbing constantly into the tissue of my heart. Unbearable.

"Lucy! Come here!"

Wiping the tear of pain from underneath my eyelid, out I came from the shadows, my excitement to see him again mixing with a sense of dread. Inside of me, I knew that something was about to happen I would never wish to see.

A muffled voice from up above pushing a sense of urgency into my movement. "Take two! Light this mother up!"

"Argh!" In clear agreement, the few sailors left on board chanting and stomping preparing for the blast, nobody caring that we were down here. "Up! Up! Up!"

Repetitively they all banged on in calling growing far more aggressive. "We need to move! Lucy, come here!"

"I am he—"

"No time to waste! Help me carry him."

On the floor he lay, blood pouring out from a shot wound to his thigh, clearly in agony, unable to speak, articulate any words at all. "He... is too heavy."

Straining, my voice becoming a blur, nothing at all. Each time I tried, my arms became weaker, hoping my will to bring him to see daylight again could help us both bring him back with us.

"I will not be able to carry him on my own, his body is limp. Try again!"

"Ugh!" Stretching my arms to bring him up into the air, we managed to bring him about halfway up the staircase until my arm collapsed, repeatedly throbbing over and over. This was happening. I was losing him.

"We need to leave! The ship will explode anytime now, we need to go!"

"And leave your son! Are you insane!"

"What would he want for us, Lucy?"

"To be safe!"

"Then come with me! Now!"

"No!"

"What?"

"Leave! I will not leave his side, go on!"

"Lucy—"

"Go!" By this point I was choking up, tears, uncontrollable, heart evidently broken. Three people. Four if you include me. Dead. Dead to everyone. Lily would be better off without me, surely, she would be okay. "Tell Lily, I love her! Please! Take care of her!"

Saying nothing, Samuel continuing to go. Here Theodore lay silently next to me, there had been an attempt to stop the bleeding in his thigh through a ripped-up piece of fabric from his shirt, stuck into the wound from a rolled up trouser leg with a bullet hole through the top. "Theodore…" Sobbing into his shirt, I lay down beside him putting my arm over his chest, feeling the heavy heaves from his chest rising and falling with my head on his shoulder. "You have to wake up, open your eyes, please."

"Ugh."

A groan. He was definitely alive, barely conscious, it was all I needed as an incentive to carry on fighting for him to awaken, help us to survive. There had to be another chance, another place, another life, another way. Anything else other than the thought of dying so easily after everything I had worked hard to achieve and fight for.

"You can hear me… soon we will no longer be here. Despite how many times you would have told me to leave by now, there is no going back. Just listen. Okay."

"Mmm."

Small, barely audible, able to bring a smile despite the

doom and gloom. "I really want to say that, without you so far I could not have coped. There is definitely something I want you to know…"

"Hmm."

"I—"

Only my scream shook my body, not as violently as the plummeting cloud of smoke, burning ashes along with pieces of wood flashing past my body, sheltering Theodore from anything else. Those from outside holding a torch for our survival, albeit minor in the grand scheme of things. Surviving? What a miracle that would be, miracles do not happen in real life, they happen in fairy tales. Maybe that was all my life ever had been. On replay, day after day, I had to go through it all with somebody beyond this world playing a game. Myself and everyone else puppets on strings. Manipulated, twisted, writhed together, spoken for, depicted in particular ways. A story. Below, the ground tilting downwards in a diagonal motion… the end of a lifetime, my life flashing before in a beam of light clutching the body of dear Theodore in the deep-seated hope and desire that he could survive because of me. Warmth… Spreading down my arm, tickling me, meeting the cold as my ankle gradually absorbed the sea waters. Tinging with red. Why? Absorbed into a trance not even I could snap myself away from, stuck in a time period, everything seeming frozen, stopping. Drifting around, my eyes, twisting gently, careful to not miss a single detail of my surroundings. Fire. Lighting every single piece of wood inside, including all else it came into contact with. Waters below us illuminated so that everything was ducking, tucking and hiding away from the roaring flames heating the side of my face, burning the skin on one side. Still, I could not snap away from my trance. Calls of people from the boats telling those beside them, front, back, left and right that they could see me in the flames holding onto Theodore, crying tears mixing with sweat, gripping his body tighter to me hoping to save him.

"There she is!"

"Sit down."

"Someone has to get her!"

"No. Stay put."

Searching longingly in the boats of people beyond my view, none of them daring to meet my gaze, perplexed that I remained down there, with him. Theodore. If not now, more than ever, people now are able to understand what type of woman I am, what I stand for despite the standards others set. This is me. If you try to change my beliefs, pull me away from what you believe that should not be witnessed then you will face a lifetime of guilt as you watch me die in the flames, never change. For one day, you could be me, I might be you... call your shots, let me call mine. I burn in the flames, you burn in your heart.

"Lucy! Lucy!"

Beatrice. Calling for me, realising that I was never how she anticipated me to be, this girl who loved, still loves, her son with all her heart, not after him because of just his looks.

Beyond the appearance I give, my personality traits are those which no one can ever understand — complex. Just behind me, land lay in sight, seeming not so far away if it had not been for the burning wooden rigging that luckily missed us both. Unfortunately, he was still in pain, agony now that he had awoken, no longer stuck in a sleeping state, crying as the burning terrorised his skin, aching every inch of his body seething.

"Listen to me, stay here okay."

"Lucy... what is happening to me?"

"You are in a dream, just stay with me, as soon as we get out of this, reality will come back. Okay?"

"I can feel shooting in my arm." Reaching to put his hand on my arm, where a shrivelling sleeve wrinkled back. "You are real, where are we?"

"Real as I can be."

"You're crying. Stop crying, Lucy."

Despite him telling me to stop crying, the tears flowed heavily on my cheeks, each of his fingertips just about reaching to wipe them away. Stopping the staining process.

"Easy to say."

"For me. Stop crying."

Crackling of fire around us burying any other sound, screaming deeply into our ears as a child's screeching, burying all other things. "I will try."

That smile I had once believed was lost forever, resurfaced, stopping the aching in my heart. All had not been lost thus far. Hope remained.

"Mom!" Shrilling of my daughter, across the sea getting closer to the shoreline. "Mom! Mom!"

"Baby..."

Stretching my hand towards, the fingers quivering, curling into a ball from the light skimming off Theodore's hand across my forearm, telling me I had to stop fooling myself, survival was the main thing now.

"We need to go." Ignoring him, he had now sat up, stuffing a piece of material from his shirt into the wound on his thigh, giving me a smile of pure fright. "Now!"

Wrapping his arm around my waist, expecting his touch

to send shivers coursing through my body. Instead, survival instinct kicked into motion, preparing me through anxiety, butterflies, memories, all that I had worked hard to live for.

"Let's go."

Steadily standing up on the loose floorboards, managing to help me stand up, slightly rocking from side to side in the imbalance of the sides.

"Give me your hand, Theodore."

Holding out his hand for me, I held on tightly unwilling to let go unless absolutely necessary, shuddering under careful touch, icy cold, lacking life or any circulation. Still, searching his eyes for a sign he was still the same Theodore I had grown to love, ignoring our first initial meeting. Down where the injury of the bullet penetrated his skin, the leg trembling violently as an earthquake would tremble an entire country.

"You are not okay to stand, are you?"

"Not really."

"Hold onto me."

Nodding his head towards me, I saw a massive impact coming to my right, one of the masts heading straight towards us, seemingly larger than when the ship was intact. Pulling Theodore back towards me, his body thudding into mine, sending him flying to the ground with the weakness in his leg. He lay down watching the curling flames of fire begin to roll toward us.

"Get up! Theodore!"

"I cannot."

"Why?"

"It's my leg, it's bleeding again."

"Shoot!"

Pinching my lips inside out, my eyes darting at all angles,

tightly wincing my eyes together repetitively, resting the palm of my hand onto my face, squeezing back any tears arising.

"I don't know what to do."

"I do. Go on without me."

"No!"

"Yes, just go!"

"No."

Theodore's breathing began to gain heavily, it seemed the dense thickness of the air around us began impacting on the condition of his lungs. We had only minutes before he was dead. Now or never, those three words repeating in my mind like a hymn embedded into me.

Creaks, cracks, clicks. Something was about to break… where? "Thedore, remember to stay with me."

"I—" Coughing and spluttering everywhere, some of his saliva spewing into the flames igniting it ever so slightly. "I do not think I can."

"Of course you can." Cupping one side of his face into my hand, feeling the heat of his skin sending waves through my body. "You cannot disappear on me now, you have to stay awake."

Below me, the wooden floorboards moaning under our weight as they weakened in strength.

"Grab my hand."

Taking my hand once more, he held tighter than I had done, still getting some of the power left inside of him. Mentally begging for his eyes to stay open for longer than the time he had left, it was impossible for me to imagine him leaving me now. My life appearing so dull with him no longer alive to mimic me, giving me unbelievable names that I never understood the meaning behind.

"Something is happening."

"I know. Do not leave me! I cannot live without you now."

"There is not time, you will be fine without me, save you—"

A brief scream, his body hitting the waters, the splintering wood falling in with him as he fell into the water. Then, the horror I wished to not see, every split second my brain had fooled me into thinking he would survive this, surely not… it could not be the end of him. Of us. "Theodore!" Bellowing into the sea, the sound of my voice absorbed by the waters. "Theodore!"

Rubbing my furrowed brow, I thought about diving in after him. I could swim, it just scared me what was down there. Seeing his body sink to the bottomless pit of the ocean tearing me into shreds. Could this be the end of me if I go down there? Caught in my eyeline, I saw the figure of a body caught on the rocks, Theodore was drowning while being unconscious. Maybe I could save him, I could try to save him one last time. Would I make it towards him? Could I even dive through this hole? Do you know something? Theodore is one of the few I would die trying to save.

"Here I go."

Arching my arms straight, pushing my body from the burning surface causing some pieces of wood crumbling into the waters below just as my own body had been minutes ago, plummeting water rising upwards extinguishing at least some of the flames. Not nearly enough, as they continued burning onward with no sign of stopping at any point in time.

Saving Thedore was my goal.

Watch me burn in the flames.

Watch me sink to the bottom of the sea. Watch me save the
ones I love.
This is me

Fixed in my view, Theodore lay on the rock about to fall away
to the even deeper depths to be eaten, demolished over time, a
life gone to waste. The last thing on my mind, had been to
waste such a young life. Especially someone I truly cared
about so dearly. How could it be that this is the way everything
would be destroyed, all the love in my heart turning into waste
despite it always being there, forever. Water consumed me,
surrounding my every move making it feel almost impossible
as the thickness did not even try to ease away, gaining further
thickness the deeper I swam. Lungs burning, eyes wider than
when I strain them to look out to the sea in the black emptiness
in the night-time. There he was. Each strand of his hair gently
flowing as the bubbles from out of my mouth surfaced to the
top, illuminated by the blazing fire floating upon the surface.
Gritting my teeth, attempting to ignore the burning sensation
in my arm's muscles which had become corrupted through
strenuous use over and over. Little bubbles, ever so tiny, arose
from his lips parting minutely with water inhaling through his
mouth. Only an arms-stretch away, the will to keep on going
shooting straight into my veins, pushing me towards him just
as my tears pushed away underneath these waters weighing me
heavily. Wrapping my arms around his back, beneath his
armpits, pulling him with me to the surface through extreme
heaviness in my arms which castigated me for going after
Theodore, my Theodore. Beams of light came from the sun
just on the water's clear surface, feeling its warmth absorbed
in the water which had been cold in comparison to the burning

wreck just a few hundred metres away from where we rose from beneath.

Heaving for air, the lungs inside of me expanding and contracting rapidly, begging for mercy of the oxygen from outside although contaminated with the wood fractions inside the burning ashes. Deafening ringing sensations imprisoning my ears instead of allowing the normal ability to listen to everything else. Despite this impairment, the cheers and screams of the people from the boats ahead of us calling to have somebody come over to help me in my endeavours to save the one we never expected to see fit for saving. I saved him. Miniscule, the chances to keep him… was he still alive?

"Lucy…"

In between heavy breaths, I barely heard his inaudible word, calling to me unaware of what had happened. "Theodore!"

Before I could even start swimming to shore with him in my arms, Jonathan had swum his way out to take Theodore away from me, relieving me of the responsibility.

"I have got him now."

"Thank you."

Chapter 8
Why did you save me?

Torridity, surrounding me. Sudden onrush of mildness. Sinking, below somewhere, somewhere dense in capacity, thickness... why? Where was I going? A dream, it must have been as I woke up surrounded by a few people on grass near the beach where nobody dared to move the bodies. Inside of my head, a dull aching migraine pounding repeatedly without let-up accompanied by a thudding in my thigh. Ah. Bullet wound. Where did that come from? With no idea, it felt as though everything had happened so suddenly without my knowledge or company, happening behind my back... yet, I still felt as though the different places I had been with Lucy seemed far too real to be a lie. Asking her might lead to an awkward silence in thorough thought. Although, the last word I supposedly spoke had been her name. Far too many questions rounding in my mind, written into a long form directly addressed list to her.

"Hello..."

Trailing away into the evening breeze, torches starting to be lit, a fire pit dug out into the centre of the grass with wood burning in the centre, large tree logs sitting around looking like designated areas with everyone's items around them.

"Someone, can you tell me what happened?"

Briskly a person walked past, carelessly not even

acknowledging my presence apart from answering a minor question I hoped somebody would be decent enough to explain the answer to.

"The girl saved your life, ask her."

"The girl?"

Ignoring the follow up question, he turned his attention elsewhere, preferably someone other than me. Craning my neck around to see behind me, Lucy stood there with the colour drained out of her eyes, her skin, everything. Maybe it was never a dream after all? Usually, in circumstances where I could walk freely, then I would reach out to her.

"Lucy." Widening my eyes, a slight huff, and a quick realisation of how quiet I was calling her name. "Lucy!"

Still she could not hear me, despite my attempt to shout higher hoping to gain her attention with no success in my enterprise. Through brief memory, parts hazy in certain times, her tears refraining from being held back, they had been perfectly real; the flames, the water, the sinking, the lack of air, the choking, death was evidently near. Underneath my armpits, a woman... man... picking me up, whoever felt the need to help me out from the predicament that I had been so desperate to escape from. Who was this *girl* mentioned to me? Highly I doubted that it could have been a *girl,* maybe a woman? Silent speech between Lucy and Jonathan piquing my interest, guiding her to sit on the wooden logs helping her through something she was traumatised by. At least the hearing inside of my ears had not been compromised over the period of time when I had been accustomed to the dark. Warmth flooding through my brain as a hand placed itself upon my shoulder shaking me awake out of the daydream my mind was wandering off into.

"Theodore. You should have called for one of us."

Christopher took his place by my side, arching his left leg up, leaning his head onto the side. "Lucy has been through a lot since you went..." Mimicking circles around his head, highlighting how I must have turned crazy. Through the minute raise of my eyebrows, he soon noticed the confusion. "You know nothing of what happened, no memory?"

"All I remember was a girl crying. Someone saving my life?"

"Wow! You should ask Lucy, she will tell you everything."

Turning to leave, grasping hold of the last piece of his sleeve bringing him back down to meet my eyeline. "Leave it!"

"Do you not want to know?"

"Well, I just do not want to hurt her more than I already have done that much, several times."

"Just let her explain everything. Hmm?"

"Fair enough, I will never win, not with my banging head."

"Okay."

Off he went, leaving me in silence, viewing the little waves bashing against the shoreline gently wetting the bottom of my shoes overcoming any fear that I had. That was until the sun became lower, knowing rather clearly that Lucy would have to leave later on, speak to her father. It was best for her to release everything now, rather than having it bottled up when she meets her dad after years of believing he was dead. Already traumatised from her previous way of life, this new way of living was already enough. Still, I was worried about everything she was about to open up to me regarding the time when I collapsed. Perhaps you are wondering what it felt like? Truthfully, I felt as though I was dreaming, suffocating, sleeping peacefully all at one time, but I was choking on my own breath... spluttering out water from my mouth, soon after rising above the waters. One word tingling on my tongue, my name itching to be spoken out loud... Lucy.

"Theodore..." An unsteady voice came behind me, followed by a tight hug around the back of me, all the way around my shoulders. Lucy's warmth. "You're awake!"

"If I was not awake then I would not be having this conversation with you."

Pausing, I idly watched her biting her bottom lip, choosing her words particularly carefully as though they had become a matter of life or death.

"Do you remember what happened? Christopher told me that you did not. I was unsure. I just do not know what happened, or what you want me to say, how you want me to explain it."

"Calm down."

"I cannot be okay, I am just so glad you are alive." Grabbing my face with her freezing hands, she let go, realising that they sent a shock through me. "Sorry, I just did not expect us to survive."

"Survive?"

"Right." Rolling her eyes, a smirk grew on my face which she must have mistaken. "No. No. That is not for you, I am rolling my eyes at me being ridiculous and stupid and everything wrong with the world."

"Please shut up." Pressing my finger against her lips, she soon quietened down, mumbling for me to remove my finger. "Promise me that you will not call yourself things that you are not."

"Mmm."

Lucy positioned herself comfortably on the ground next to me, crossing her legs, patting her hand on the inside of her thighs, pulling her dress further across to cover any skin.

"Maybe it is best if you go from the start."

"That might be a good idea. Okay. Well. I first noticed that you were missing, no longer inside any of the boats that had been set sail to leave the ship before it had been obliterated into smithereens. Your father came, running, telling us as we had been set to leave that he was unable to find you."

"Because I was shot in the leg."

Before she was able to carry on, I soon added up the dots that she had decided to come in search of me! Why did she have to put herself through so much? To me, she would always be beautiful. However, the way she looked, I hardly recognised the woman that I deeply adore, her skin whiter than snow, nearing a sickly porcelain, yet far lower in its tone. What had happened to her? To us?

"Exactly. In the end, despite what your mother and father wanted me to do, I jumped from the longboat to come in search of you."

"Why?"

Instead of answering my question, she carried on feeding my desire to understand how we ended up here at this moment in time. "Your father held up Chrsitopher from blowing up the boat, I heard you on the lower storage deck in agony. We could not get you up and out of the deck in time, you could not walk with the wound on your leg."

Lucy paused, leaving us in a silence that hung heavily in the air, lasting for a second despite feeling as though it had been going on for a longer period of time. "Did you leave me down there? Is that why you are so… colourless."

"No, Theodore, I could never leave you."

"My father did."

"He hoped that it would force me to leave with a tight sense of foreboding."

"You stayed."

Nodding up and down, my fingers began scratching away at the dried blood around the wound to preoccupy the guilt coursing through my veins.

"Stop scratching at that!" Slapping me away from the wound, her eyes sternly locking onto me. "We had to stay for hours on end trying to stop the bleeding, if that opens again we have barely anything. Just stop."

"Tell me the rest."

"All the way through?"

"All the way through."

"Okay. Umm, I, after that I laid by your side not wanting to leave you, counting down the seconds till the ship exploded."

"You were crying."

"You remember!" Expressing her surprise, a slight head dip and rise she pressed on as the sun fell. "Yes, I cried, many times. I thought I was going to lose you."

Tears built up into her eyelids, wiping them away as soon as she caught sight of me, her cold finger pressing against the bottom to dry any excess.

"Look, if it hurts you this much to tell me, leave it."

"Strangely, it gives me the release that I needed, nobody has dared to even ask."

"If you are sure."

"Yes. Yes, I am sure, Theodore, you deserve to know. Soon after that the entire ship was set ablaze, I was attempting to stop the bleeding on your leg, protecting you from the flames, hoping we could survive. We did, thankfully. You had become delirious, not knowing whereabouts you were, sweat pouring uncontrollably off your skin, barely any audible speech over the roaring flames. Everyone screamed from the boats, including my daughter, and nobody decided to help, leaving us for dead. One of the masts came down, nearly severing your head."

"How did you manage to get us back out of those flames?"

"To be honest, it still remains a blur, the brief things I can remember are quite hazy. In short, the wood collapsed beneath you, having been weakened by the weight piling on top of it."

"You really believe I am that heavy."

That was not the correct time to make such a joke considering the circumstances forcing us to engage in such a deep conversation. Whilst listening to her voice, the salty sea air, the light brushing of the wind, the cold against the soles of my shoes, calming down the nerves I felt inside, the guilt profound.

"Not the right time."

"I know, sorry."

"It's okay. You sank to the bottom of the sea, you can guess that I dived in after, seeing that you were drowning, strangely peacefully, usually when someone drowns it is less... silent. But you were so calm as though death had not been drawing near. To be honest with you, I had been lucky to pull you up from the sea, at least getting down there. There had been so many times whereby I thought you would not have been able to survive."

This time Lucy had made no attempt to hide the fact that

her emotions overpowered her strength for once, her powerful elation of me still being alive mixing with the dread of losing me. It may sound self-centred, yet, through those gorgeous eyes of hers that information had become overly evident. Even the most uneducated person could tell.

"We have survived, Lucy."

"I still cannot feel alive."

"What you have been through for me. I do not know how to express my gratitude greatly enough. You must know that. I will always be indebted to you, I owe you my life, Lucy."

"No, you will never owe me your life, just promise me one thing."

"What would that be?"

"Never, ever leave me again, or scare me into thinking that you are leaving me. Never leave my life Theodore, I would not be able to cope without you now, never ever go."

"I promise you ba—"

"What were you about to say?"

"I promise you."

"Okay."

Pulling her shoulders over towards me, resting her head on my lap, careful to not hit the injury or lay on it, watching the waves roll in and back out again, seeing the sun disappear beyond the horizon. As I cast my eyes downwards, she had fallen asleep. If only I didn't have to wake her in a little while, to go and greet her father up on one of the cliff sides.

"Why did you save me?"

Putting one of her pieces of hair behind her ear, her head shuffling slightly, listening to my words in her sleepy character.

"Because I love you, Theo."

Chapter 9
I do not know who you are!

"Lucy, wake up, you need to get going."

"Five more minutes."

"You need to go see your father before the morning comes, we will have no way of knowing if we can escape."

"Stop nagging me."

"Just because you are a heroine does not mean I can't stop nagging you."

Rubbing my eyes, pouting my lips angrily, Theodore felt that it was quite humorous and amusing as he turned red with lack of air.

"Hey! Just because you called me a heroine does not make my waking up any nicer for you." Pushing his head backwards, messing his hair with my hand, I pushed my body up getting rid of any sand and dirt off the front and back of my skirt so that I would not be messy greeting my father after all these years. Softening down the creases on my skirt, combing my hair with my fingers, it seemed to make no difference or impact when it came to getting rid of the knots.

"Your hair is an absolute mess."

"I can see that."

"Just wet it in the water, it should wave like it usually tends to." Waving my hand at him sarcastically, it had been my turn to laugh. "Okay. That just teaches me to not mess with you."

"Exactly."

Wading into the water, rolling up my skirt so it would not get too wet, my one hand aiding my hair in becoming wet, dipping it in and out, over and over. Removing it one final time, brushing my fingertips through carefully, ruffling it up in the end, it started to wave.

"You seem ready to go."

Inhaling one deep breath, the jumping in my stomach, thudding in my heart as though someone else was living inside of me… it had been time to face my inner fear of the moment. Meeting my father after believing he was dead all these years.

"I should get going. Which cliff should I climb to?"

"The left, someone is up there already."

Pointing his finger towards where the silhouette of a man stood over the cliff side wearing a cape blowing in the winds rapidly sending shivers through my body. "Thank you, will you be able to walk?"

"Hopefully. Do I need to watch out for Lily?"

"That would be wonderful, thank you."

With that, I took off in the distance with great gratitude for having Theodore to support me through this time since both of us depended on getting out of this ridiculous situation, feeling as though there had to be a place beyond this place. Somewhere that did not involve this sense of entrapment, caged like animals in a holding cell as though we were violent, to be feared.

"I hope he can get us out of here."

Mumbling to myself on the way, I realised that this walk would take me much longer than I had bargained for. Burning sensations tore straight through me, an ultimately painful feeling, as someone glared and blazed each of their eyes into me, ingraining a treacherous trembling into my soul. Surrounding me, dark greenery rooted deep into the ground searching for nutrients, water, soil, to keep it living for the rest of its one hundred years. Sometimes I wondered if death was really the end of it all, if it was the end of your centuries filled with lack of hope. Maybe beyond the grave there was something else, somewhere else that you go to instead of rotting away in a meaningless grave that nobody decides to visit all that often. Eventually you fade away as the trees disintegrate your shadow through their own towering above your head, protecting drops of water from harming your oh so delicate head. Each of the bushes surrounding the trees luscious with berries that you dare to not touch or eat for, the time you do, there may be a possibility of death, increasing chance of death, prolonging death and more and more possibilities where death is all inclusive. Apart from these merciless plants, you have the luxurious scent of fresh grass waiting for the heavenly dewdrops to fall onto its delicate sprouting pieces, reaching for the sunlight. Looking towards the large ball of fire bursting its anger to provide for those underneath its control. "Stop thinking, Lucy, I know you are worrying about meeting me."

Shooting my gaze around continuously, a voice I had become familiarised with, linking it to treachery I was yet to be accustomed to. Upon the cliff side, the male figure still stood awaiting me. Why was he there? What did I hear? Walking would be the best idea, with barely any light to enable me to see in the thick darkness apart from the slight glow of the moon, the less impactful twinkling of the stars above to guide me. Brushing fingertips skimming my shoulder, back, forwards, back, forwards, similar to the movements of a paintbrush.

"Whoever you are, playing this *sick* joke, it is certainly not very funny."

"You think it is *sick*."

Spinning around on the ball of my foot, my feet moving me backwards up the hill, ready to attack the person in front of me, now they had not been able to scorch their eyes into my back. They could do the decent act of looking me dead in the eyes.

"Yes, I do. Whatever you believe it to be, I warn I never take kindly to the actions of a rude, insolent man."

"I have been watching you, who you are, how you act. At least you will have made your father proud."

"Yet, I can still make him proud."

"How?"

Rising my head proudly, closing my eyes together, able to examine the figure now he had stopped in the moonlight, able to see his body clearly, the cape. Everything.

"Hello, Father." Removing his hood, pulling it over the back of his head, seeing his features once again. "You have not been dead all these years."

"Maybe it is time I explain."

"I think you should." Rolling my eyes as he mouthed the words *just like your mother,* our laughs penetrating the awkward silence, closing my eyes while we did so.

"Hang on… where am I?"

"Atop the cliff."

"How? One minute we were down there, now we are here."

"All in good time, daughter."

Just a minute ago, my eyes were wandering across the sumptuous greenery lining the grounds, decorating the skies so perfectly. Then, in an instant, feeling nothing, we had moved swiftly up onto the cliff, looking down over everything appearing so small and delicate in time, moving about easily in slow motion. Time up here creating a world impacting how I viewed everything.

"Up here everything seems so insignificant."

"Everything seems so lifeless."

"I remember when you were a child, your wooden dollhouse and little dolls."

"Are you comparing that to this?"

"It would appear so, you agree with me."

"I have missed this, Father, me and you talking about everything, understanding, knowing exactly what the other person will say."

"As if nothing ever changed, but I had to leave you."

Heavily sighing, knowing the answer to what my heart longed to know and understand would completely change when I had been told the script I had been reading from all this time.

"Did you really need to leave?"

"Yes, I did, I received this letter. Just the day before you had been told I had passed away." He was holding a crumpled sheet of paper in his hand that had resisted his attempts to renew and reassemble.

"From unknown?"

"Yes, I never actually found out who it was."

"About Mother?"

"Just read it, out loud, I need to know that I give you everything you deserve to know."

"Okay…

Dear Henry,

We hope this letter finds you well. Since your wife, Elizabeth left, her life has not been too good. Due to prolonged ill health we fear that her guilt shall cause her further complications, death is on the cards right now, holding the aces. Every night she calls your name, you do not answer, she cries, she screams begging for your forgiveness over and over praying of your return in her life.

Since she came to us, beyond the world you are living in right now, her knowledgeable information and foresight for the world has provided many advances in many areas: technology, medicine, livelihood, helping young children to deal with their issues, and many more things.

Because of this, we decided to make a simple and short exception, you will leave where you are now to come and be with her, her mind is so brilliant that we cannot afford to lose it.

Therefore, the next letter enclosed will provide you with all the information you require on how to leave. We are watching you very closely, all will become clear when you arrive.

Yours Sincerely,
Unknown.

"I never left you and lied to get away, it was all for you mother."

"Did you leaving make everything any better?"

"Slightly."

"What do you mean, slightly?"

"No longer does she call out my name, it is you who she needs to be with."

Everything that Father was telling me felt plausible, entirely true, he had no reason to put on a facade since the truth was out. Whether or not he liked it, knowing my mother was still here in my life felt joyful, frightening, intense, a whirlpool of emotions combining horrifically. "There is no way of me getting out of this place."

"Of course there is, you can come with me right now and take one person with you."

"Do you expect me to leave everyone here behind, everyone who has welcomed me with open arms, taken me away from a world filled with people saturated with the pains this disease has brought. I would not do it even to humour her, just because she wants me, I will not come."

"Why? Look, Lucy, your mother needs you."

"What about when I needed her? Where was she? Elsewhere."

"She understands what she did was wrong, you know I would not be here if not for needing you to come with me now."

Laughing hysterically, I held my hands on my hips, dropping them down by my side putting most of my weight onto one side. "She has made her bed, Father, now she can lie in it."

"You will not leave because of these people." By the time he had spoken up, by the time he had figured out one of the main reasons as to why I was not leaving, I turned on my heels to leave him standing there. "If you think that leaving me standing here will take away my desire to have you come with me, then you are wrong."

"Look, if these people adore Mother as much as they do, they shall do anything to save her. Will they not?"

"Not everything."

"What if I let you think about it, will you?"

"No. There is *nothing* I need to think about, *they* need to think about it." Glaring with my eyes, they shone like diamonds, the white luminescent in the glowing moon. "Where will you be going tonight?"

"That is something I have been forbidden to tell you."

"Well then, I see how things are going to be, I am done."

Turning back towards the lengthy slope in front of me, the cliffs descent daunting in size, either side waves violently bashing against the rocks with the heavy gravitational pull of the moon. Never had the sea scared me until now, seeing how the temperament can change so quickly in a blink of an eye. Warmth from the cooling down waters reaching my ankles as they sprayed with rage, smothering the rock faces below me. There was something quite unsettling about the way in which the innocent one can be taken by surprise, harshness empowering the weak to fight back to the daunting devil below. One swoop under the ankles, down you would go, underneath the crushing of the water atop your body. After trying to save Theodore, I could understand completely how it feels apart from when the entirety of its passionate indignation kicks in.

"Lucy. I am not done with you, remember your place, woman."

"Twice, I have been told that. Remember your place, woman. Remember your respect, girl. Now you."

"Now me."

Picking me up by my collar, dragging me back up towards the cliff's edge weakened by our weights atop its crumbling point. Pinching my lips together, unable to pierce them with my teeth, the pain took away any anxiety in my stomach… not my head. Widening my eyes, they began to make their bets at my survival if I dropped down into those waters riddled with rocks, owning whittled points ready to pummel the skin off my body, preparing to destroy me through one sharp push, drowning me into the waves, washing any trace of the blood. "Murder."

"Murder? Who mentioned murder?"

"With you dangling me over the edge, I would say attempted murder."

"That would be if I let you go."

How could this be my father? The man who in my past, loved me, he would be there for me despite anything that would arise, he would die for me. Now he wanted me to die, possibly for the reasons of me not wanting to come with him. Since wanting to leave, there has not been a day going by where I had not been threatened by the arms of death ready to accept a corpse for them no matter how bloody, how clean, how innocent the life might be. Despite how many times I attempted to release myself from its clutches, release other people from its imprisonment, it found a way to rip through the life I had been living in for twenty-six miserable years, a few moments of peace. Now, when faced with homicide, me the victim of the murderous intent, I was not prepared for death. When being ready to die for others, the tables turn quite quickly, the process of being able to consider the consequences of my actions. However, there is no time to prepare yourself for someone else to kill you, there is the moment of realisation, no way of escaping, no time to say goodbye, allow others to accept everything that will take place.

"You are my father!"

"Do you realise that this will be the only way of getting you to come with me."

"Voluntarily. Never. Pressured. Never."

"Let me drop you forwards further." Dangling me further over the edge, the breeze from the winds came past me. "How about now? Change of heart before it gets pierced."

"Maybe I will survive, Father."

"Shall I drop you?"

Despite the strength he decided to show me, a different story had been portrayed through his hands as they shook against the fabric he held, frigid hands against the skin of the neck which could be punctured severely any minute if his weak hands let me slip downwards. "Why would you kill me? I am your daughter!"

"You will come with me. If I have to force you to, even if I have to drop you, then they will take you dead or alive. Your mother will know then."

"Know what? That you murdered her child, your child."

Weakness. Fear. Disquieting thoughts inside my head, expressing outwardly for anyone to see. Underneath each breath, the fear crept up, squeaking.

"Drop me, drop me, drop me."

"I enjoy seeing you like this."

"Sick! What sort of father enjoys seeing his daughter in fear of him?"

"I do, clearly."

"They changed you, what for? An experiment, to see how

long he could last in a world where everyone hates you apart from them, those who seek enjoyment from other people's pain."

"Lucy… you should stop it right now."

"Stop the truth? Never!"

"It will all come out eventually, every little detail."

"The truth! The truth! You are really one to talk, holding me over the edge of the cliff to prevent me from ever finding the truth."

Embedding in my thigh, a tearing of my skin slicing straight through causing a whelp to cry as a dog begs for food, attention, love. I was not begging, neither did I want food, love, attention, this pain crucifying my body through to the last detail. Where was the blood? It felt like it was running down my left thigh, the contents winding around to my ankle, burning yet another mark, this I could see briefly as my blue skirt was flipping up and down in the wind.

"You have been marked."

"Marked? Marked with what?"

"Something you should not have… you cannot know."

"Your voice is shaking. Dad, why are you scared of me?"

"You have what they need, they will come for you, be careful."

"Dad…" He relinquished his grip from the top of my dress collar, bringing me back up from the fear of death. Entranced by the sea, my eyes burning, whirling around seeing destruction of a city vastly expansive. "Who are you really?"

The surroundings of this island had changed to a city, how did I know what a city was? How did I recognise this place? Dad was not Dad, everything that I had just become accustomed to had changed, memories slightly coming back to me that had been incomprehensible even to me.

"Seriously, who are you?"

"Sergeant Liam Fernsby. Commissioned by your father, Captain Henry Simpson, by order to bring you back to him and your mother."

"Not happening."

"You must meet me here every single night until you decide to come with me, or find a way out of here for you and your *friends.*"

Liam was medium height, possibly six foot one, maybe taller, blond hair ruffled slightly under his khaki hat, medium build under the uniform I seemed to recognise all too well. Father had to have told him a message to pass on, he would never just send someone to keep coming to me day after day to coerce me into coming back to him. He was dead!

Maybe one day we could get out of here, beyond this place where they had cooped us up like chickens in a pen, ready to be slaughtered to feed the king.

"He must have told you that I would be like this, did he?"

"Over and over. Apparently, they have been watching you very, very, closely."

"Seriously, I am not coming with you."

"They say you can see the world from here when you are burned with that mark."

"How?"

"You saw it just then, something you figured out."

"Of course, fear for my own life."

"Yet you would willingly give it to someone else."

"I should be going okay… I don't know how much you know, to be honest, I do not care. Stop watching me."

"Tomorrow, you come back here, do not be late."

"Or, what?"

"You will find out."

"I do not know who you are. Okay. Stop trying to mess with my head!"

"I'm not messing. Go on, go back to your boyfriend then."

"Then I can be happy, much happier than if I stayed with you."

Pushing the letter into his hands, I ran back down to where we had made our camp for the evening, the fire had been lit and no one seemed to have noticed that I was missing for so long. Perfect, no more questioning, interrogation. End of story until tomorrow came.

Chapter 10
Where did you get that marking?

How many hours she had been gone for? It had to be inexcusable considering her child, Lily, needed her mother. Although, it seemed to me that her daughter had taken a keen liking to my mother, in turn my mother to her. Whether this was what mother intended as an act to get back at the new 'dragon lady' on the block, then it would only be to her detriment for Lily never stopped asking about her mother and I. To be quite truthful, somewhere deep in my mother's heart she approved of us, whether she decides to admit it one day would become a separate story. Finding someone to share your life with is a big deal. Over the years you are forced to become couples with other women of the town, always having rich fathers, noble fathers, notorious women of the household. Everytime the exact same kind of girl. No love in her eyes, cold, deeply vain; materialistic, always talking about the next diamond ring to fit her finger. Obsessions of having a fairy tale wedding, glamorous, extravagant, far more lavish than her friends. Lucy was beyond all of this, a simple girl who had a far from simple mind, caring, knowing that money is never everything just needed in small amounts to get by. Still, my mother tasted dislike around her, Lucy could not tell all of the time since she had a skilful way of keeping her emotions shut tightly in.

Fortunately, my father seemed to approve of us if ever it came to it, including courage unlike the Dutch courage he had when proposing to my mother... it always made me wonder why she laughed at him the way she does. This all made sense when she finally let out with the secret kept tightly inside of her.

"Lucy!" Watching her trudge her way down, a lot less elegantly than she usually did, changing the mood in my head completely, a limp in her left leg showing me injury.

"Hey!" Coming closer towards me, a vision popping into my mind, carrying her bridal style, to take the weight of her feet, just when I remember the injury in my own leg. "Missed me?"

"As always, what did you think?"

"Charming, always ridiculously charming."

"Yet you enjoy it, do you not?"

"Shut up!" Giggling, her own happiness returning, saving the very life from draining me dry. Her happiness means more to me than most things, only now after meeting her had I been so glad to have carried on living, never becoming part of the memorials that had been held high for those losing their lives in battle. Steadily breathing life into my lungs, a grateful smile crept onto my face as she took her place next to me. "I am fine, stop giving me those concerned eyes."

"Your leg. What happened?"

"Nothing, nothing much, I accidentally fell on a large rock up the cliff."

"Come on, Lucy, I know you better than that, you have no scuffing on your dress. Tear. Gravel. Dirt. Nothing. What really happened up there?"

"Can we talk about it tomorrow?" Her eyes pleaded with

me to not discuss the matter any further. "Please."

"Okay then."

Digging into my pocket, my hand searching for the leather canteen I had filled up earlier. Once my fingers laid their touch upon its soft case, they wrapped around its neck, pulling off the cap, handing its contents to Lucy.

"What is in here!"

Catching a strong smell of its contents, a whiff caught up her nose tickling her senses as she sneezed tiny amounts repeatedly, it caused her to go bright red from either embarrassment or warmth.

"Rum."

"Rum! I thought it was whisky or something along the lines of that."

"Well, it was the only thing I could find to cheer you up."

"I cannot drink this stuff, it is putrid in scent and probably tastes far more disgusting than anything I would rather not drink."

"Go on, it will not harm you. One swig."

"One swig."

"And?"

"It's enough to kill you."

"Hey! I never drink alcohol, just this once." Thumping me in the arm, her head tilted back with the canteen, taking a gulp from the bottle, handing it back to me willingly. "Your turn." Coughing with the strength of the alcohol content, I took it from her.

"This is how it is done."

"Let me see then."

Taking a larger drink than she had done, a few trickles of rum remaining in the bottle. "Done."

Spluttering, most of the rum I had tried to swallow down the hatch, came out onto the floor just missing my shoes. To hear her laughing once more had been a miracle, patting my back violently hoping it would do the trick.

"I win!"

"No, you do not win, I was just laughing when I was taking my drink."

"Why?"

"No reason."

"Of course."

"I have an idea!"

Lighting up her eyes, appearing to me quite childlike, the moonlight reflecting in her eyes shimmering like glitter. Stunning.

"I am all ears, Theo."

"Never mind."

"No! Tell me." Whining down my ears, she shook my arm, making it wobble up and down like jelly. "Theodore!"

"Do you want to go to the beach? Sit on the sand, talk about life."

"Sure, why not. Two cripples walking to the beach."

Picking up a blanket from the ground for us to sit on, her daughter smiling at me noticing that I truly cared for her mother. It sounded so strange to me that she was a mother. Why, I will never know, yet it took me by surprise so easily. Maybe it had been due to the fact I never chose to contemplate her story and who she was, her company, her time had been enough for me so far. She saved my life! What else could I ask of her, or even want to think about? Each time my mind dwelled upon the times when her life had been so simple. Without this. Without her troubles. Without suffering. Without me. For me she endured an eternity of hardship that would never leave her, for me she will never forget all she had to face on this fateful day. Seeing her father must have taken its toll, it had been crystal clear in my eyes, I understood in my own little way, albeit very small, that finding someone you thought you had lost all those years ago will never be easy to deal with. In my mind, in my heart, a vow that I made quietly, I promised to never abandon her or leave until the day death will be ready to take me to darkness. Forever she would be under my care, my protection, my love, as long as she would have me. Yes, we may argue, yes, I would let her win. That was minor, therefore, those times she could have given me the pity even if it was her fault.

"Come on daydreamer! Move your butt off the blanket."

"Excuse me?"

"You got up, picked up the blanket and sat back down again."

"My bad."

"Lift up then."

"Ah, yes, it would be a good start."

Standing up, she took the blanket underneath the comfort of her arm delicately offering her hand to me as we stood up together. My arm held in hers since I was hoping the bleeding would not come back again as the bullet had penetrated all too much for anyone's liking.

Sudden, direct force upon the wound and the bleeding would return. When Lucy had disappeared, they somehow managed to retrieve the bullet from deep into my skin, how they managed was a mystery with the evening beginning to loom over us slowly. Now it could heal correctly, the way that it should as everyone worked hard to keep fresh bandages coming every few hours, checking and applying every time. Jonathan, being the physician, offered advice, careful consideration to all that would need maintaining after the light surgery on my leg. Christopher specialises in many things, including a specialty for operating on people. At this point in time, operations had been rather limited apart from knowing where organs are situated through the work of an anatomist, physician and author. Andreas Vesalius. Magnificent work, allowing many surgeons to figure out where many vital organs would be. Unfortunately, his ideas, fact, writings had not been accepted in society very well since it opposed religious views. Those who found themselves in the minor groups of this country, having no religion, adopted his views willingly. The arguments when I had been operated upon came greatly, taking the thoughts away from the pain, the pain away from the thoughts. Jonathan, his entire family, many he knew who had decided to come along on this trip had to be religious. Christopher only invited him along since they had been long-standing friends, offering to take one family that he found favour with on this trip. The family of Hamiltons have always been far away from the ideas of religion, you can tell by the names they gave their two sons and daughter. Bethany, Lucas and Julian. In my father's younger days, he had been religious, soon falling away from the idea of faith, God, heaven and hell. Everything seeming confusing, at least that is what he admitted, giving me a name that did not sound a single bit Biblical, still he carried on portraying to other high officials that he continued serving in loyalty and faith. Vowing on the Bible in front of rulers whenever he needed to, hoping he could fool them all, which it did. To others, such as the families he brought along, religiousness flew out of the window, never a topic of any conversation.

Snapping back to reality, I found Lucy laying down the blanket on the golden sands, ensuring none of the edges had been turned over or creased. Her eyes had soft tears rolling in them as she reminisced on a memory so painful, even she could not hold back any emotion. Unless she had decided to open up to me, then I had not noticed, or she was just crying with happiness, I could not tell.

"Lucy, are you okay?"

"Huh! Yes, I am fine, thank you."

Offering her hand to help me sit down on the grass, keeping the injured leg straight, the other arched to support my body getting down onto the soft touch fabric.

"Let's hope your leg will ease up soon."

"I am sure it will, what happened when you were gone?"

Taking her hand in mine, the warmth had been saturated out leaving lifeless blood in her veins, still keeping her heart beating in her chest. When her eyes left the world, I left the world, only living for the words she waited for me to hear. Watching her pupils widen, her body reacting with the anxious waiting inside, not knowing whether to stay and fight, or go take flight. Placing my hands around both of hers, the most of the energy pouring from me into the pale skin that held her structure so easily.

"What happened when I was gone?" Spitting the words out, her hands slid out of mine pulling her skirt over her knees where she sat on her calves. The laugh which had once filled me with joy, sarcastically cackling wickedly with ever forceful breath. "Who cares what happened when I was gone! Nobody does."

"I hate it when you turn like this. Lucy, when will you

understand that I care, I want to listen to every word you decide to speak. Adding salt to the wounds, pushing me over the edge of a cliff in an argument, you mean so much I cannot even begin to explain."

"Pushing me off a cliff. He tried to push me off of a cliff." Quivering, jittering, high emotions obliterating her normality. "Trying to force me... force me to go somewhere. With him."

"Did he do this, to your leg?"

"No! Theodore, you cannot understand, really you will never comprehend. My insight."

"Your insight? Lucy, look at me." Holding her face in my hands, she gently smiled, shrugging away the touch I gave her, wandering over to the waters. "What is happening to you?"

"There will be a way out of this, for us all, if we find the way out of here."

"Do you even know where it is?"

"No. No idea. Where did they put the bodies?" Her eyes peeking, lighting up in realisation of something. "Where did they put them, Theodore?"

"Over there." Pointing towards the far end of the beach. She shook her leg testing its durability, she seemed to cope with the pain all too well. The stretch to the bodies had been far away, the time it had taken them to move down there... hours. "Where are you going?"

"I just need to take a look. One minute."

Taking off into a sprint, her shadow casting alongside the rocky cliff side as she went on her way to the bodies, albeit rather faint in the minor light of the moon. To my surprise, she tossed the bodies in a line strangely not bothered by their gory nature, lacking blood, rotting skin, washed away mostly by the sea water helping to decompose the flesh.

"Lucy! You need to come back."

Repeatedly, she scoured the bodies, back up, back down, time and time again but it was not enough as she gathered notes that had been pinned onto the bodies. Everyone had frozen in time, including her daughter. Nobody appeared to be alive, besides from us. A darker shadow coming over me, shudders spreading through my skin as everything came into a complete view.

"There will be no time. There will be no time. There is never any time. We will die. We have to die." Two men seized her from behind, putting her in chains and manacles ensuring her wounded leg had been wound up tighter, why? "Let go of me!"

Despite the distance that she had been away from me, the sounds of her screaming words had still been audible even to me, the many metres away could not deprive me of her words. "Get off of me! I swear to goodness I will use this thing on my leg."

Pulling up the left side of the dress, a marking revealed on her left thigh, alongside a marking on her ankle; the red tattoo destroying her perfect skin. Upon her thigh there was a shape in the detail of a dagger with blood dripping from its edge. It looked far too real to be true. Around her ankle, a detailed set of words wound around it in four separate rings, darkening into a black solid shade.

"Ah. See here, I told you she would have it, Fernsby."

"We can make a deal here, Lucy, you tell me why you have that marking, and we will let you go."

Pressing his hand across her mouth, she wriggled and writhed, trying to get out of their grips, her eyes begging me to come and help her. I could not walk. Despite the willingness

I would have to save her, I wanted to tear my eyes away from something I could not control.

Still, they remained fixated on the situation that my eyes could not bear to continue watching. The muffled screams just about escaping her lips, unnecessarily blocking her from even being able to have the opportunity of freedom once again. Everyone behind me, sitting around the flickering fire, standing still in what they were doing, laughing heartily halfway as though nothing had happened, frozen in their motions all the same. Nothing seeming alive any more apart from the sea, sand, us, and them.

"Let me go!"

She never gave up in trying to get help. From me. Beside me, two sticks similarly sized lay separately apart on the sand. Then, it clicked immediately, as if I had never realised it before. Instead of it being someone else's support, they could help me in walking, even speed walking if I found my rhythm. Fernsby, who had already been named in the tussle of Lucy's capture, had not realised I was here and I would take him on even wounded. For her freedom, she had already been so brave when saving my life that this was the way I would repay her. Picking both of the sticks up, weight pushing upon them heavily, I shook my leg checking how it would be able to move.

"Okay... let's go." Mumbling under my breath, many places of the rocks had dents in them where I would be able to hide inside them when their attention came my way. Fernsby and his companion had already focussed on her leg for long enough. Taking this moment to move into the first dent of four, I could hear the conversations far more clearly.

"The mark of survival, Daniel, here, see the blood

dripping down from the edge of the knife carving. It represents her sacrifices that she makes when willingly dying for others."

"And the intricacies around the handle of the sword."

"The complexity of her thoughts, she is definitely not just a pretty face."

"We all know that." Daniel winked at Lucy, eyeing her beauty knowing that she was a stunning woman. "What do you think, Liam?"

"Certainly fine, she has a boyfriend on all accounts. Where is he?"

Loosening the grip on her mouth, they both grinned devilishly seeing how she had not backed down from them, accepting the sinister, sickening compliments they had given her. Standing here, watching them stroke the carving of her thigh with their fingertips, ensuring it was the mark that they had been looking for all this time. Her eyes screaming for them to get away from her skin, knowing through her eyes how their touch caused her to scream in agony. With it still being red raw, the marks around it, appearing to be those of fire murdering every piece of skin that encompassed the markings.

"Where is he! You have no right to touch my thigh, you have no right to have me cuffed. Do what is best for you and let me go!"

"Miss Simpson, we advise that you do not become so resentful towards us, it will not be in your best interests."

"It is fine, I already know exactly what I need to do. Remove these cuffs. Nobody will get hurt."

My dragon lady mark two had been released from its cage, the flames rolling off her tongue, all eyes directly focused on her. Each moment I wasted watching them arguing, I could have moved to the third checkpoint. Despite not being so light-footed on these makeshift crutches, nobody apart from Lucy noticed where I was, her eyes lighting up with a bit of hope every time I crept to the next corner. Third base, readying for number four, I would need to be stealthy… far more careful than I had been prior to this, cracking branches underfoot, coughing, gasping nearly slipping in the sand. All these efforts with no goal in mind whatsoever.

"We will not remove these cuffs until you tell us, where did you get that marking?"

"I have no clue where it came from. Leave me alone." Screeching at the top of her voice, a sudden change in character switching like a light, her eye colour changing almost instantly to a furious fire-coloured amber, the igniting rage beginning to thrive in her soul. Unchanging, their acts did not change at all, still keeping her tightly cuffed. "Get away from me!"

Gritting her teeth in pure aggression, her mindset, the locking system on the cuffs breaking free as they became hopeless in trying to hold her any longer. But they had been unaware, they grew too confident to notice.

"So then, Lucy, where did you get that marking?"

"Where did I get this marking? Explain to me where you both got this mark."

Swinging her left leg into Liam's head, he fell backwards onto the pile of corpses behind us just as the tide drew in, her foot pushing into Daniel's chest pushing him into the wall, close to where I had been. Picking up the crutches that were leaning against the wall, knowing full well, clearly and brightly that we had to go. Right now. Before they sent reinforcements to capture us. Her.

"Lucy!"

"Theodore!"

"Come on, we need to go right now. They will send more people to come and get you if we do not move."

"What is the point? They have been watching me all this time, it will not take them long to hunt me down anyway."

"There is a point in trying, okay, just do not give up just yet."

"We will be getting out of here soon enough with everyone else."

Still she had not realized that everyone had stopped living, solid in a fixed state where they could not move, as though they had been manipulated and controlled by someone else, everything else continuing to live besides the group of people that had arrived with us on the journey. Through the crowd of people around the campfire, I found myself searching for anyone who could come away with us, to hide and protect Lucy. She deserved it. Jonathan, frozen. My family, frozen. What if they had never been my family in the first place? Maybe I have been manipulated myself, to believe certain ways of living. Brainwashed?

"Wait…"

"You just said we need to get out of here! Make your mind up."

"It is Christopher, everyone else has been put on pause, they cannot move. But Christopher is absolutely nowhere to be seen."

"What about my daughter?"

"I'm sorry…" Downcast, her eyes lowering, heaving a heavy breath weighted with emotions even she could not control. "Maybe you have a daughter outside of here that will be real."

"My son, if he took my son, then he must be real. Right?"

"Well, if this will be the way our lives shall be, then we

need to consider every kind of hope. Lucy, you did not want me to leave you. I do not want you to even consider straying from my side right now, not with these idiots lurking in the shadows. Grab what you need and go." Blinking back tears threatening to show, she dipped her head up and down, releasing a few of the tears that she never wanted to be shown.

"What shall I grab? Where shall we even meet?"

"Meet me at the old ruins, I checked earlier, there should be a path to your right which is far more complex. I will need to take the one to the left, make sure to not even think about stopping, just grab water supplies that we have brought. Stuff them in a bag, then run, grab blankets, anything you can find."

"What about you? Will you be okay?"

Lifting the makeshift crutches, I smiled, trying to give her the best reassurance that I could. "I will be fine. Promise. Come here." Walking over to me, resting her head on my shoulder, listening to my heartbeat. If only we could have stayed there for longer, the warmth radiating from her, the comfort she found within me. "You need to stay safe, it is you they will want. Not me."

"I will be careful."

Planting a kiss on her forehead, my hand stroking back a few strands of her hair which took her back quite a lot since we had never been this close. In that moment I felt a connection with her that had never been felt before, as though she wanted me to comfort her in that manner. I had been quite right to believe so. Parting her lips ready to talk, she closed them, smiling awkwardly to decide what she would say.

"Are you okay?"

"Yes, I——"

"Go on."

"Thank you, Theodore, not just for now."

"Then what for?"

"For everything." Kissing my cheek gently, her hand stroking the skin on the back of my arm. "Always being here when I needed someone, despite how we originally felt. See you over there."

"See you over there."

Chapter 11
Ferell Lucy Berrel, that rhymes.

Tender touch of his skin on mine, albeit very small and minor in somebody else's eyes, considerably small. How could it be that we had turned from people of two very different natures, hating each other very passionately, to wanting to save each other's lives. Maybe I had been correct all along, in mind only, that we had a connection I did not want to admit. Ever since meeting Theodore, coming on this expedition, if you will excuse the dramatic use, everything in my life has been turned upside down and on its head. Afterall, finding out that little Edward had been real yet my little daughter, Lily, had never been real in the first place.

Henry, my father, appearing one time as a murderer with intent on killing, then my father, then Liam Fernsby! Everything had never been how it seemed, especially not now, not here. Something had to be truly incorrect with this place, even if it had not been real either. One solid goal, in mind, in heart, to escape this prison once and for all even if it meant injury and wounds. It would happen. Theodore set off on his path promptly to the left, I on the other hand took a quick detour to the right where they had used an old abandoned building with a dilapidated structure to store food, water, supplies and all sorts of other goods. Taking up one of the bags, already having its weaved tie undone, emptying all of its contents onto the floor where they had moved all the large bricks, tools, wood, anything that stopped them from being able to have enough room for everyone and everything. Outside, the hum of animals inside the woods stirred, no noise, not even the slightest coming from those within the centre of our campsite, stopping in motion completely. Not blinking, breathing, speaking, looking, thinking, motioning for any help. Statutes. Glued to the ground in their habitual movements and acts, facial expressions and feelings. Me and Theodore have been the only ones living, or so it seemed. Despite him noticing that Christopher was nowhere to be seen within the group, it was impossible for him to not be alive like us, he had to be frozen in time.

Inside the abandoned small housing, they had neatly laid out all of the food supplies in one corner, water and liquids in another, building materials, followed by tools, weaponry and all other things I cannot explain being here. So, one by one, I took liquid supplies, consisting of mostly water, followed by perishables, knowing that they would turn disgusting in just a few days. Bread, jams in jars, liquid butter having melted in the heat, some fish wrapped in paper. Some of these things, the way that they had been kept, was very questionable. The sunlight would not be rising for a while, neither would anyone outside. My hand deciding to take extras, praying that the strength I had could take the weight easily. Bit by bit, my head edged towards the empty gap where a door would have been to see if anyone was waiting for me outside. The coast was clear. Striking a flint and steel I had found near the tools, the fire lit up a lantern that I had managed to scavenge from the pile of items the others had left behind from a while back. Sliding a knife into my sock, down into my shoe with its sheath, I knew that it would keep me safe if I ever needed to defend myself, loading a gun with bullets, hiding it inside the pocket of my apron. Even though part of one of the protective doors had been shattered away, it seemed to work perfectly fine, especially for the purpose I intended to use it for.

"Psst! Lucy!" A hushed shout called from behind me. A man, the look of Christopher with a cape around his body, a hood over his head. "It is me, Christopher!"

"What are you doing here? Never mind that, why are you alive?"

"I could ask you the same thing."

Dangling by his side, a gun, a lot smaller than the ones I thought our country had made, resting with a lot of bullets inside of which I could tell. "What is that? Why are you wearing that?"

"Before I answer, put those items down and put this black robe on you." Tossing me a robe similar to his, I placed it over my body as he picked up the hood from the back tossing it over my head. "This is what they call a handgun, nasty little toy. I am wearing this robe because they wander about this place, if you are not wearing it then you are shot dead."

"What about Theodore?"

"I met him on the way, ensured he put it on, do not worry."

"Who are these people?"

"They are called the silencers, sourcing a robe that had been dumped around the tree, if you speak or even try to speak you die."

"Basically, you die whatever happens?"

"It appears to be that way." His eyes darted around, ducking underneath one of the window ledges where the glass had been shattered, pieces remaining on the ground, still in place at the corners. "Shh! Get down."

Despite the hushed voice, his hand caught my arm dragging me down, the bare knees where my dress had lifted scraping against the gravel, off cuts of woods and sand.

"Do not look at them directly in the eyes, it is said that they will kill you."

"Where and how did you find that out?"

"I took a detour around this place, found a little note somebody had left pinned to one of the half-broken wooden doors that still hang on the hinges."

"And… what did it say?"

Picking up a letter from the back of his trouser pocket, he handed its delicate form to me as the torn edges, tattered corners and browned sides had started to crumble away through years of being untouched, then handled with a lot less dignity and respect. It had many contents, full of many different thoughts, emotions, ideas about this place. Hopefully instructions would follow, even though I had a fairly good idea as to what we needed to do. When Theodore questioned my whereabouts, events that had taken hold on that clifftop it acted as a decoy for me to examine the bodies at the end of the shoreline, knowing full well that my inquisitive questions as to where they had been tossed could leave him in the dark. Everything he said, everything he did, indicating to me that the decisions I had taken, certainly managed to prove to me how gullible he could be, not even thinking about what I was doing. Just why. In all honesty, I knew that Liam would turn up soon after our first encounter, it had been on the cards all along. An inevitability in the grand scheme of things. What had truly puzzled me from the offset had been the chain breaking free? Where did my ability to be able to throw such powerful acts of violence? In all my life, I had been a person highly against violence. At least all that they had told me had been real. These things had never come together completely, Father had been against me fighting the bullies who decided to torment me day by day, in the hope one day I would buckle underneath their pressure. Not one time did I touch them with a finger, expressed a decision or thought that could have offended them, I was defenceless. Within all of this, I felt an emotion, gave myself a thought I wished had never crossed my mind… it haunted me day after day without giving me any warning as to when it would hit. When it hit, it hit more harshly than any bullet wound could give to me, burning flames seething my skin. What was that thought you might ask? Well, to be quite truthful, at times I wished he was dead. My father. Every single breath I took, my tormentors had stolen away, father did not do a single thing to help me, help it to stop. Apart from when I was bleeding, bruised, broken hearted, left with the souls that slide in the corner ready for death. If anything, it had all turned me into a fighter. That thought haunted me so much for when I wished he had been dead, in my mind, never spoken, we awoke the next morning to his dead body. Whilst it looked real to the supposed doctor, at this point in time I cannot even begin to state whether or not he is alive, whether he is still in his grave. *In loving memory of…* shading him from the harshness of the sun.

"Lucy, we need to go, right now. The coast is clear."

"Okay."

Stealing a glance to my left, his hand gripping my jaw turning it to the right. "Remember, shut up, stay close, do not look."

"Mmm."

"Not a word!" Without responding to his commandment, he pulled his hood over his head, holding the lantern outwardly in front of him as I carried the supplies on my back, ensuring that the gun still remained in the front of my apron, knife in my shoe. "Good. To the right."

Nodding, without speaking, I saw the point he had been getting at. Since they had been after me, it would be clear to them who I was if at any point I decided to speak, his threats of me dying could possibly be all a hoax. I was not ready to just dismiss them, right now had not been a good time to. So, I kept my head down on the ground, eyeing the different sized pebbles, stones and rocks lining the dried mud on the ground, hiding amid the grass.

Pathways had been lined out where many people had walked countless times, trampling the greenery with the dirt on their feet, setting a pathway just like this.

Whispering gravely under his breath. "Raise your head, they are all gone."

"How can you look at them, but I cannot?"

"Do you want them to recognise you?"

"No, you are right."

"Right then, we just need to make it up the path without any trouble."

"Can I talk?"

"Did I say you could talk?"

"No."

"Be quiet then."

Twiddling together my fingers in an attempt to calm my anxiety, we entered a wood filled mostly with tropical trees, everywhere you turned there was a different colour. Despite it being dark, I noticed the different colours that surrounded me, tainted by the black of the night, coloured by the shining of the moon on their surfaces. They danced, they swayed amid the warmth of the moonlight breeze. Each colour glorious in its own way, scented with fantastic smells that could not compare — especially with the smell of London. Most of the time, we would be choking up back home, the air dense, thick on our lungs, still it had been all I had ever known. Now the smells of this place, thinness of its texture remedies the broken hearted, gave help to the poor, opened the eyes of the unbeliever, gave me a reason to heal. Without this, I dared not to think about the scary place I would be in, no longer able to keep a level head. Something felt wrong, as though something had happened. I was unsure whether to believe my gut, or carry on walking. Something felt wrong with Theodore, I feel his emotions as he feels mine, connected in some way, I dare not to imagine who we are, what relationship we have on the outside of this place.

"You are silent. You are never silent, Lucy." Ignoring the sly comment he had made, I made a mental note that this was his way of coping with anxiety, stress, in a hope that it would give him some relief to take his pain out of someone else. "Cat got your tongue?"

"No."

"Ah. She speaks."

"I cannot talk and I will not talk."

"You have something on your mind, might as well speak before your thoughts eat you up."

"Before *they* eat me up, you mean."

We both chuckled heartily, breaking the tension that had built up between us after the long trek we had taken, the deadly silence bearing heavily on the mood between us.

"Go on. What have you been so vexed about? Is it

Theodore?"

"Yes, I have a feeling something it very wrong, something has happened, I cannot put my finger on it wha—"

Stepping forward in front of me, we both became ensnared in a hunting trap, disguised under piles of leaves, hanging us up into a tree with its crisscrossed bamboo wires. "Get me out of here!"

"Shut up, Lucy, if there is somebody here, and they hear you, they will not release us! They might release us thinking it is just another animal."

"Okay." Sliding my hand into my shoe, pulling the knife out of my sock, proudly displaying it. "I brought a knife with me."

Removing the sheath that held the dangerous metal, its cold blade sharp, began its unintended purpose as it cut through the thick bamboo stringing us in the air like puppets at a show. Biting the bottom of my lip, holding onto the knife for dear life in case it slipped my grip, my hands shaking from exhaustion since the material was thick to cut through. It wore down every strength inside of me.

"How is it coming?"

"My arms ache, especially my hands... this stuff is thick to cut through."

"Give it to me."

"No, I am nearly there." A little closer to us being free from this entrapment, the bamboo had definitely been on its last legs. "Be prepared to drop in 3... 2... 1."

A great thud onto the ground, making next to no sound apart from the crunching of leaves underfoot. Our hoods had dropped down, we immediately ensured that they returned to be on our heads just in case. We did not know where anyone had been, let alone Theodore, I had to find him before they did. Whether it had been pure instinct, knowledge, somebody telling me mentally that something had to be wrong, I could not tell for the life of me.

"Listen to that." Christopher held a hand to my lips that prepared to speak telling me all I could hear. "Is that Theodore! He sounds as though he is in pain."

"Theodore! Theodore!"

"Lucy…" His agonised voice called out into the pitch black where no man could see, despite the mediocre light of the lantern. "They have me strung in a tree!"

Even though he was far away from us, Christopher and I clearly knew he was in agony, possibly bleeding. Meandering through the density of the forest, he held the lantern high above his head where a row of trees were set out in a line clearly placed there by hand, grown over many years for a purpose. What purpose that they had in mind had definitely been clear as day. People. Dead people strung up in the trees not hung, left to die in the snares lining the thick growth of trees, held highly above all as a prize, first class in their opinion. Sick.

Many more people of all different ages seemed to be dead — young children, wandering from their parents disobediently wanting to investigate all kind of things; adults, young mostly, holding harvesting tools that they could have used to cut through; elderly, clearly very oblivious to what had happened, unfortunately not having the means to slice through.

"Theodore!" I cried at the sight of seeing him in the lamplight, his bloodied hand stretching out to me in his time of agony. He could not stand to reach the top to rid himself of the ensnarement. "Stay calm I will get you out of there."

"Okay, hurry, I am losing far too much blood."

"I know, stay with us." Pulling out a drink of water from the bag, unscrewing the tightened cap then pulling it away, tearing off its top so he could drink properly. "Here, drink this, leave your hood on."

So the hard work began, with Christopher taking hold of the care for Theodore ensuring he stayed awake, holding the bottle of the canteen to help his weak hands from shaking since it had been heavy. How they had managed to make these snares so thick to cut through? Not even the greatest craftsman, builder, constructor could comprehend the workmanship.

"I hope you're proud!" Gnarling into the black space, spitting the words with vigour unable to control the strong overflow of upset, aggression building a storm inside of me. "Oh yes! Do not forget how you killed most of the people I love in my life! Taking my son! Go string yourself up in this tree, at least then justice would be served on you!"

"Maybe I will, maybe I will not, it depends on your next choice. Lucy."

"Liam Fernsby."

"Sergeant Fernsby, please, humble yourself."

"Okay, Sergeant Fernsby, what are you here for?" Continually cutting through the strands in hope of a large enough gap to remove Theodore from this prison. "An offer I presume, what can you even offer me!"

"You can be very nasty when you're scared."

"Scared of what?"

"Scared of losing lover boy, right? Well, I can offer you an awful lot if you listen."

"Go right ahead, I am all ears."

Shining a light onto Theodore's face, revealing blood dripping from him, hand marks where he held them to his face in order to let out the tears of pain come down his cheeks. He wore, not a smile, but a clenched expression with his teeth, blood from his hands having caught on his pearly whites.

"He has not got very long left to live, before he bleeds to death." Shining my light, I held my arm above my head squinting with the sharp brightness. "You will come with me, for a full day to see your mother, then we can help your boyfriend here. Deal."

Torn. Torn between what was right for Theodore, what was right for me, I saved his life once, I had the power to save it again. Dropping the knife to the ground in sheer shock, Theodore looking to me with loving eyes, unable to contemplate the situation befalling us. "Just let me die, Lucy, you cannot keep saving me."

"Or I can save you again."

Christopher remained silent, the narcissistic Fernsby making sound effects with his tongue tapping his wrist. "Tick tock. Tick tock. Tick Tock."

"Shut up! Do not speak, do not say anything!"

"Ah. So you are considering it. Tick tock. Tick tock."

"I told you, *Liam*, to *shut up*!"

"Okay, okay. Tick tock. Tick tock."

Growling, feral emotions overtaking me. "Liam!"

"Feral Lucy Berrel, it rhymes. Hah."

Tapping my foot against a leaf on the floor, I bent down to pick the knife and sheath back up, sliding it into my shoe.

"I have made my decision."

"What would that be?"

"I will come with you for a day." Pulling the gun out of the front of my apron around my waist, aiming it at his head. "*One* day, that is it. Any longer, I will not hesitate to shoot, I have pretty good aim."

"Hmph. Of course, put the gun away."

"Why?"

"Be a good little girl and do it."

Without a fuss, I put the gun back into the pocket of the apron, walking towards him. "Try anything and I promise you it will fire."

Pressing my two fingers against his head in the shape of a gun, locking my eyes onto him, I pretended to fire one with a fake gun shot. "I get your point."

"What was that!" Something stuck in the side of my neck, sharp, flooding a liquid through my neck. Woozy. Everything went blurry, nothing was visible as I turned to just about view Christopher lying on the floor. "Chrissy—"

Falling with a heavy thud, everything began tingling, feeling numb… nothing at all could move, stiff, a dull aching. He poisoned me!

"Good, take their bodies out of here."

Eyelids fluttering shut, after fighting to keep them open for a short amount of time that felt longer than reality had portrayed. I felt dead, but alive.

Chapter 12
How does it feel knowing I will never love you?

"Ugh. My head."

Above me bright lights drew me to a state of awareness despite the heaviness weighing down my arms, feet and chest. Why? Throughout my body, a cold liquid spread throughout me, something that could not be described. Attempting to sit up becoming a challenge upon seeing I was bound to a bed around the ankles and wrists. Pipes, tubes pushed underneath my skin as many different coloured substances pushed through my body. A headache. All of this white, an angelic shade around me. Slightly yellow lights flickering ever so slightly, not noticeable, detectable to a trained eye, looking ever so closely with the time. Pain. Stabbing in my feet, then my hands. A shrieking condemnation escaping my lips, an unpleasant wail killing away any other thoughts. This pain was on my mind, until, through the corner of my eye on the right, a few figures walking outside the grey, silver, metal room on the outside watched me pull against the metal encasing my ankles, writing down anything they noticed about me. Wearing white cloaks, all of them focussing on the work at hand, careful to not miss a detail with their beady eyes scrutinising each sound that escaped the lips which remained sealed for compromise.

"Sick! The lot of you are sick in the head! Find another hobby! Before you do that, get me the hell out of here."

One of them closer to me clicked something on a panel full of different buttons, holding a clipboard to her chest, placing a visor around her ears, tapping a pen against the wooden material. "Hello, Lucy, I see you are awake."

"I see you enjoy torturing people." Repeatedly tugging against the metal on my ankles and wrists, gritting the tops and bottoms of my teeth in agony, managing to free the left arm. "Ah. One arm is free. Now I can get this rubbish out of me!"

Tearing away the needles stuck in my right arm, holding each of them out in front of her eye. Her gaze unwavering as I tore them out, watching her flinch slightly. "Did that not hurt? My monitor says that it did."

"You are one annoying, little woman, I have been through enough to tolerate this little chit chat with you." A smirk grew on my lips, ensuring she could visibly see it, the wickedness embedding deep inside of me beginning to grow. Everyone has a wicked side at some point, unlike these people here, it is not a daily thing. "Unfortunately for you, whilst I was speaking, I am no longer attached to these wretched things you enjoy watching me under."

"Hannah! Take note! Take note!"

Standing up straight, shaking the feeling into my arms and legs, I snatched my eyes back to focus on where I was, my surroundings, who they were. Finding that I had been dressed in another dress which was not blue, instead a white skater dress with a smaller white apron around it, containing all my belongings from the old one.

"Oh! Oh! Thank you, Sergeant Liam Fernsby."

"How do you know Fernsby?"

"I know him well enough to say he is a narcissist, and you should shut up talking right about now. Take note of that!" Pulling the gun out of my pocket, aiming it four times, each of the corners of the glass, shattering the entire screen in front of the floor as they all took cover. Without shoes I could not exit this place, to the left of me, a pair of trainers sat in the corner, sliding on simply, no hassle.

"Someone get help!"

One man spoke up in the corner of their investigation room, locking with me, not scared whatsoever. "Maybe start crying for it."

Shooting a shot just above his hairline, ducking underneath the computer desk taking cover, begging me to not fire again, I would never. Still a woman carried on taking notes on the opposite side of the room, trying to secretly take notes without me noticing. Another shot!

Fired through her clipboard, destroying the notes she had been taking. "My notes!"

"Sorry, you should have made a copy."

Taking a bed sheet from the pile in the room, I threw it over the edge of the wall so I would not cut myself on the remaining shards of glass protruding from its lining.

Inside myself, the big facade I had put on terrified all the women and men in the room, no longer able to gather the words for the situation at hand, unable to put into context what was happening. One minute I had been peaceful, civil, as they watched my chest rise and fall with every breath I took, noting down new information, readings that they had taken from the tests performed on me.

"Call for help, I promise you, I will find you, I will hunt you, I will make you regret the day that you were born!"

Despite the dishevelled mess that my hair was in, there had to be no other place I would rather be than in Theodore's arms, the memories of what had happened to us still firmly fixed in my mind that no one would ever be able to remove. So many things did not add up at all, nothing able to be pieced together, the mentality I was currently facing leaving me feeling hopeless, broken. Hands trembling at the trigger, aiming it at anyone who looked as though they would attempt to take me down, ready for a fight. I was a master, they, my servants.

"You! There! Get up."

A young woman, possibly my age, stood up with her hands in the air, eyes quivering unable to lock eyes with me, completely shook up by the situation. "Wha—what can I do?"

"Listen to me, I want a whole map of this place, exits, everything."

"Now?"

"Now!" Growling at the top of my lungs, a remorseless narrowing focus on her, watching her eyes as she moved. "Move it!"

Cracking the gun in line with her head, I was not in the mood after being watched for however long I had been there. Taken note of, hooked up to medication I had not given permission for them to hook me up to, locked into a bed without a choice. None of it. Still, it violated every bit of freedom a human could have. Every. Last. Bit.

"Here…" With trembling fingers, she pointed to the different place where I could get out of here, identifying where I could run into trouble, guards would lie in wait for me since they have cameras everywhere. Someone would have to come eventually having heard the many gunshots having been fired.

"That is all the information I have."

"Good, thank you, now be a good girl and come with me."

"I have given you everything you wanted!"

"Unfortunately, I have other plans for you, you are my ticket to getting out of here, Hannah." Tapping the gun on her laminated lapel by her heart, she failed to meet my eyes, fearing the worst, not daring to speak any more. "One wrong move… and you know exactly what will happen."

"Or you will let her go, daughter."

"Mother."

"Yes, Lucy, it is I."

Pushing Hannah away into the wall, strolling towards Mother with confidence, cockiness, arrogance, all in the walk, smirking as I did so, swinging the gun on the tip of my index finger.

"Hello."

"Hi. How have you been?"

"Cut the chit chat, the pleasantries, I do not care for all the *how have you been* malarky. What do you want from me?"

"To start over."

"Turn a new leaf." Nodding along in agreement, I tut tutted her. "You need to do an awful lot better than that, Mother dear. Maybe talk a lot less here, and somewhere more private, unless you want me to let all of your dear colleagues know what a cruel person you are."

"You would, I know, I have watched you."

Since how I turned out, the tempest that had risen calmed down. What she had yet to learn, was how truly furious I would become, in an instant and over time. "You watched me!"

"Very closely, how did you manage to move on so easily from your first husband, then find your next."

190

"Because I do not leave them selfishly."

"How does it feel knowing you never had a daughter in the first place?"

"How does it feel knowing I will never love you?"

Unable to control the movement of my hand making contact with her face, palm completely slapping her across the face, skin on skin, as she covered the side where I left a mark with the complete obliteration, I brought on her. Red, bruised, pained. Across her face, she wore a mark of upset terror, that her only daughter, only child, struck her with upset, for not wanting to know her. It had gotten to the point where I did not care less, she never blinked an eyelid when leaving me, why should I give her another chance.

"Lucy, I want to tell you why I left."

"Why you left! Oh! Of course there will be a plausible explanation for this."

"Yes, Lucy, there is." Putting her cold hand on my back, she wanted to lead me forwards. Instead of backing down, I shrugged her off, reminding her I had a gun. "You would never fire it."

"Who said I would not."

"You are a smart girl."

"Certainly did not get that from you."

After walking in silence for at least five minutes, we came to a room with a modern, brown wooden door. A gold handle pushing downwards to the floor as if backing away, leading me into an inviting room with comforting colours. Welling inside the corner of my eye, it reminded me of the family home, everything in the correct places, as they would have been in my childhood. The money that we had, ample enough to provide for the necessities and more.

"I see you missed this place."

"I did. At least there is one thing I can agree on."

"Two things."

"What would be the second?"

"We missed each other, every day for the past sixteen years since I left, you have read the letter I sent to you day in day out. Every day since I left you, I watched you grow, twenty-four hours a day, not wanting to miss a thing." Pulling out a chair around a table, I sat down on the opposite side, her hand taking mine. I had let her. For now. "I know you have been through so much, I was not there. Just know, I am proud of you, always have been. Always will be. Even if you decide you do not trust me, love me, want me in your life. There is not a second I go by, where I regret the decision I made. You have questions, you want answers. Maybe it would be good for us to get to know each other. I want to live knowing I tried." Considering carefully all she had said, I felt a connection there, this was not fake or a pretence she had put on for me. Her genuine motherly instincts kicking in, grabbing my hand tighter and tighter as though I could leave her for another time.

"To be honest, I did not believe I would say this to you. Yet, I cannot live without the closure. I want to get to know you again, Mom."

Her lips thinning out as they widened on her face, crying with strong passion. I had accepted her words, taken them onboard and wished to act.

"So do I, baby girl, so do I."

"First off…" Squeezing her hand to indicate I was not leaving, giving me comfort that we could still restore what she had left behind even though there might still be prejudice against her. "Where is Theodore?"

"Do you mean husband number two?"

"He is not my husband." We laughed together for the first time since I turned ten. From the moment it turned one minute past in the morning, we celebrated the first decade of life through love, laughter, tears I was growing up and many more happy cheers. This felt right. "Just tell me where he is, if he is alive, survived or…"

"I know what you mean. He came out of surgery five hours ago, recovered from the anesthetic three hours ago. Fernsby told us you would be here for a few days. Then, if you like it here, you can stay. Or, go back to the way things were, in that wretched place."

"Excuse me!"

"Did I say something?"

"*Fernsby* said something. He said only for a day."

"Oh, well, that is all he told me. Just give yourself a rest from fighting, you never stop."

"Ever since… you know, you left. I changed. It made me this way."

"How?"

Lifting up part of the wavy hair, I revealed to her scars on both sides, another ranging from underneath my hairline to beneath the dress, slightly yellow as it bumped out of my skin. Returning memories from so long ago, so near, so close that I felt as though I would be able to feel the blood pouring out of me on each of those occasions. Persecuted for not having a mother, pushing me down the grass hills, bashing my head against a tree, a lump forming on my scalp. Further followed by a stronger shove into the stream where a river washed away my tears, the blood from the scar turning the water yellow as the rock waited for the blood to dry on its whittled point, having cut the back of my neck tremendously.

"For years I was tormented by bullies for not having a mother, never giving me a break, it felt as though I would break at some point. Pushing me, shoving me, hitting me, dragging me by the hair, name calling, tormenting, locking me in a room that proved inescapable. Until I learned tricks to get myself out of a locked room, breaking free from locks, escaping the fate they had for me."

"All this time I was here!"

"Mother, you leaving was for the best, in a way. I did not understand at the time. You could have left when I was in my baby years, toddler years when a mother needs her child more than ever. Yet, you reached out to me, now releasing the mistake you ma—"

"I am just so sorry, baby girl!" Her whimpering shrieked in my ears, audibly deafening me for a brief moment. "Please! Just forgive me, I never understood how I left you but, I want to try, make things right."

"Then, if you want me to forgive you, I want to know where people are? What that place is where they have had me cooped for the past twenty-six years of this hell-bound life I have lived!"

"Who do you want to find?"

"My father, not Liam Fernsby disguised as him, my real father."

"Your father died two years ago."

"He left me as well!" By this point, I gave way to tears after trying to suppress the lump in the back of my throat. It still returned time and time again. "Why does everyone want to leave me?"

"People left you because they did not believe you to be

real. The descriptions are far too complicated to go into, but, there is something different in you. Compared to everyone else. Nobody believed me when I came here, that you had an ability, a different type of blood that allowed you to be so strong, capable to help those around you."

"Is that what this is?" Pulling up the skirt slightly, revealing the knife carving on my thigh, then pulling down the side of the white trainers to reveal my ankle markings as well. "Do you know what these mean?"

"We all do. Apart from those who decide to not believe."

"Believe in what?"

"You have a marking of survival. A marking that allows you to survive anything, you recover, you remain young... unless someone finds a way to destroy you. That is why we had been running tests."

"To find out why this happens."

"Everybody wants to remain young, forever, do they not." After taking all of this in, a migraine came over me quite quickly. Taking in all this information at once would not register whatsoever. "Are you hungry, I could make you some food if you would like?"

Listening to the loud rumbles of my stomach, I must have not eaten in days; I had been far too intrigued in the matters of life, solving the problems of others. "How I have survived this long without feeling hungry... is a miracle."

"I told you, you have the mark of survival, you could live without food for the rest of your life."

"And water?"

"And water. What would you like to eat?"

"Can I test you?"

"Sure. Go ahead."

"Make me my favourite meal, or food for that matter."

"Cheese sandwich coming right up!"

I was grinning down at the table, replaying the memories of my childhood in my mind when lunch came. I had been home-schooled for the first ten years of my life, and twelve o'clock in the afternoon, a chiming clock in the hall following by the thudding steps of me charging down the stairs for the prized cheese sandwich. The wafting of the fresh hot bread from the bakers as the butter spread across the beige surface, cheese delicately placed onto the sandwich, cut into triangles.

"What shape are you cutting them in?"

"Squares!"

"Squares!"

"Just kidding." Her chuckles sent a wave of relief that I would not have to eat squares. Pathetic I know. "So, this Theodore, what makes him so special?"

"Nothing much."

Placing the sandwich in front of me, licking my lips uncontrollably after living without these kinds of luxury for so long. "Come on, have you truly moved on from William?"

Drumming each of my fingers on the oak table, a smile formed as I shook my head in utter disappointment that she asked, having pushed the sandwich aside till our little matter in question had been solved. "How long did it take you to get over Dad's death?"

"I am still not over his death, to be honest with you."

Taking a picture within her hands, she held it as though it would break if let go, if released from her touch. "If you want to know how I got over William's death, I still have not for the time to consider it has yet to dawn on me. I cannot, I will not let the feelings take control of me."

"You have to at some point." Pointing to the sandwich I had left to the right hand of me, taking a large enough bite to satisfy her. "Eat it all, not just a bite."

"I am not the ten-year-old girl that you left."

"I am not the mother that left you all those years ago."

"I am not some fool."

"I am not going to let you go back into that jungle island."

"I am not going to leave till you answer my questions!"

"I am not going to let you go without finding the answers then!" By this point we stood opposite each other, my height a few inches over her, the shrinkage of old age bringing this fate to her. "If that will be all it takes. Sit your backside back down."

Obeying, for now. Nothing was certain, especially not then, never. I wanted to trust her, I truly did, right then, right there, everything seeming so unnatural, I still hurt realising how she had left me.

"Mom, when can I see Theodore?"

"I do not know, he pulled out of surgery and that is all I know, okay."

"Can we go and find out?"

"Not until you finish eating."

Soon enough, I stuffed the sandwich in my cheeks, smiling with the bread protruding out of my teeth, spraying my words out. "Can I go to the bathroom?"

"The door behind you."

"Thank you." Chewing down the rest of the remains in my mouth, taking my hand to the golden handle, similar to the one on the door just outside of here, confused in the toilet that befell me. "How do I use this?"

"Just sit on it, and do what you need to do."

"Can I shut the door?"

"Yes, just shut it, I do not want to see anything untoward."

"Good point!" The door closed behind me, doing what I needed to do, still nosing through the items in her bathroom. "What is this? Oops!"

"Are you okay in there?"

"Yes! Just fine thank you."

What was this? At that moment I realised she had been a distraction, my own mother had been used as a pawn in Liam's games. Sorting out myself, I found the intrigue to begin a thorough sweep of this one room, all sorts of items stored in here: needles, filled with an emerald serum, clearly to be used on herself or others, possibly for her aging process; a white label with a doctor's writing scrawled on them, initials inscribed 'LB' possibly mine, possibly not; inside the make-up bag, a few things checked out to be ordinary apart from the notes kept inside... my notes. Taking them back, placing them back into the apron tied around my waist, ensuring nobody would take them. Good.

"You have been in there a while, Lucy."

I had been in there for less than five minutes, clearly, she did not want me inside for more than a minute of time, knowing everything that had been going on. Clearing away the few crumbs on my cheeks ensuring there had been no fault, straightening the edge of my skirt, slight clearing of the throat, straightening everything in the bathroom to avoid suspicion.

"Can we go now?"

Opening the door wide, her hum showing she had been scrutinising, leaning against the door with her looking dishevelled. "Yes, of course. This way."

Putting the gun into my hand, the handle reminding me of

the mad actions I had taken to get my way just an hour or so earlier, the fear people express, the things people will go so far as to do just to spare their lives.

"What made you put me under those high levels of medical investigation?"

"You may have been unconscious when we brought you here, but, my goodness you do not stop fighting."

"So even when I was unconscious, I put up a fight."

"Yes."

Grinning with the purest feeling of delight with myself, the first commenting coming out could not have been more narcissistic, striding with pride as we entered another corridor.

"I'm cool."

"Boosting your ego?"

"I never had one. Just felt like it. You understand me?"

"You have changed your tune?"

"Because you injected me with this stuff!" Holding the needle into the light, spraying a little onto the ground. "What does it do?"

"I am not allowed to say Lucy, I thought that we were okay now."

"Just lead me to Theodore. That is I want right now."

"Sure."

Tension. Personal hatred, sense of loathing, refining issues I knew I should have trusted. How she had managed to inject me with this was unknown considering I would have noticed. Unless…

"How did you inject me?"

"I did not." Unveiling the notes from beneath the bottom of the pocket, her eyes immediately widening, gulping a massive amount, stopping still in her tracks. "Where did you get those?"

"Your make-up bag. So, tell me the truth!"

"I will not ever tell you!"

"Because you are not a real person. You are a test designed to make me trust everything around me, this is all a big hoax, when is the grand movie opening?"

"No, Lucy, I am real."

"Why was it planned to inject me with this serum?"

Her silence pause depleted my hope in her telling me the truth, it had never been far from the innocence of an adult who is fully aware of their actions and the consequences that would come over time after doing such things. You wither away, wilting to the touch, wilting under the poison injected, for in reality you know such things have to happen. I was untouchable unless someone came along to kill me. A wound. I could recover. Hunger and thirst. I can recover. Why then would my own mother seem to have an underlying displeasure with me being this way? Surely, it is a mother's duty to love her child no matter what, no matter the cost. You. Love. Them.

"I had not planned it, this was just for your own good, can you not see!"

"That you despise me, for being this way."

"For being like me."

"Stop lying!"

"I am not lying!"

"Yes, you are!" Pushing the serum into her arm, I started down the hall, throwing away the serum through a glass window that had been blackened out so no one could see, stealing a steel look at my mother, before turning back again. "How does it feel knowing I will never love you?"

"How does it feel knowing I will recover from this serum,

you injected me with. You will have to find your own way out, if this is how you feel."

Taking out a dart gun from her pocket, she blew her life-giving air to it, only poisoned at the tip, shooting into my neck with a thwump! Oh... no. Thwump! Thwump! Thwump! Clicking on heels, everywhere around me figures as I start spinning around, unable to control my feet, control my breath, the heart rate in my chest pounding like a beating drum to the rhythm of a thousand feet in a marching band, pulse heightening, feeling it straight through. Entirely through.

"Where am I?"

"In a room, listen to the voice, follow it home."

"Where is home?"

"With me, Lucy, follow it!"

Another voice deciding to pipe in, both male, both wanting me to come to them. "No! Do not listen to him, Lucy, come with me, our children!"

It was Theodore and William. He was alive.

Chapter 13
When you marry someone, you do not lie to them Will!

Watching her for these past few days has been one of the hardest challenges ever to be faced. Most of the injuries I had to endure were real, others had been fake but in ways real. All too confusing. No wonder she would choose to go with Theodore. I lied to her, I lied to my wife whether I choose to accept this fact now or never. I lied to her, we only had one child, Edward. Another lie, he was taken forever, all this time he was with me being told countless lies. For her sake. After all this time, I truly believed she would never move on from our marriage so swiftly, at least some more mourning, it never happened. How would she be able to mourn? We both had unfinished questions to ask each other, wanting explanations for everything that had become of each other, knowing how the other person was doing. Only her side. Now she found herself back where she originally came, a place that did not really exist but it did, inside the jungle wearing her black cloak, listening to mine and Theodore's voices, a gun in her hand, shaking with such lack of control. A test. To see if this stronger, more pure, potent substance would cause her to turn like this. It worked completely. These types of people we need with the outside world, a situation unlike any other where war is out of control, nowhere untouched by nuclear weaponry, bomb, gunfire, littering the ground with dead bodies, rotting in the smoke and toxicity from the gases, flames, smoke. Killing all life within abrupt, forceful contact.

"Okay, Lucy, listen to my voice, you must."

"William." Her gasps of surprise, her tears irreplaceable, rolling down her cheeks. Seeing her cry for me at least once more was enjoyable. "You stupid idiot! You are dead!"

"No, Lucy, he is alive trust me, I have seen him after he sliced a gash in my arm."

"Theodore!" Her gasps exceeding those she gave for me, she had more of an inclination towards him. Convincing is all it would take to get her on my side. Surely. Play with her mind.

"He is not who he appears to be, the countless lies he has told you. Focus on me, on me." Pulling up her hood, her arms becoming steadier than a surgeon's, cracking the gun to the left path in front of her, aiming for my figure standing up on the top of the hill.

"Okay then, William, give me one reason to not shoot you. Trust me, I will do that in a heartbeat!"

"No need, I have all the answers you have been searching for, surely?"

"It depends, tell me something I do not already know before I shoot." Everything that came off her tongue shocked me to the core, taking me aback, she was no longer so innocent in need of protecting. "Come on! You can die twice. One... two... three..."

"Fine! Your son is alive, your daughter was never real!"

"Knew that already, give me something else. Three... two... one."

Raising her eyebrow to me, I began walking from the distance to an easier eyeline for her to see the man she used to love, hoping, praying after everything she would still have something. Nothing showed, dropping the microphone to the side of me, my footfalls making clicks, thwumps in the background as I went. Click. Click. Click. Thwump. Thwump. Thwump.

"You are back inside the place you only ever remember, but it is the jungle, this is not a real place but… it is."

"I knew that as well."

"How much do you know?"

Sliding the top of the gun backwards, aiming it at my head, her hand held still, ensuring to give not a single emotion away to me, a blank canvas waiting to be painted, with her blood. "What I know should not concern you!"

Contorting her face aggressively, her eyes gradually narrowing so I could no longer see the emerald in her eyes, just the dark black pupils radiating the heat of anger towards me for lying. Truly understandable.

"What you know always concerns me, Lucy, what you have been through concerns me, a lot of things concern me."

"Theodore concerns you, why?"

Putting my hand on her shoulder, gently feeling the warmth of her skin against my hand, she shivered to my touch pushing away the hand that still loves her. Deeply ingrained inside her mind has been an ever-growing tendency to continue throwing me away to the side, as if I meant absolutely nothing to her now, as if I never had.

"Theodore does not concern me, why should he? We are married, Lucy."

"When you marry someone, you do not lie to them, Will!"

Throwing a forceful push into the shoulder on my left, she knew exactly where I had been wounded by Lewis Peterson, still wearing off the after effects of the medicine he had been injected with on that fatal night. The night she actually felt something for me. Now, her eyes coldly staring darkly into myself begging to rip every last piece of my heart from its beating place, wanting nothing more than to hurt me. Hurt me. Bring me to justice. How could I blame her? Why should I blame her?

"I know, I had to lie to you, I had to do that."

"Well tell me! If you want to undo your guilt then tell me, as my husband what went wrong!"

"Firstly, quit pressing the gun against my chest."

Unknown to her, the end of the gun was practically wedging into my skin, where it hurt. Untangling the mess of hers, they examined my body tearing off the right side of my shirt, unveiling where she pressed the gun too far into me, now bleeding, seeping into the white shirt. Dripping.

"You're bleeding… I need moss."

"Survival expert?"

"Something like that."

Lifting the back of her black cloak, she replaced the gun into its pocket, casting many a gaze towards the handsome man on the hill, held back by guards not bothering to resist since he would get his turn with her. A few signals from her hands came her way, giving him information I could not understand. I was an outcast in her life. Still, she cared, she had not even requested to get back to how we used to be, instead of this undeniable distance weighing us down, if only a simple apology would suffice for us. Bars. Intensely raw with the cold, frigid conditions. An outcast. Being locked away inside prison walls, no privacy, no nothing, an animal kept there just because of a few things committed, only one person can let you out, let you be free. Everything that you say is accounted for, everything you do, the actions you take continually scrutinised by the unbeliever who examines, develops a stronger opinion of you as the seconds, minutes, hours tick by on the clock. Tapping of finger. Against an interrogation table, in the chambers, cherished so much that you will never understand why they risk everything to be with you. Inside the walls, entrapping, confining you to the manacles on your ankles, on your wrist, even around your head as a dog on a leash. Barking. Growling. Lewis Peterson. After all that had happened on that night, all that had been said and done, reliving in his mind like a record on a repeat, not knowing how to stop it from playing, unless he decided to smash it to pieces, break himself into pieces. Countless times, he was put in restraints, tying him to the bed, not allowing him any bed clothes, bedding, belts, anything with shoe laces since he became so suicidal nobody could understand. His wife, he was constantly missing her every day, not knowing that she had never been a real person in the first place, a figure in the mind put there by force, a fantastic scientific discovery whereby you could change someone's perceptions, memories, imprinting another person's perception and memories... swapping bodies to test if that person has the skills to survive everything going on in the outside world. When Fernsby visited Lucy on the top of the peak, hanging off the cliff side on the Isla de Diseath that night, he injected her with a potent substance which would take minutes to react whilst he had her there. She would be numb inside, fighting to ensure nothing would ever happen to her, so she would continue fighting to find her son, save her daughter... save him! For most of my life, I have made displeasing decisions, none like this, hence how I want her to hear, see how I still feel, know I never wanted to hurt her. Not like this. Coming back to me, a mossy pile delivered in her hands, taking small pieces from the pile, applying pressure on my chest each time. After putting the last piece on the wound, her hand deciding to take a rest there, feeling the heart inside my chest still beating, growing faster and feeling her touch on me again.

"Still thinking about killing me? Killing my heartbeat."

Delving into my eyes, I saw how she wanted nothing more but to deny the sincerity in my eyes, she could read them, a born gift. "I wish I did, you're being honest with me."

Pulling across the red shirt, having a big dripping stain where by blood had been, her hands fumbling with the buttons sealing it shut, her hands patting my chest two times before gazing into my eyes. One smile, for the first time since I had seen her again.

"What?"

"I should talk with Theodore now."

"Why?"

"I need to make my decision, who I stay with. I come back to safety with you, or I face the danger with Theodore and try to escape this place, just know I never take it lightly. Ever."

"No way, I can help you make that decision."

"No there is no—"

Cutting her off, closing the gap between us, I reminded her of everything we married for, why we got married in the first place, as she put her arms around my shoulder, my arms around her waist. Kissing her. For the first time since I left her life, to me it was easier, for her it was harder as she was calling all the shots, not truly knowing how she would cope as a single mother. Now. Right now. Her touch with mine may have rekindled the flame between us, this was just the reason we had been together, this is how we always were. United. Apart. Drifting on driftwood in the sea, unsure of whether a monstrous beast would rise from the murky depths of the blackening sea, ensuring hunger would not kill us but the lust for blood of the body, feeding them for a few months until they found the other one of us.

"Will..." Trailing off in satisfaction, her hand coming up to my face, cupping the jawline, stroking the lines on each side, smiling down to the ground. "Just like when we were married."

"We still are married." Walking backwards with two guardsmen dressed in cloaks, dragging me away from her. "I am listening to you through an earpiece, say nothing you would not want me to hear."

A handsome young man began his walk down to her, Theodore. He was intimidating to any male considering his good looks and brilliant way of understanding. Much to my surprise, Lucy's greetings welcomed him far more pleasantly than me. Throwing her arms around him, untangling his hair from the man bun kept neatly with a band, shaking it up with her hands.

"I prefer it like this."

"Please, Lucy, do not beat around the bush. If, and only if, you want to go back with your husband I completely understand, after all he is your everything. What am I? He helped in giving you a beautiful son, little Eddy, who loves you so much. Please. Save me the pain of dragging this out any longer, I realise it is not me."

"Do you know something?"

"What?"

"It is funny, everything you just said."

Mentally, serving a prayer to God never appealed to me, talking to someone you cannot see, asking for help and guidance always seeming so ridiculous. I had always, will always, find it incomprehensible to the mind that you are speaking to someone not in your eyesight. Here I was, atop the brow of the hill to her left, seeing her every move, hearing her every move as he had been able to hear mine with her... chances on both sides of the story. The lack of interest with me, the lack of liking towards me certainly did not lack with Theodore. What had he done wrong to her? Lost. Engulfing myself in an overwhelming state of panic and emotion that cannot, will not, go away, not for a second until you feed the desire to take away the problem completely. For this, she would not forgive till the day I brought him back, still resentment would remain no matter how often begging occurred, with me on my hands and knees in front of her.

"What was funny?"

"Understanding. That is what is funny Theodore, now, I know that my husband is listening, I know you heard and saw the conversation. Do not think for one second that you do not mean anything to me. Okay, just hold on."

"You should go back, with him, stay safe. I will find a way out of here for us, when I do, we can be together, you deserve to be warm, not cold."

"That is the point. I can only die if someone kills me in one go, there is nothing malnourishment can do to me, nor the cuts and infected wounds. Nothing. I heal."

"What if someone kills you, completely."

"Then they will have you to contend with, right?"

"Of course they would, it is just... never mind."

"I know." Pressing her pale pink lips against his cheeks, his eyes examining, counting every single freckle on her nose, joining the dots I had often done when looking at the stunning wife I could call my own. She was longing for him to call her his own instead of me. "Do you know how long I have to decide?"

"No. Your husband does."

"Will, do you know?"

Sternly, her whispers freakishly echoing down the microphone in his ear, biting her lip down, feeling the dryness; backlash of the sound ringing down my own, screaming intensely. "Tell. Me."

Eyeing the ticking in the mechanics of the gold watch on my wrist, its perfect shape showing the inner desires of my heart, slightly materialistic. Lucy has never been a fan of watches, clocks, anything that has a timepiece. 'You are just watching your life tick away'. To be fair to her, she was correct. On this item of metal, many numbers consisting, alongside hands, choosing when we breathe, when we die, when the hands stop. For we have been given a beating that others could not compare, the timepiece, the glass, spreading across the floor as other people tread upon the shattering remains. Of my heart.

"You have till the end of the night, Lucy."

"How many hours?"

"You never like to know how long, why now?"

"It matters more so now! I can either stay in here and die, or, come with you and possibly live."

Behind me, one of the guardsmen that Fernsby had to escort me down here, took one of his hands, prodding my shoulder till I chose to look him in the eyes. "William, Fernsby has given me the orders to escort you down there, where they are. He has given you the choice."

"How long do I have to decide?" Smirking, innovation creeping to my mind, thinking of how to gain her on my side. "Do you have Edward on your radio?"

"Your son?"

"Yes."

"Let me ask Liam. Mr Fernsby, I should say."

"Nervous around him?"

"He is dangerous and he has a certain feeling towards your wife, I cannot even pinpoint. He likes her. He hates her. Something like that."

Throwing down the earpiece from inside my ear, stamping down the plastic with my foot, I knew now none of them could hear me, responding with full confidence to his slave."Unsure. She has that effect on people. Get Edward on the phone, see if she can contend with this."

Chapter 14
Sick. Twisted. Evil.

Life can give you some good times, some bad, you always need the right ideas, the right mindset to pull through. Mentality is where it all starts as decisions are thrown at you continuously. One thing that is the most challenging, can be the decision of following your head, which knows the best way to go, or your heart, that provides the moral way through. After a while, you figure out if your heart gives you the best judgement, or your head. For some, it can be harder to deal with, harder to grasp, you just find it difficult to make things fit back together again with the glue, the material just gives up being fixed. Upon the hill, I began to read every single tell from William's body language, he had been my husband for a few years so I can easily tell what he is up to, right now. It was not good. A trick up his sleeve. Out here, in the woods, I felt as if everyone had a vendetta against me, nothing appearing as it seems, so many times where I swore things were real but they were not. For example, the fire. Fire burns you, screams at you, tells you that it will kill you if you do not move. You will be burnt to a crisp if you do not get out of its path. Your body will have a complete smothering of flames across your skin. Never mind the screams, it integrates into its torture, your screams shall be added to the painful increase in heightening pressure of pain, of stress, anxiety being higher than the silence of a grave.

"Lucy, are you okay?"

"No. Not really. He has something going through his mind, I cannot think what the hell it will be."

"We can be prepared, okay." Theodore started tying up his hair, into the man bun, pulling it backwards.

"I wish you would leave it down."

"Why, what does it remind you of?"

His voice quaked in worry, the small talk as a mask for the nervousness embedding into him. I had made my choice long ago. So had William, I knew exactly what would happen, how to escape, especially with the notes I found in my mother's make-up bag, inside her bathroom. "Not right now, I know how to get out of here, we just have to find something."

"You know!"

"Yes."

"I do not want you to think I am pressuring you, but, have you made your choice?"

"I have made my decision, neither of you can change it."

"Lucy, it is your choice, either way I will never influence you any more than needed, unless it involves other people besides ourselves."

"You're understanding!" Blurting, I never understood understanding, why people wanted to make the load lighter on my shoulders, helping me to keep fighting. No longer fighting on my own, with someone else to cover me. "I have never been able to fully figure out why people wanted to make my life easier."

Rolling back the green iris' covering up the branches of black, shielded with pale umbrellas, gazing to the luminescent glow of the soft moon, reaching for the eternal blackening mysterious crepuscule.

"Maybe it is down to the fact you roll your eyes like that." Brushing back a piece of my hair, shivers shooting around my body, till I found the courage to gaze into something other than the moon. His dark brown eyes, so gorgeous with the colour that they exceeded my view of any other brown eyes, they are so perfect. "Maybe you just enjoy everything to be hard, tough, dangerous."

"That sounds about right."

Giggling in amusement of his theory, there had to be some truth to it, every time danger arises, my body feeds off the adrenaline, taking the emotions I feel to another level, setting aside everything else. Forgetting responsibility, I often did such with my daughter, finding great relief with others taking care of her. They knew. Those who never had been real in the first place. Feeding off the adrenaline that those people who will always own a place in my heart, never really deserving to be there, for they did nothing, they were not real. Why did they not have to be real? Pulling me out of my personal thoughts, William deciding to interrupt my peace with the sound of a voice I had been so hopeless of finding ever again, after losing him to my father. Who was not my father. To Liam Fernsby, who masqueraded himself as someone he was never actually breathing as in the first place. Wearing a mask at a ball, winding around in circles with me, a dance partner. Each of his footfalls bringing me to the edge, bringing me to the breaking point until I was close to breaking the edge of the cliff face. Wearing a look of terror on his face, reflecting onto my own as soon as a realisation as hard as a boulder smacking in the face, breaking every living tissue attaching itself to my remorseless body for being negligent to my children at times. Out of my mind with terrifying feelings never ending inside the corrupt state others had brought to my heart, smashing the bones, my teeth into smithereens. His voice, it never could be.

"Fernsby has Edward."

One of the guardsmen standing next to William, never tearing his eyes away from the radio holding in his steady hands, playing a voice of a boy appealing to the help of my voice, not enjoying knowing I was still alive.

"Mommy! I tried, I tried to be brave. I could not be Daddy!"

"Baby! Where are you?"

"I do not know, Mom, please come before he goes for me one more time."

"Before who comes for you?"

"Mr Fernsby."

"Mr Fernsby. Get your hands off of my son."

"Oh! What will you do?"

"Anything to blast your body out of this earth, till it comes raining down."

"All talk."

Knowing Liam, knowing his temperament, he would never hit a child despite how nasty he could get, the fire inside his eyes could tell me all I was needing to know. He would never. He needed me on his side, in the fight the world had to face to keep other people alive with whatever had to be going on outside of this place. Further outside of the laboratories they kept people like me under constant examination. To keep their research ongoing, far more detailed for the next generation.

"You need me!" Burning each of the eyes filling with anger and frustration to William, I caught sight of a smirking guard, a smiling William. "Sick. Twisted. Evil."

Wrapping both of my hands around William's neck, I

never saw this coming, in all of my fury, not this. Applying pressure to his Adam's apple, pushing it in his neck, gasping for air, furthering the push into his skin. He managed some words. "Stop. Lucy, ple—"

"Never! You are so sick in the head that you had my own son lie to me, you lied to me again, as for Fernsby, he needs to apologise in five seconds."

"If… if he does."

"I will release you, I will be on his side. Let us see how far his ego goes to protect me, to protect you."

From the microphone wired up to the radio, Fernsby's voice crackling due to the bad signal burying us in here, managing words I knew he would say. Every time he spoke becoming more of an incentive of growing frustration. Liam clearly never had any idea of the mindset I could be in at times, despite how often he chose to watch my every single move, playing each chess piece carefully, trying to put me in checkmate with no pawns, queen, bishops, rooks, knights. None at all. I could win. All the time, every time, after a few simple movements to switch up the play, he would be destroyed each game.

"Never in a million years will I apologise to you! What for?"

"Since you and William concocted a plan to make me come with you, one of you will have to make up for doing. Trying. To do this to me. That person is Fernsby. Go ahead." Awaiting a response, having the upper hand right here felt so empowering I was on top of the world, a queen to the world of every single country. Power. They want me, need me. "I am waiting, Liam, does it look like I have all day."

"You certainly make it easy, don't you."

"Easy? You think that it is easy for me to stand here, strangling my husband, hands around his neck. There has only ever been one occasion where this has happened, not to William."

"Who?"

"You should know."

Remaining in silence, I felt all else drop, realising everything all at once, nothing mattering other than the reality of a point in time, just coming back to me. A flashback. Painful, torturing, demonic. When I switch. Occasions that Theodore and William have no idea about, an explanation I never wanted to give them, not for the world, unless the world came near to closing in on me where they might end up seeing the other side of me come out. The demonic side no one would believe happens. Push comes to pull. Green eyes, to black.

Whoever sat on the outside of this place had control of my thoughts, sometimes, only allowing the optional memory to come resurfacing, then disappearing to the possessive pit of emotions from the past. Emotions that allow me to punish myself every time for the results they watch on for, until this happens. I came out. Pinning William to the tree, feeling the switch flicking off and on in my head, my head, my heart in a battle against one another. My heart has a sword, my head has a gun. Is it not clear to all who will win?

"Lucy, we both know this is not what you want to do."

"You know this is not!" Immediately after hearing the dark growl in the undertone of the voice causing William to quiver in his feet, begging me to release the hand I held firmly around his neck, unrelenting in my purpose. I killed a man. Before. Not in recent times. Eyes blackening, understanding that change will come, is coming to me. "You know I cannot.

Will not switch it off."

"Listen, I will not apologise, right now you are scared to feel so alone, you have every right to kill him. By all means do it." Calmess. In his voice, no sign of fear that I was about to murder the husband who gave me two, no, one child. Right now, I was out of my mind, controlling the thoughts winding up in the mind incapable of backing down to a fight. "Just know what happened last time."

"It seems they are giving my thoughts back, will they?"

"Will it switch you off."

Switching another focus to the other hand against the bark of the tree, wafting across to the guard who was allowing me to fight alone, against the monstrous being still pushing against the rough, soon to be stained brown tree of life. The irony. Something providing us with life, about to be the place where life is taken away, how funny, how strange.

"Shut up! Shut up! Shut up!"

In the background Liam began calling to the doctors behind the scenes, asking them to give me this one memory from my true past, instead of the ones that they gave to me previously. No. Too much. Everything was beginning to be too much to deal with as the patchy memory, becoming so clear in my mind. Like a night of being drunk, waking up in the morning half sober, not knowing whether the truth of the night before was really the truth or the way your mind work in that second will be the reality of it all. Point being, you are left with so much agony in your head, everything is a mess, nothing complete, no one can really understand if you are giving the full story, a story that you dreamed, or the fake news. You can never truly know. Right now, it felt like torture, all flooding back in one swoop, coming back to the basics, bringing me up to speed with my past. Held down in my bed, pinning me against the bed, crumpling underneath my body, creasing at the edges until I was being allowed to leave. Would I ever? Until that time, the intensifying flames invigorating the flames within the heart that had been punished more than just a single instance in the past. All for what? Hitting me. A wave crashing over the heat, cooling down the curiosity no one could dampen until the full truth, the truth that was real, given to me through playing with the memories they can control, something on my brain. What was it?

This is what these separate personalities can do to me, change me, twist me, manipulate me, turn me into somebody that no one can contend with as I rip through the lives of those who cross me. I had done so in the past I could do it again. When Mother left, left me for a better life, I found myself not wanting anyone around me, no friends for they would only divulge the problems I had to the gossipers of the town. Enjoying the suffering of your family goes down in the ranks among people, absolute pleasure, a show they never had to pay for or leave their homes to mix up, make up, create. So many people, taken into my life to be taken back out again, changing the rhythm of my life to something more temperamental, the arguments becoming so fragile, teaching me that no one deserves my tears, unless they are happy tears that I had on the wedding day. Blissful. My first child. Lasting inside of me.

Pushing me to the limits, can cause me to entangle myself into a long-lasting state. A beautiful blood coloured rose, wedging between thorns, keeping it away from the sharpening thorn ready to yield a rising case against the beautiful rose, punishing it until it feels guilty for being so stunning. For me, it was never that simple, never had been and surely never will ease off the pedal, full speed ahead, whenever the feelings of guilt overwhelm for something I did not intend to do, cascade before plummeting straight through. Life is never so gentle, so simple, it has to crucify you for the very least of the things you do. What goes around, comes around. What is lasting now will not last in the future. It is true. Far more truth in those sayings, than the explanation William was giving to me, bait to hold onto his arm like a petrified young woman, unable to handle herself in the big bad world. Well. I can. This is the difference, ever since the day Fernsby had pushed me to my limit, on the day where my hand met skin, skin meeting pressure. Slow. Not steady. Shaky. Liam's best friend. Before anyone corrupted the thoughts, memories embedding into the brain constantly memorising every last detail. I was living elsewhere, outside of here in a sunny town near the sea before all of this, casually attempting to fit into normal life. My mother did leave me, that was true. For another reason, besides finding a better life, a story well scripted for me to believe, biting down on the lie because how would I know any better with no recollections of the life before? Until now.

Liam gave me a little freedom to figure out my own way. When we were younger, Liam and I used to be the closest friends could be. Girls never caught onto me, never having a girl best friend to have slumber parties, make-up, partying, hunting for the 'the latest catch'. I was basic to them. Liam always enjoyed my company, his family always looking out for mine when mother went away to do what she needed. She had to. Why? Why did she have to go? The surgeons controlling every detail of the memory, deciding to leave out the main pieces I would want to know, knowing the strength of my brain.

"Oh, you let that one slip!" Wiping away the sweat off my brow, wiping off Will's, wandering in the perplexing gaze in his eyes. "You do not understand since they took our memories! The thing is, my brain is more powerful than them, I have a chance to heal the world!" Truly ludicrous. Out of my mind. The inability to stop these continuous thoughts, I could feel the smile spreading straight across Liam's face as I started recalling everything repeatedly, with something they did not know running through my mind.

"You are scaring me, Lucy, remember what happened?"

"Oh yes! I know a lot more than that."

"What did you do?"

"This." Pulling the gun out of my back pocket, releasing my grip from William knowing I was in desperation to pull back the top of the gun, cracking it against the underneath of my jaw. "Now you cannot have my brain. Suffer!"

"Lucy! No!"

Backing away steadily towards the pathway, pulling over the hood so nobody could view the dark eyes meeting everyone else's screaming faces. "Sick. Twisted. Evil."

"Lucy, stop this madness!" Running towards me, wanting to pull the gun away from my grip, Will understanding if he came any closer, I would fire a bullet straight through my head. "What about your son?"

"This is all for you, baby. For you, Will. Your last words, okay." He was not paying any attention, his eyes constantly begging for support from Theodore who became my only confidant for this matter resting on the shoulders of us both. They would have to bury me in here. "Listen to me! Please, just listen. Your last words to me had been few and far between, but you spoke two words telling us to use them as we die."

"I did not expect you to use them!"

"Well, you can now." Pulling my hood back down, revealing the black eyes like a hollow doll, empty from any emotions, still finding some fear in the lack of being alive, that is what I would be now. Tears leisurely caressing my cheeks, imagining all the times when Will did the same thing. "Just know this was never easy, trying to hide who I was, they gave me back my memories, they gave me too much!"

Laughing in amusement at this, Liam knew exactly what was happening, predicting it long, long, ago, speaking from the hiding place behind the comfort of a radio.

"Remember all those years ago, when I told you that you were special, when I said this would happen."

"Yes. Now I know why I have to die."

"Good."

"You knew about this! You crazy, idiotic, fool! You knew!" Creating a scene, ripping away the radio from the guardsman's hand, the laughing of Fernsby becoming a rampant display of his intellect, happy that his prediction came true. "Listen here! You knew that my wife would die, and you just accept this."

"Yes."

"How?"

"Death came really easily for her in her past life, if only you truly knew how brutal she could be!"

"Would you all just be quiet for a second. Please." Choking up on my words, the surprise that everyone became quiet showing all over my face. New tears overlapping the dried ones on my cheeks, pasted with dirt from when I picked up the moss for William's wound. "There is the right time to die, I feel like this is the best place for it. In front of the two people I love."

"There is never the right time to die, Lucy."

"Listen! How many times, listen to me!" Pleading for him to not say any more, Theodore remaining silent, the heaviness weighing down the burdens. Watching me take away a life both of us wishing we could keep. Not forever. I had to die. "You do not understand, I have to go now. There is no time."

Cranking the gun closer and closer into my jaw from underneath, I was sure it was starting to pierce the delicate, thin skin underneath. This would go straight. Yet, I felt no fear, I was ready to die. Die like a soldier. "Take away that gun, Lucy."

"No. Your mother said it, you said... it is my time, tell Edward I love him. Use these words, as the last on your tongue. Theodore. William. Liam. Remember me!"

A shooting pain began ripping its way through my skull, immediately dying in the hands of death, a few moments of noise with the ringing of the bullet going straight through, the bullet going in and getting stuck inside. Blood. Flooding the place. Darkness.

Chapter 15
Mia Vaile

Secrets. Everyone has them, telling other people will be a matter of personal decision, no one can force them out of you, when you are weak, then they strike. With Lucy, she had her fair share of secrets, even ones that she did not know, these people she spoke of, giving her thoughts back to her, controlling them for the past so many years of her life. For just one second, I was in disbelief that she would pull the trigger! Eventually, I and William, her husband, began forming an alliance in order to protect her body so that the silencers would not seek out the blood from her body any longer, they had spent days scouring the woods for the corpse. After the incident, long debating where to place her body, lay it to rest one last time; crows, insects, announcing that she was officially gone from the world. Why would we need an autopsy? Liam concluded that it was best for me to stay with them, in the laboratory buildings, where they were keeping others under observation, to check the wound I had on my leg. Sitting, the white walls covering themselves in a heavenly glory, surviving walls, allowing others to recover within them, like the arms of a mother. Holding, comforting, wrapping her son or daughter with love, true passion, the kiss on the forehead, rocking in her arms, bobbing them up and down to ensure calmness would ensue all else. A knocking bouncing off the walls, echoing around the room, alerting me that someone was beyond the safe fortress.

"Who is there?"

"It is William, Theodore, I need to talk with you."

"Come in."

Pulling over the light blue bedding covers, my body having barely any clothing from the waist down after they performed the last surgery, enabling me to be assured that nothing else would take place where another pit stop would be required. Widening, a crack of light peeking through, the lack of windows dawning on me with a claustrophobic atmosphere, strangling the breath out of me. Why was there never any windows in this place?

"Let me sit down first."

"Why is there never any way to see the outside world? I mean, if there is, why can I not see it?"

"No windows. Huh. Figured you would never notice."

"Lucy did." Handing him over a note Lucy had given me before her death, reading.

They are lying, the world in there is safer than the world out there. No windows.

"She obviously suspected something to be wrong."

"Always intuitive, fell in love with you, clearly." Turning over the note, giving it back to me, she wrote:

Theo will always be in my heart, liars can lay dead.

"Charming much."

"She certainly had a way with words."

Reminiscing on her past, the way she used to be, memories entering left, right and centre till I was about to explode. A bomb with no off switch, unable to keep the smoke, the death toll down as I spread to the corners of everyone, every room, every lung, every human body... until they die. She was my life, everything I wanted. Gone. Only two weeks ago we lost her by her own hand, not anybody else's, despite how much I will consistently blame the doctors and Fernsby for not allowing her memories.

"That is what I will always miss, about her, the ridiculousness of her choice of wording."

"Never hesitating to tell you if she hated you, had an opinion, it is why we... became what we did."

Recalling the time when she wanted to save poor Bethany, only, at that time I did not have the understanding that Lucy gave me now; to help those, even if they cannot help you. With everyone disappearing, I had never seen Bethany since that day. Dissipating, gone with the wind. One minute Lucy was tending to her wounds, the next moment, remembering her children, then onto something else. Nothing was real. Ever. No wonder she kept moving away from one thing, to the next and so forth. Motherly instincts, a wound on her heart, always weighing her down in moments, where needing to move would determine survival, determine whose hands our lives would end up in. Life, or death? Chance. Fire, ripping through bodies, never ripping through ours, so close to dying by burns marking our story on our arms. Remember me. Two words. Those two words, where she had not given me an explanation, just to use them when I die, when that day comes. William's appearance was not deterring me from asking any questions that I steadily started conjuring in my mind, wanting to know certain things, like: Why was he here? Since Lucy went, we did not speak, only when discussing her memorial, saddening. His fidgeting, why was he doing it? From what I know he never gets uncomfortable around people, rather proud, liking to never show nervousness to anyone. Did he know anything of the silencers finding Lucy's body? For hours after her shooting, we watched them forage for her body, on the cameras that they had on the place inside the trees, observing the encirclement of the place. No wonder they knew all about us. Breaking the silence, seemingly inevitable that someone would have to crack the ice one way or another, collapsing the sombre tower shadowing over our minds, hearts, souls.

"I presume you are here for a reason? We have not spoken since she… you know."

"I know. It is just our cameras picked up something last night. Liam appears to have let his guilt get the better of him, watching to see if she would arise from the dead."

"And?"

"That is the thing, strange as it seems, something happened last night none of us can explain."

"Carry on? I presume it is to do with Lucy considering we would not be having this conversation if something else happened."

"This girl…" Handing me an image of a girl, a girl I knew who Lucy tried to help on the ship. Bethany Hamilton. "I can see you know her. She was supposed to be dead, at least, through the mechanical structure of the inside of this place. Caught her wandering about the place last night, rummaging around where we buried her."

"Did she find her body?"

"That is the point, silencers only find the body, eat the flesh and leave the remains. If the programming went wrong, then she would not be able to eat or pick up the body. Let alone turn into one of those silencers, she would develop the characteristics down to computer programming."

"But something more than that, as per your twitching, scratching, constantly looking to the right."

Persisting to develop his own characteristic traits through stress, a crinkling brow furrowing to the confusion inside the heart so whole, so broken, knowing her beauty returning to the dust. Thudding of his heartbeat against the panicking, sudden urge to flee, to take flight, knowing that one day this would all be in the past, the pain no longer there. The grief passing by day by day, still there, leaving me stuck inside a maze, tall, mountains higher than I could ever reach, no vines or a ladder to help me escape these never-ending corridors of pain, each with a challenge harder than the next. With so many to contend with, it would wonder of my survival, without her. Lucy.

"The grave we had Lucy in was left open, dug up, just last night as the cameras had caught."

"Is Lucy's body still whole or, is it just bones?" Hanging in the air, a knife could not cut through the tension, unless breaking with a few words.

"Come on, William! Stop pretending to me, come out with, for goodness' sake."

Heaving with exhaustion from the tiring effect of these unusual circumstances, no longer able to breath fresh air, just the second hand oxygen others had been breathing for many, many, years by the thickness of it. He brought light onto a wrinkled piece of brown paper, dirtied with wet mud on the edges, dog-eared and torn in places. An envelope, filled with multiple pictures of people, dirtied with earth.

"I know who these belong to, she looked upon these every single day of her life, she found something none of us wanted to know."

"Why do you have them?"

"We buried her with them, they could only have been left behind if she chose to leave them behind herself."

"She is *dead.*"

"Yes, she is dead. But, these would only be left behind if her body was transported elsewhere."

"What are you trying to say? Get to the damn point." Rubbing my thumbs under the crooks of my eyelids, William held a letter underneath my bowing head, stress controlling me. "Who wrote this?"

"Read it out loud, please, something happens when you read it…"

"To Reader…

You may be reading this after finding your friend's body gone, well, wife, girlfriend from espionage on her so much. Well, we took her body since it had a use to us far greater than it would have had for you.

She deserved to die. She deserved to die. She deserved to die. So do you. No matter how hard you try to bury her properly it shall never work, we will always find her.

"There is no name at the end of this?"

"Why would they leave one?"

"Can we not match the handwriting to anyone here?"

"With at least one hundred thousand workers, I would say you are setting yourself up for a task so impossible you will die before you finish the last scripted handwriting."

"Thank you. Way to make me feel better."

Pushing my body off the bed, dragging the medication on the tall metal pole to the sink, turning on the running water in the tap, icy cold. Splashing the water all over the heat on my face, hoping if I did this over and over everything I knew would dissolve.

"No matter how much you want to try and change everything, Theo, it will never happen."

"I know, that... that is the part I hate the most."

"Why?"

"I never got to tell her something. Something I should have said a long time ago, something you got to say to her every day until you *lied* to her."

"That would be?"

"I loved her, still love her, for as long as I live."

Wearing one of the hospital gowns tied around the back, nothing else on me, apart from the gown, so light on my skin that nothing could compare to the soft yet rough fabric brushing against the skin. Inside the underneath of my eyelids, salty water began welling at the thought of her knowing how I still feel towards her, not able to relieve the swell of pain beating inside my throat, stomach, heart, knowing she will never know. Suppressing the thickening lump at the back, choking down the remnants of its infectious aching pain. Clearly the silence of William taking him aback by my words, not able to even begin to consider someone else loving the woman he called his own at the altar. To be with her through sickness, death, ill health, everything. The 'I dos' for what? Nothing now that she took herself away from the world, taking the most precious person in my life, leaving her son to the uncharted course of our life.

"Come with me for a second." Pulling away from his

thoughts, hand gesturing for me to follow him. "Bend down and you will be the death of us all."

"Okay?" Bending down when he left the room, I felt something bare round the back. "Ah. Wouldn't want the sun to go in, would we?"

"No. Be quick, Fernsby is off duty."

Taking the metal liquid holder with me, holding the back of the dressing gown so nothing would be on show, I felt the embarrassment of others possibly seeing something by accident, I never wanted anyone to see. Trauma. For them mostly, for me as well, it could be argued for the whole room. No one needs to see that surely. Just about empty corridors, the silent hum of machines, light feet movements, squeaking of the wheels on the bottom of the trolly coming along with me for the ride. Theo's glancing becoming a little annoying, constantly over-checking every bend, corner, twist that we made to get to this small room at the end of the hallway, down the dead end. Just inside, a creaking of a door widening to allow a clearer view of where Fernsby must have been while on the radio to us during the time when she removed herself from everyone one final time. After that, two weeks on from then and problems still could not cease, as if they never really existed, this was just the way things were supposed to be, for the rest of my life. Now, instead of two to fight the demons of imperfection, there was only one. Putting my life in the hands of William is something a fool would do, knowing how much a sense of loathing clouded his judgement of me. Only wanting to seek revenge that Lucy was putting her trust in someone other than him, taking sides with a stranger because that is all I was in his eyes. Controls surrounding us, lining each and every single wall, ensnaring us in a trap of surprise with cameras lurking in the darkness outside in the inner areas of where they kept us. I was on the inside, in and out, back in back out, seeming to be the only reason they could allow me to live just as long as they knew that I could not control them sending me back around to the inside of hell.

"Sit down there."

Pointing to the chair, it was irrefutable that staying standing was an option. The day I met Lucy I knew for a fact offering her a chair would be an impossible action to make her take, especially with her stubborn persona. The way in which she acts all the time never keeping you away from standing on the tips of your toes, feeling punishment for trying to show her sympathy or pity. Not allowing one single person to show her that. Occasionally me, how could she trust a person like me, after all I was nobody that she knew or came to know, people only telling me about her past, little bits by little bits, miniature bites still too big for me to digest. The past of her life certainly made mine look so insignificant and puny. The challenges with men in her life not something I appreciated when talking to her, having someone else hold her unless she was comfortable with them. Snuggling her head into my chest, she was comfortable with my personality, reading that my intentions were purely for her benefit.

"Why have you brought me in here?"

Clicking most of the light from outside, surrounding ourselves with an ominous pit of darkness through every corner, the buzzing pixelated screens lighting just about everything simply by a ray of light tilting them around.

"Just so you could see the footage."

"The footage of Lucy's body?"

"Trust me, you will not be disappointed."

"Play it."

Around her, everywhere around her, darkness embodying places I never thought could be overcome by the shade of black, capturing the last details to the finest points, everything barely visible until the manufacturing lights built in the shadows shine a natural appearing light to the places needed. In the background the voices of those on the night shift being heard as we both picked up the headphones from the desk in front of us, slapping them over our ears in uniform, watching the recording so intently that someone threatening us at gunpoint would never be able to tear us away. Since the thick feelings we allowed inside of us for Lucy kept us away from each other's throats, both would have equally weighting arguments for why they were at the other person's neck, preparing to kill no matter what. I with a knife at his throat for lying and hurting her, leaving her, him, at mine with a gun to the head for stealing his wife. How stupid? For my argument, being able to go on and on forever until the day death comes, knowing how right I am, other people can make their own judgements, it is not mine to make.

"See that Tommy, ol' Fernsby is never going to be happy."

"Luke, you need to stop thinking you are seeing things, as much as we enjoyed watching her, it is the end."

"Tom how can you not see that?"

"See what exactly."

Pressing a few of the keys on the control, a storming noise of footsteps burying the muffling voices of those in the seats screaming with cloth gagging their mouths, a voice of Liam clearly wanting to kill them for not notifying him quickly enough to stop this.

"You need to talk, Luke, hurry up with it quickly because I have no choice but to do something to you after seeing this, send Thomas out there since he knows nothing."

Footage of two cameras came on the screen, this second one showing us Fernsby ridding of the rag keeping his mouth apart but his eyes growing in fear that would never leave. This violent outburst from Fernsby was certainly unexpected for him. The look of trepidation swelling a feeling of growing anguish of what he would do.

"What do you want to know, Liam?"

"Sir! To you. What did you see on there?"

"I saw that girl's body, being moved by that other girl who went doolally, the one with the thing you put in her neck."

"Bethany?"

"Yes. She took her body, and she did some stuff to it."

"What stuff?"

"Watch it back."

"Okay. Shoot him."

Immediately the camera was being shut down as it was fizzling after a bullet bang shot through the speaker of the headphone. Looking at the ones I had been working with sitting on the right-hand side where Luke had been. I was using a dead man's headphones. It was obvious that Thomas still lived, I would need to speak with him just for more information on this matter. An overwhelming feeling of pathos towards Luke who had been shot dead in this room, a ghastly thought that I was here where he was shot dead. Hearing a voice close to me, still sounding distant and familiar to me, until the realisation that he was talking to me. William.

"Theodore, are you sure you want to watch this?"

A spine-chilling feeling from a gust of wind caught up my bare, but hairy leg, wafting all the way through me to feel the goosebumps starting to line every piece of skin of my body, skinning me with blister-like bumps, each with a reason to be there. Unknown. A feeling of unknown, not sure what to expect from these recordings, not being able to understand the reason this was happening now, trying to ease the feelings embedding into me from the loss of an amazing woman from this world.

"Unpause it, it's like ripping off a plaster, do it once never again."

"Okay then."

Clearing up his throat, exchanging a look of comfort for each of us to seek refuge from, both loving Lucy ever more. Placing the headphones back over my ears, warming up the coldness growing on the empty skin.

Even the luminescent moon could not bring this scene to justice as four of the silencers crept around the burial, we never bothered with a tombstone or somewhere to mark her name just in case they could read, or, had an idea of what tombstones actually meant. Each of them holding a different object: a knife, a whip for lashing, gun and a spade. The first crept up around the area with the spade, marking a rounded rectangle around the area where we buried her, digging it harshly around the corners. The fake natural lighting casting over the area allowing them to see and us, horrifying trauma as the one began spading up the area to uncover the dirt over her body. Following from the side of the shadows a woman, stockily built with muscle, hardly natural considering her age, and the fact she did not look anything like that when we

arrived. Now, I could hardly recognise Bethany as she pulled
her hood down, removing the black cloak, chucking it to the
side as a piece of unwanted litter, taking out her torch so she
could count the four corners.

"Dig!"

The faint shrilling of her voice, the effect of the tip from
the lethal weaponry they had been using against us turning her
into a monstrosity, no longer the innocent, young, soon-to-be-
married lady, of a very wonderful family. But she was not real.
As far as we knew, just as everybody else but me, Lucy, William
and Christopher. We were always mere game in their trials for
whatever they were testing and I am yet to discover what
exactly that is as soon as we find Lucy, well, her body. If it is
still actually here, hopefully it is still complete so we can give
her the right, proper burial she deserves. Around the body,
these things kept kneeling and standing in unison humming a
tune being picked up by the microphones hidden amongst the
canopies of leaves, among the crepuscule in the sky shining
down on each and every one of them: a spotlight on a stage.

"Keep watching Fernsby, I am sure nothing bad happens."

All rising at one time, the uncanny resemblance of a fake ritual
to create a worrying seemingly endless pit of pure evil,
jumping down his throat, being spat back up as an unwanted
visitor in his deeds. Only supposed to be a spectator rather
than getting involved and halting his plan. Knowing the power
of good it would do to the world, the wreckage and havoc it
would create with the manipulative planning of his mind,
creating a new world of terror, a whole adventure trek to take
part in. Bethany's hand produced one finger, licking it, holding

it to the sky with a face as normal as it could be, given where she was standing. In the centre of the grave we had dug for Lucy, examining the particles of air brushing on her skin carefully to not cause damage to her, not even a slight scratch for the fear was real that someone was watching her every move. She was correct. We had been watching her for as long as this recording had even been real, closely conducting searches into its contents well before I had even become aware of its physical existence on a screen. Do they have recordings of us being on the island Isla de Diseath? Back in London? Possibly. More so of Lucy than me, she has been far more interesting than any man like me.

"Exhume it. Be quick. We do not have all night."

"Yes miss." In one collective, they responded all in time, on time for each and every second that they decided to spend with the psychopath calling herself Bethany. A human being completely and utterly intoxicated with the lethal weapons being used against her chemical defect to fight anything being absent from the body since birth. "Where are we digging, miss?"

"Around the body,"

"You are standing on the body."

On the surface, their shovels digging absentmindedly. Not at all careful to not damage her body, so beautiful when full of life, he smiles so contagious that when she smiles the whole world smiles back, on cloud nine despite her moaning and complaining about so many different things. Teasing. Annoying. Winding us all up till the point of arguments, spitting at one another with meaningless, empty insults, falling to the ground in feverish fits of happiness in each other's company. Gone so fast. In so little time. Not knowing when the last time, each other's company would be the last. Watching someone remove her body from the resting place we thought nobody would ever think to open back up again, turning the pages of her book, reading the contents with a scrupulous mind engaging in the life as they read the speech, the mental thoughts she was feeling at that time, knowing everything far more than I ever had the chance to get to know. Bethany on all fours, digging a pile just behind her, rummaging energetically to the bottom, carelessly uncovering the pain of the past till the point of no return. Thinking this would all just be a figment in my imagination, a careless whisper of a coma keeping me tightly bed bound, nobody thinking I was alive. Escaping this place of dreams, I wake up and she is by my side, no longer dead, no longer being removed from her pretty grave. Deserving so much more. Not so little. Not so little at all.

"Hang on, pause it there!"

Fernsby's voice shot me awake as the recording began to rewind, spotting a man standing in the shadows with a body in his arms, however fully cloaked he was. He looked so much more similar to Lucy, definitely an older man.

"Who is that?"

"I would not know, sir, if we circulate his image around the different sections, someone might know!"

"Who?"

"Anyone, I suppose?"

"We cannot just allow this face of this man to be circulated, chances are he is among us, we all know who we put in there and who we do not. He was not one of them."

"Well, there is only one person we should ask."

"Lucy's mother, we ought to tell William and Theodore."

"Agreed, leave this running."

The recording continued as a double click, Liam might have entered, I could not care, finding myself intently gazing at the empty grave. Someone else had taken her. Cutting out, the camera stopped, nothing but black, then some writing, writing showing something I did not understand or able to even think about, why it was there. A name of a woman presumably.

Mia Vaile

Chapter 16
How long has she been missing for?

"I have been staring at this name for the past few hours, William, there is absolutely nothing I can make out about it."

"Well, knowing Lucy, it is a person linking to her body being moved, she always knew certain things that nobody else did."

"You are right, maybe she is letting us know something from her grave."

"A message from the grave? Always reasonable to expect with her."

It is true, you can always expect the unexpected. One mistake and she can rectify it by knowing earlier on that this was the case. After months of trying to piece together a one-thousand-piece jigsaw, we hadn't been able to discard the truth Having let the last one go missing in the infinite dust, lining the unused room, like a tomb never being opened, gathering dust from the skin of the remorseless corpse lying for an eternity of time, till the hand casts upon the edge of the golden rim ready to open up a new avenue of adventure. Just one time to seek the remaining pieces to allow others to fall into their fixed position.

"What if we are looking at this all wrong, try spelling it backwards."

"Aim Eliave, the first part is a word as for the second... I have no clue."

"Different language maybe, run it by the computer one second."

Liam Fernsby still has not returned, sticking tightly in my stomach as glue sticks to skin. Superglue can burn and be quite fatal, ripping off pieces of skin after tearing a removing it to keep blood circulation of crimson crippling the body and satisfying the deed, keep the pulse moving and the heightening need for someone to repair the damage done. Sitting inside the disliked swirling of the stomach, churning all of the insides into one smoothie wanting to just empty from me, leave me bare and hung out to dry. A bug on the market place, left to be dried to a crisp, shrivelling in the infiltrating heat, baking the living to the living dead. Instead of acting like the normal, the heat begins to disturb the mind in a sick frenzy of feeling, and feuds so futile and full of friction, you begin to wonder if sanity was ever the issue. If it was really just you in the end? Not being able to perceive the area in which you are being perceived by others, as someone so incredibly different that they separate you from the meaning of reality and a fabrication from someone else's mind.

"Where is Fernsby?"

"You are right he should have been back ages ago."

Clearing his throat, the dominant man we knew to be Fernsby must have been looming over us for a period of time that we had not noticed in the slightest. His quiet breathing never coming to our attention, his tall shadow bringing a shadow on the monitors. That must have been the breeze I felt earlier, when we were watching the recording. Our minds leading other lives elsewhere in the recording sought the comfort of finding the truth other than our lives in the hands of someone who could have plunged a machete in each of our backs. The numbing of the temptation to keep watching never making us flinch an inch as the life would be drained from the already dying.

"How long have you been here?" Questioning him being here, one eyebrow raised in confusion. "You came in while we were watching the recording, didn't you?"

"No, rubbish, Sherlock. That name has to be an anagram of some kind, she obviously left, she obviously wants to tell us something."

"Unless you are in on this, Fernsby, I see no way in which she could have done this."

"She was clever, you do know that right, Theodore." William was clearly angered by me all of a sudden, switching on and off like a switch, he just changes as though it is okay to be against me all of a sudden, making Liam smile. Trying to impress him.

"If you think this is funny Liam, this is your fault for even letting her have those memories of hers back again, you *did* this. If she was not dead, she would be here, her body would not be in the hands of that man in the woods."

"Good point, nice story, not a nice ending. Where is the point in pointing fingers, naming names, and glaring at me with your demon eyes, when we could be decoding this."

"For once, I agree with Liam, you need to stop acting so self-righteously and holier than thou, when you are just as bad as anybody else, quit being so idiotic and move past being all over yourself because you hurt her." Gripping the back of my throat, straining every muscle to stop me from plunging my hands around his throat, honestly, wholeheartedly thinking he is a hero and a saviour, pointing his finger this way and that when he is far from a perfect man. Especially in our case.

"Liam, did you help her?"

"I know how this may look, but you have to understand, I do not just offer up mine and Lucy's past like this."

Gasping in unison of surprise, we briefly knew they had some kind of meeting before but, hearing it outright as a thing of the past gave it a whole new meaning in the grand scheme of these affairs. "You knew her before?"

"Yes, we did, we made a pact with each other. If either of us died before realising our life goals, then we would do anything for the other person. In her case, she wanted to display this as another riddle for her, one last puzzle to see who would stick by her in the end. Discover what she wanted us to do."

William seemingly allowed his body to calm, his mind to relax and stabilise since we all needed to think rationally. I know that she could throw us all around the place in search of what she was after. Whatever it was, she was still in need of us to help her in discovering what she could not, whether we had to go back out there and find what she wanted. I would die doing it for her. For us. We never stop fighting for each other. Tapping the pen against the desk writing out Mia Vaile over and over writing it with force, a lump swelling on the edge of my hand from pressuring the skin to harshly. It clicked.

"How long has she been missing for?"

"By the remains we discovered, Theodore, that recording was faked and it is now a week of a missing body."

"After a bullet wound how long would it take for someone to recover?"

"A week."

"How long for someone like her?"

"At least two days, why? Have you got it?"

"You bet I have got it!"

"'I AM ALIVE'!" With a triumphant cry, my hand scribbling down in large letters with the yellow highlighter the solved anagram of 'I AM ALIVE'. She was still alive. I knew she would never die without telling us, she must be out there, this was all a ploy for her to be able to figure things out on her own, buying herself a little longer than a week. We would have to seek her out without attracting trouble. She sought out the help of someone or multiple people from the inside without the knowledge of anyone important. These people she let help her would never know where she is, life is a very important concept for her to uphold, one of her morals to protect life unless it deserves to not be here at all. For killing others or being full of hate, a torturer or something more. Every single thing made sense now, everything she is, still here. How she heals, when wounded she heals unusually quickly and can never be affected by doses of medicines because she does not need them and her body can never need to respond as they never try her body with the effect of high or small dosages. A slight bullet to the back of her neck would heal, everything would heal leaving her with the chance to be knocked out for a short period of time allowing us to bury her with the minute means that we had. Barely any soil covering her body, giving her the strength once she woke up to take herself from the resting place and leave, cleaning herself up on the inside and out with the water down by the sea. Whoever she had met gave us the idea that she was still gone, lost, taken to her last destination whether that be returning to the dust, heaven, or hell. She was not religious one single bit, not even one part of her heart held a candle for it so… it seemed correct to conclude she would not ever end up in the resting places a religious person might seek comfort from.

"Well, this is all swell, Theodore, but, if she is alive how are we supposed to find her."

"She is clearly not here, William, so she has to be out there, always searching for something that none of us could ever figure out ourselves."

"So, you are thinking that we need to go back out there."

"Well, we left Christopher out there on his own since he is yet to realise that he is not a real person, technically."

"So, we should?"

"Nice to hear you listening to me now, and yes, we have to. We both love her, and in the end, it matters if we at least try to help her through this. She has been there for both of us, through thick and thin so tell me are we going back out there?"

"You expect me to go back out there, in the jungle, it is absolutely freezing!"

"Well, she is worth it."

"You will *die* wearing that measly hospital dress, you will also kill anyone if you go to pick something up, those silencers won't know what hit them."

"Maybe I can test it on you one day, give me some peace."

"Shut up, Theo. We have to ask Captain Fernsby first."

"Sir, yes, sir."

Penetrating the glorious grinning of our faces, childlike and so unlike the pair of us, realising the woman we both loved could still love us.

"Well then, we best get you ready to go back inside. Find her and bring her back, there is no place for her out there."

"Fernsby…" Cutting off the speech he was about to over exaggerate, how it might end up being this perilous journey following each footstep we take into the density of an abyss of jungle. "What if she is long gone now, made an escape off of the island, find what she was looking for. What if we never find her?"

"You will, I know Lucy was looking for something, most likely in the abandoned houses up the top, we have had rumours in the past about that place, albeit a very fake place."

William became stern and uptight very quickly, upon hearing this may not be the clearest cut situation we had planned separately. These rumours not sounding so pleasant. They never can be. "Rumours of what kind?"

"Those people never wish to talk about it, ever again."

Chapter 17
Just outside of the dome.

Working together with a man my heart found no pleasure in being around seemed a much harder task to complete. The icy chills of a windy breeze, freezing all contents of my body no longer what I was wearing. Up there, alone, on the brow of a hill where nobody knows you are there, apart from the piercing, chilling, demonic gaze of the cameras swirling, encircling your every move to ensure it is captured for all to see. In so many ways I could rid the planet of Theodore, shake him up a little and let it all come out, tear up the parts of him and lay them on neat display on a red cushioning, smooth blanket of red. Lucy, wherever she is, might eventually find out. Who cares now? The damage I have done to her has now happened, she will always pick Theo over me, not that I much blame her. He is the best of us. Never did he once lie to her, pretend to die before her eyes, lie and try to blackmail her with her own son, she didn't know where he was. We missed her. Still missing her with the daily dozen demoralising memories that should have been spent together rather than apart. Coming to this island together as a family, seemingly whole, without her world being torn apart by the minute with so many challenges. So surreal, an inevitable fate. If it is meant to be, it will be. If it is not, it is not. Finding and decoding the message happened so quickly it remains so blurry, a television screen with a terrible aerial connection. This I now knew after they gave me the necessary details to continue living in their modern, laboratorial life screening and examining those they put into these places, watching them die one by one. The best of the best survive, like Lucy, to be put through much more harrowing trials, discovering the understanding her body had to adapt to the world, set to die from the outside, none of which she realised was out there, or what was going on. I did. Yet, it is not my place to say just yet, there will be a time. She saw the burning during her first meeting with her old friend,

Liam Fernsby, we forced a sight of the world outside in her mind to see what it is like, not that she took any notice of what she was seeing. Changing into the warm clothes Liam sourced for us to wear, mostly camouflage to blend in, military wear since it was a better fit for us. Sliding into the uniform, a relief flooded my body, a sensation of great pride for no apparent reason, delight in putting on the country's colours. Still I have no idea where I am currently, for all I know, I am living in a dream and they are waiting for me to wake up.

Usually, you may feel quite bound, an inability to move, during a coma you barely do anything, maybe shift a little and breath, but the action I am dragging myself through for this woman was nothing of the kind I thought you might do. Lacing up the boots, tucking in the trousers and shirt, finding the buttons near the badge on my chest, still something not registering in the collision of feelings and the mind. Follow your heart or follow your head.

Two starkly contrasting things, one can be dangerous and the other less dangerous, one is innocent and out for the best, the other a more logical solution depending on your conscience and mind balance. Some do not have the circumstances to make decisions for themselves as they try to fix their mistakes, enabling their mind to think correctly.

"Are you ready to get going, William?"

Peering around my door, checking I was ready, before entering fully wearing his uniform, reminding me of something else I could not pinpoint without straining my mind to harshly. Giving me an unnecessary headache, banging on in my head like the beating drums of a drum. Pounding and pounding on and on invading my thoughts with only beats.

"Yes, just let me grab my gun and we can leave, have you got yours?"

"Yes, it's in my holster around the back."

"Put it around the front, someone can attack you a lot more easily from behind."

"Good point." Doing as I had instructed him, commanding him forcefully hinting a touch of a high station in my tone, wanting him to realise that I deserved the power in our little predicament with Lucy involved in our mission.

"What now?"

"We go in."

Plunging the needle into his arm, numbing the area in which it is being delivered through his system, shutting him down for half an hour so he could not see where we were heading and the journey we needed to take just to get there. From the outset, the world outside has not been what you expect, full of vegetation so luscious that the fabrications the mind might create can never be far away. Still, if you understand everything that has been happening over the last fifteen years then your perception may change to a different kind of understanding.

"Why did you plunge this in me?"

Removing the needle unnecessarily protruding out of his arm, checking all of the serum had been transported from one site to the next, in the plastic tube, through the thin metal and into his bloodstream. Grasping my arm tightly, his balance lowering onto the ground, letting us take him to a place he would forget after he was asleep, letting the power of the magical scientific tool do its work without a fuss. None of this could ever work with Lucy, unless the dose was fatal enough to kill a person, allowing us to manipulate and control her body's response to the drug. Latching my hands onto his ankles, buzzing the radio on the belt around my waist to call Fernsby to send help so we could drag him onto the train.

"Liam, what is wrong?"

"I need help getting him on the train, he's heavy and I have to carry a backpack loaded with weapons and supplies."

"Do you want me to send someone to you?"

"Two people, he looks very light but he's not."

"Just be glad he is no longer in that blue hospital apron."

"Trust me, I am more than happy."

"Good, wait there for a second, I will send my two best men over. See you on the train." Buzzing himself off the intercom so he allowed himself enough time to make his way down. Without speaking, knocking, the men he had sent my way opening the door nonchalantly, so oblivious to the fact I was standing there. I was unsure even a bullet through the head would knock even one of them to sense.

"Thank you."

Waltzing out of the room, taking one last look of reasonable normality, our legs taking us down many corridors so alike in many details, scaring me with every single mark out of place, red marks. All the newcomers we find out there in the real world, they are suspicious of red marks, over time turning like burnt fat on a piece of bacon. Except, it is not so tasty, not so salty, a lot more corrupt and black-hearted and the hearts of those no longer beating any more. Charred. Still, I eventually began applying my mind elsewhere, questioning everything I know at the moment would not make for a happy journey, Liam would have to give me some form of indication or insight into his past with Lucy, if that was her real name. Is it not truly aggravating, itching away at the flesh when you truly believe you know someone but they have still time to discover who they are. You want to support them so much and you find yourself straying from their side ever so slightly. Feeling the useless echoes of the stomach you feed, not allowing you to digest your food, the emptiness just becoming heavy on your body. Running away from your problems, trying not to chase your problems for as long as you can hold your breath. You can take away the pain for a short time while sleeping, then, when you wake up, the world is a cruel place filled with mounds of people, with such greed that they would rather see you suffer. Taking one more turn to the right, the lengthy road to the end certainly taking me minutes to get down. Running with my feet and problems as a heavy burden, exercising my patience to contend with its mad significance and torture through the human mind. Those two men who had been in front of me now disappearing into the doors, with Theodore in their arms. As much as I hated Theo with all my heart, he did not understand my level of thinking nor his own, he could understand Lucy like he was reading her feelings from a lengthy book, longer than anything you might be able to imagine. Her complex life led to many questions surrounding who she was. Whether she was actually real, or just nothing, and someone we create in our own minds so we can have somebody to talk to when needing the guidance and emotional support only she can provide.

"Where shall we put him?" One of the men spoke in a strong German accent, possibly from Berlin by the tone and pitch, his arms lowering Theodore's arms to the ground, the other man still holding onto his legs.

"Lower his legs then, you muppet."

"Oh, yes. Yes." Agreeing, this man having a less strong accent, integrating with the English accent, strong Londoner slightly tinged with his old German memories. Upon first sight he is not the type of person you would expect to be strong, skinny, gaunt on the legs and arms, especially the stomach and face. You never judge somebody for the way they look or make assumptions, despite it being a natural thing for imperfect humans to do.

"I am sorry, never again. Sir."

"Good, come with me, we can go pick up the rest."

Coming my way, the much more buff man pushed his helper roughly on the back, taunting him, leaning into his ear, making him shake with worry. Sticking up for him would be the right thing to do, but somehow, going in there with a broken nose, black eyes, was never appealing to the storyline. Lucy would have to know what was happening, why it happened when we found her. That being something I could not deal with sorting out, her questions in large abundance like the grains of sand on the shoreline.

"Are you coming in Theodore, or shall I leave you to ponder over your life?"

"No, I am coming."

"Good."

Taking myself a seat in the deserted, dirty train, an old, reformed train that was being used to search and find those on the outside. One hundred miles away from here a special place had been built when they found out about what was going on in the communities. So, after many years of trying to understand the disease, causing certain issues, hideouts and high security buildings were built in order to protect the community and those without the symptoms, or anything out of the ordinary. Prone to being violent, abusive, tired, walking strangely, head flopping to the side, ripping skin off the body, sucking like a leech on their own blood. Feeding off of their flesh. We never understood what this disease was entirely, just that some people rarely have the ability to never contract it because their genetic coding is so strangely built that nothing can stop them from dying. Unless you crack a gun to the head, that would be it. The heart is repairable in one person but the mind is repairable in another, it just depends on the type of coding that you have, if you are that special type. Theodore lay on the ground, lifeless but breathing, colour in his cheeks showing a good indication. The floor beneath us was made of metal filled in grates, steady and firm in place so we would not fall through the floor to our death, run over by the rumbling movement of wheels, clearly coordinated in movement. A slight hum of the lights, reminding me of the operating table, going to sleep with an anesthetic, the dim lights the last thing you see as the curtain begins to close, drawing to their end.

"So then, I will leave you when you get to your destination."

"Which would be where, exactly?"

"Back inside the dome, William, we have been through this a million times."

"I know, I know, tiredness." Puffing heavily, heaving the air till the point where the levels of oxygen in my lungs were so minimal, I felt like I was dying. Why was I not dead already? How often I thought of that every day, plaguing everything, the spread of the disease through the body, the mind playing tricks on me when I set my head down on a pillow to rest for the night. Time runs away so fast, that when you wake, it feels as though you were away from the ridiculous realism facing the day-to-day court trials, ruling yourself as being guilty or not so guilty. The gavel hitting the wood, one final ending to the matter until the next one follows in the proceeding hour, unable to take the pressure any more so you admit to everything. Admit to Lucy that I was wrong. I am in the wrong. I will always be wrong for leaving her behind to fend for herself believing that I will always be dead no matter how often she thinks I am alive. For the rest of her life, I will be dead, as long as I am alive, I am just this person in her imagination wanting to get out of her way because I am so meaningless in ways nobody could describe to me. I get that.

"So, where do you expect to find her?"

"Well, Theodore told me about the ruins up top yesterday, after we realised she was alive. SDtarting there will not do us any harm surely?"

"No, it won't, you might need to use your protective gear up there, there are so many people dying from the disease. Watch out for them."

"I will. What do they do?"

"Only those who bear the mark will know, they have told stories of what they can do, what they cannot do. Lucy can survive but you and Theodore might not so be careful."

Sitting in sheer silence for the next ten minutes, the rest

of this hell-bound journey tearing every mortal piece of my skin from me. Substantial amounts remaining for me to feed the urge to feel pain other than the tossing and turning within my gut. A cure for this unsteady feeling within me needed to go away soon. When I was a child, going to school was something I always feared because of the number of children taunting me for the stark contrast of our families. My father held a high position as an admiral for the king, so they let me believe anyway, never allowing me to make friends. The other children mainly had fathers who belonged to the Redcoats, as far as I knew most of them had little to do anyway. The higher standing, as many of those in society, believed me to be an outcast. To be honest, I always thought that when you have an interesting life story that others would be far more receptive to you, wanting to delve deeper into your history so you then question theirs.

Halting to a sudden stop, Fernsby rising to take his stance outside of the doors where a tube rounded underneath the ground. Snapping his fingers quite quickly, each in fast succession. Stirring from the after effects of the drug in his system, a rather drunken, bloodshot eyed, Theodore rising to the oncoming challenges we would most certainly have to endure, each faster in pace than the clicking of the fingers arousing people from their sleep.

"Where are we?"

Offering him a hand, pulling his sluggish weighted body up, helping to keep him steady on his drug-bound legs, shaking faster and more vigorously as his system started to defeat the substance injected into his system from earlier on. His half an hour of resting was up.

Without any warning, the perilous chilling blast of the

wind catching in our faces, cooling down the heated dilemmas of these newly challenging phantoms, that ignoring would bring more ruin to our lives than wounding our imperfect bodies with every means possible. "Just outside of the dome."

"Not far to go now?"

"Just through the tunnel and out into the open."

"Then we can find Lucy."

"Hmm."

Chapter 18
Losing you has always been the hardest thing.

Lead weights dragging along with me through the brightly-lit tunnel, only blue all around the outside. That was never the only peculiar thing considering the depths of this tunnel which seemed quite impactful. Either my head's pounding was starting to take its toll, or we are most certainly down deep under the sea where no one would hear us scream, not ever knowing that we are down here. One piercing in the top of the glass like plastic, we would die almost immediately, the pressure of the water on our head too much for us to contend with. How we could even travel down here would seem impossible to me. Obviously not impossible for the creators of this place.

"You have questions. Ask away."

"How can we be this far down and not be dead already, because this is genius."

"Well..." Tapping his finger on this glass, responding with a glitch. "See."

"This is all just mind games."

"It is far greater than mind games, Theo, this place is as real as you see it and as fake as you cannot understand. This is reality."

"Reality is always slightly distorted anyway, now, life is

just messy."

"Filthy, disgusting and still precious."

"Precious enough for us to need her back in our lives." Running my hands through my hair to find the bobble I had been using these past few months to tie back my hair, William outstretched his hand to me handing a brand-new brown bobble to tie it all back with.

"Cheers."

Smiling in a split second, then fading the next, so swiftly that you would never have even believed me if I told you he did just so. His hand began snaking around the backpack trying to find the zip so he could take out his standard flask filled with water. Instead of one he took two, one with the initial 'W' the other bearing the initial 'T' giving me the one with my initial to drink out of. The effects of the drug draining the water supply inside me, making me dehydrated enough to not want to speak. He could so easily take advantage of my situation and let me suffer in my Saharan mouth, drying up like a beached whale.

Depleting steadily, evidently, and thoroughly.

"Why are you surprised? I am not going to kill you yet, what good would that do me?"

Laughing along with him, sipping carefully from the supply of water, knowing there would not be much more for us, dangling it by my side inspecting the surroundings of where we were walking underneath.

"Is there any life out here? I presume since you took me on a train ride that there are things you cannot allow me to see, or know exist out there."

"There are so many things you do not know, if I told you, I know it would not be pleasant for both of us."

"Does Lucy know?"

"Not a single piece of information."

"Maybe she grew suspicious and that is what she is now after, why she faked her death so she could now be able to find it out without anyone snooping around in her affairs."

"Too many affairs with her."

"I know, I know, she is worth all the drama."

Always, everything we go through together, we do it as one unit. When the skin on my body began to crisp, delicately ensuring that the tearing through the body was going to be so steady that not even I could prevent or ignore the pain, Lucy never got burnt in the flames as unexpected as it may seem to some, she is fireproof to the effects of the flames. After all this time she has never been given a nickname, shockingly. I would give her one, so strong and so fitting to her. All to be revealed. Never reveal your hand to those who desire to take you down with every passing minute your chest rises and falls, those wanting to rise and wanting you to fall. Even though life constantly passed me death warrants and execution orders, picking myself up has become all I know how to do, fighting for the one person who needs me. She does not *need* me. I need her. When I am with her, all else disappears. Weighing heavily on my mind, the thoughts and stupid human feelings afflicting with the daily trials and tribulations awaiting at the doorstep, lingering at my feet, meeting me in the eyes, whacking me straight in the face.

"Theodore, I know very little about you, apart from the fact you love my wife."

Turning my eyes into the back of my skull, returning them to the forefront to meet his, his feet stopping dead in their tracks. "Well, ask away. I am an open book."

"Well, forget it, basic knowledge of someone has no point."

"I could not agree more with you."

In turn, the conversation and small talk was something Lucy need not contend with, two arguing children, squabbling over who got there first, shouting at us to stop being like two women pulling each other's hair. Knowing how each of us react to seeing one another, the tempestuous winds of our enraging situation catching in the cuts and bruises of the long-lost challenges scarring our skin. Before Lucy, before this, before us things would never have been so hard. Committing fake suicide in front of us, never having any say in the matter eating away at my soul, eating away at the fleshy parts still alive, guilt having already accomplished most of what it needed to accomplish beforehand, never showing remorse. The devil lies with the liar.

"Here we are." William's hands clutched the turning handle, winding it around clockwise, pulling it as soon as he heard the click, signalling it was ready to be opened. "Can you swim?"

"Yes, why?"

"Well, to get out of here, we have to swim twenty metres up there, so we can reach the surface. There was a cave entrance where you saw Lucy take the notes from the bodies, we will rise by the side of there, meaning, me might need to find another way to the jungle."

"I thought this was not even water!"

"Well… hold your breath, hold onto the door, and go when I tell you to go."

Inhaling as much air as my lungs could hold, expanding them to sink my stomach down, keeping the air in so tightly so as not to let go of such vital oxygen.

"Go!"

Keeping my hands tightly on the door, the bobble from in my hair getting lost in the onrush of water crashing into my face so rapidly. Half of the air in my lungs getting washed away in bubbles of trepidation not knowing if it really was twenty metres up, considering how far down we seemed to be. The bright, crystal-clear water filled up the tank we were in, keeping us there like fish, only hearing the water in my ears gargle with the signals from William to swim.

Unleashing my grip from the thick metal door, leaving William to shut it with every last heave of breath, to allow little to no water entering where we had come from. So there would not be an overload, drowning the sight of Liam waving goodbye on the other side, hoping we could find her although it could be quite dangerous. Below the moving of my feet and the bubbles escaping my mouth in the water, all of the corals appeared so beautiful and bright, full of colour, awe and wonder, watching the array of different fish swimming by, some hiding in little gaps and crevices, crabs retreating. Among the magical life of the fish you could see death in the dark blue, heavily lengthy drops in the water where the sharks roamed, not coming anywhere near the shallower waters where we were swimming, keeping us both safe. Admiring the sea life below us took my mind off the fact I needed to swim and keep my head above the waters, a little nudge, tap, on the shoulder as William kept swimming to the surface, gasping for air as we reached the top of the water's surface. Breathing in the fresh air far more easily after coughing and spluttering inhaled water on the sand, becoming more aware of the surroundings of bodies. Reaching the conclusion that these were most certainly the bodies that Lucy found the notes from.

"These must be the bodies Lucy examined."

"They are most definitely the ones. What if she left a note here for us?"

"She cannot be that smart."

"William, you have been married for numerous years, I have no clue how long we have known each other, I have not been able to count the days. Yet, I do know how smart she is."

"Right…"

"Never mind. Firstly, are there any people around?"

Scanning our surroundings, stretching his head, moving backwards to look up on the cliff face to see if there might be anyone to spot us, kill us. "Up there, one of those silencers, after Lucy they must have placed them a lot more around this area to stop anyone coming to the island."

"Why would they do that?"

"Because they know something we don't."

"That may be so, how do we ever even begin to figure it out, this is never an easy task. Is it?"

"That may be true, so, we just need to make this easier, instead of harder."

"Well, usually islands like these have networks of tunnels, underneath the water."

"How far down will they go? That is the problem."

"What supplies did you bring with us?"

"The basic camping essentials, weaponry, torches."

"Any gear for swimming?"

Dragging himself from the edge of the water, pulling his body to the service, bringing himself on the sand to ring out the water in his shirt, releasing a lot of weight in the masses of accumulated water in his body. Doing the exact same, choosing each trouser leg to begin with and then my shirt, wrinkling in the places where I had scrunched up the material, now clinging tightly to my body, defining the chest and torso. William did not have the muscle I expected him to have, he had slight definition but not much, evidently having trained before, lost the touch after the current situation.

"You clearly know the stories Will, what are they?"

Standing on both of his feet, the backpack not heavily weighing with water, the waterproof material holding quite well even after the maelstrom of water coming onto us just moments earlier. Many of the silencer's kept checking around the areas they patrolled, thoroughly cleansing their minds of disbelief that we could be anywhere, that we were not hiding secretly in crevices or holes, tunnels in the grounds. Every surveillance scan they made, evidently masking the fear that we would find her, keeping them satisfied that we are not fooling them by jumping between walls, trees, abandoned houses. Leaving their minds at rest.

"If we are going to make it past these, Will, we have to cooperate, no more of this time wasting with us bickering, we have much to do."

"Well, what do you propose?"

"That one of us creates a distraction, then the other runs. Vice versa. What do you think?"

"It won't work, these people will know where we are, they will hunt us and kill us, before we can say, *Hello, Lucy, lovely to see you alive.*"

"Okay then. We swim."

"What if we die… drown?"

"Say your goodbyes, I know I am being so placid and calm about this situation, relaxed that we could die, then… that is because I know one way or another those from the outside will come and save us. We both have something they want, you know what it is, so they cannot allow us to die."

"Good point, either way we will have to suffer. We will be out for as long as need be, Lucy will be gone. Count that."

"Would you rather try and make it, make it or nearly die. We could just attempt it and make it, attempt it and get out for a few days or weeks depending on our recovery."

"Sounds logical yet insane."

"Maybe one of us should go check out below the water and take it in turns, to find openings. If one of us does not come back it means there is something wrong, or, we come back because we have found something. Okay?"

"I will go down first, then, in this whole problem I have hurt Lucy the most, so I should be the first to go."

Even though I know William did something so wrong, I felt a pang of distress in my heart that for something he had no choice in doing, his guilt never left him. Everything in Lucy's life was a mess. Now mine too. Usually, I never feel compassion towards those who may have spited me or would prefer to be holding a knife to my neck ready to crucify me. William would love to hurt me, he sees me as perfect because I have done nothing harmful to Lucy, and he has. Truth be told, I am far from perfect, never have been and I never will be. We are all imperfections and our imperfections are in different aspects of life, some of us could be imperfect with a fiery temper that we cannot control, other imperfections. Medical defaults of genetic coding coming from our parents' combined DNA strands continuing to disrupt our lives every day in every way.

"Lucy does not think of you that harshly, you know, I

know what you did was wrong, yet you had no choice, it was for the best. Too many questions would have surrounded the *why,* you would have been led to all kinds of trouble for you, Lucy, Edward."

"You really think?"

Creasing the indents on either corners of his mouth, making his lips straight in a frown unable to register me being nice, nothing can be accomplished by constantly bickering and fighting on petty subjects such as who Lucy liked the most. Who she truly cared for. In her defence, speaking on her behalf, she cares for us both, even William. No matter how hard you try, you can never fight feelings, unless it is a painful break-up after years of love. Their separation and reuniting has certainly been one of a kind. Bowing his head in disgust, thinking of what he had done in the past, continuing to linger and weigh mightily in his head, a fully armed army, guns all ablaze in the air.

"I know so, love does not just disappear overnight you know your feelings for Lucy still exist. They must still exist for her."

"Maybe… anyway, I still hurt her so I have to go first."

"Let that bear in your shoulders, I suppose you must go, good luck."

"Luck is something that will only bear more pain for me, detach any sentiment or feelings because it is only going to cause more grief, leave it be."

"If something happens, I feel I should know the truth about what's going on in the outside world, you clearly know, I need to know."

"You can find that out without me, if I die, please just find Lucy no matter how long it takes you. She is hell-bent on finding whatever she has sought for so long."

"Answers."

"Precisely."

Taking off his camouflage shirt, removing the backpack, placing it next to my side with all the supplies heaving the air in and out of his lungs, as if this was a one-way trip to the end, one way tickets the only ones left to buy. Further removing his shoes, I saw the opportunity to make a joke, hopefully making him feel a little better.

"Please do not take any more clothes off, I am not Lucy."

"I know that! It would be better than seeing you bend over in the doctor's gown."

"At least it would be a nice sight for sore eyes."

"Oh, shut up!"

Chuckling like schoolboys, thinking of the different scenarios, not really wanting to view these images in our minds, sticking closely to the memory. For once, I felt happy to be around William, knowing how he might still dislike me or have changed his opinion about who I am. Just because he was about to go on a kamikaze mission, just to make sure I was not going to die and upset Lucy more. Would she still love me, if she knew I let him do this? That answer would not be able to be known unless Lucy was asked personally.

"William, I know if we had met under better circumstances that we could have been friends, we still can. I am never usually someone for soppy goodbyes but if anything happens, I pray not, that I did not just let you leave without saying something."

"Well, you are a great guy, Theo, Lucy never likes anyone unless she has a good feeling about them." Holding his hand out for me to shake, my hand collided with his, shaking it tightly, his hand loosely slipping, with a mix of his sweat and water. "Take care of her, if I do not come back, make sure that she lives to fight another day. My son, ensure he lives a long life."

"Stop saying this because you might return."

"What if I do not return, I would regret not saying anything."

"Can a dead man feel regret?"

"You know exactly what I mean."

Our eyes chartered the ground, counting the millions of sand granules on the floor beneath us, harvesting so much oxygen into our lungs I felt they would explode with overload and emotion. A lump was forming in my throat, screaming for me to just cry, cry in front of William, let him see how I feel. Pointless. Utterly a waste of time, showing him how I feel would just destroy both of us, his mind certainly only focussing on one task at hand. How did it come to this? Through everything so far William had been out to protect me, solely me, just before letting me out first so I did not have the task of shutting the door with such force that it would nearly cost me my life. He did that. So I would not be forced to reconcile with the devil, showing me the tempting end of my life, allowing me to rest with peace of mind that nothing bad could happen to me. Such a fate would become destructive to anyone, the tales of those who lay at the bottom of the sea, seeing their lives flashing before them, the heart threatening to stop beating ever so soon if they move a single muscle, so the lethal force of decomposition could begin in the weakening strength of the human body pounded by the ideal that silence would bring. Laying in the grave so the crow can cry, for the single bullet wound to go straight though, in one end, out of the others. Stopping everything. Just like my words, my portrayal of emotions would go in one ear and out of the other with William, possibly sticking closely to his mind's sickening thoughts deteriorating the mental findings to search out and devour the single feeling of being alone, screaming under the water. Held under. Not by a human force. Mother nature being targeted solely, for what reasons? No reason at all, leading the questioning to persevere over and over. That bullet might go in, it might not come out, you may survive for a short period of time unless someone removes the bullet. Infection will strike and kill you instead, giving it the time it requires, to multiply inside of you so that your emotions can grow, allow you to give your goodbyes. William had to survive. For Lucy. Knowing that he would be definitely dead this time, two times being dead, twice as hard for her to come to terms with him being dead. Ever so sure that he was still alive even after thinking this is not true. Far from the truth. Down by the river tearing up in the corner of her eyes, wanting to give it all for herself this time, doing so by a water ritual to her husband, they might as well die twice together. That would be her ridiculous reasoning as her chemical defect of emotions overshadow all correct thinking to keep her sanity focussed, to allow her more time to figure out what it was she wanted from life exactly. Whatever she was in search of, hurting the two main people in her life would have taken her a lot of strength and courage to pull off. She can hurt people *if* she wants to, not us. Not me and William.

"I know what you mean, what shall I say to Lucy, if… you know."

"Tell her I love her, I love our son, all the time I spent with her I will never regret because she was the only one, and the only one I will ever love."

"You might come back."

"It's a one-way trip…" Wading into the water, not even thinking about how far he was going into the waters. "Eventually I might come back, I always come back."

"How can you be so sure?"

Tracing his finger along the scars on his neck, stomach, wiping them all off with the salty, warm water, comforting like a support blanket, yet deadly the further down you go.

"You hid them from her. You should have just told her!"

"What is the point, I never had a choice, either way I get hurt, it's the way life treats us all at some point, bites you so hard that even the sound of someone feeding on your skin becomes enjoyable. I. Am. Numb."

"If you are going down there to do this to yourself, I will not let you go."

"And neither will I!" A woman's voice cried from behind us both, none of the silencers bothered that she was down here, maybe they are just fake after all. "Because losing you is the hardest thing. I never got over your death. I never will. Don't expect me to do it again."

"Lucy…" We both gasped in surprise, goosebumps on our backs, surprise overtaking our speech. Stunned to silence. Here she was, covered in blood, small scratches and large gaps in her arms, no matter how much help we would offer, I know it would be no use.

"Stop standing there like a pair of idiots, I am alive!"

"We figured that much out."

Getting myself steady on both my feet, a newborn learning how to walk after coming from the comfort of the womb, finally being able to stand by myself. Wrapping my arms around the woman I cared for, feeling the embrace so tight and full of care that a tear came to my eyes. She made me soft. William was still lingering in the waters, not coming out from the different kind of embrace he was feeding on, the one he was getting a strange thrill from. "Will, what's wrong?"

"No, no, Lucy, no."

"I'm back, you are okay now, we are okay."

"How are we going to be okay, ever?"

"I knew you didn't do that by choice, you had no choice, you chose to save me every time. It was me they wanted so I would be burned with this mark."

"I don't care, I do not care. This world does not need me."

"I need you."

"No, you don't, no one needs me."

"We need you, Will, you have to come with us." Chiming into their conversation, Lucy's expression evidently shocked by me even begging to care. "Of course I care, he's your husband, do you really think I'd let you see him die again."

"I—"

"I'm not coming out, Lucy."

"Of course you are!"

We both edged our bodies closer, stealthily so he could not move, catching our prey but in order to save a life instead of killing him as many wild animals would do. "We don't want to hurt you Will, I think you will find that we want to save a life."

"You can't save me."

"We can!" Lucy ran forwards, wrapping her arms around him, balancing by swaying left and right to calm him down, trying to make him see sense. "I need you on this journey, I can't see you out of my life again, I never had time to mourn

270

over your death and now I have that time. Do you think I want to do it?"

"Do you?"

"Of course not!" Ruffling his shirt with her hands, feeling a tinge of jealousy that he was getting attention even though I encouraged it. Letting him die again in front of her, once again, would haunt me that we let him die. "I've missed you. I've missed you so much, Will." Burying her head into his chest, turning my head away to not witness them kissing so much. She still loved him, getting involved in a love triangle would bring ruin to all of us. Distancing myself from the feelings I had towards Lucy would become a prominent part of helping her in what she was trying to find. Any attachment is only a harmful thing, bringing it upon her, Will and myself would just be foolish. One thing I am not is foolish, we need to see. Getting to the ruins would be our main goal in trying to figure out the secrets, the reasoning behind this place and why they were keeping us like prisoners, testing us for their own research.

Whatever we had, they wanted so desperately and strongly, to harvest two people at a time, three, wherever Christopher is. Since that night they saved me, my leg bleeding, gushing with blood pulsing to my heartbeat one after the other, dripping, encompassing the vines tying me high in the air, caught in an animal's snare.

"We should get going, it's getting dark."

Turning to face me, William was calming down a lot more, his thoughts more positive than minutes before, when life seemed unhealthy, he felt unwanted, and was lacking the desire to keep it going.

Chapter 19
This is the start, and the end

Back. Feeling the intense desire to be back has been overwhelming me for so long that this time apart from those I love to be around has left me feeling dry. Left me feeling hollow and empty of life without filling the void with the love and care of others. Theodore has been playing his part well, for me, all this time with me playing dead, he never fully became aware of the plan I was going for. No wonder William loathed Theo so much. Caving in every time danger comes, he understands well enough that each time we come into the face of trials and tribulation he must stand still and watch it all pass, letting me do what I have to. Increasing the chances of understanding within my mind deemed to be a powerful subject.

Twists and turns in the luscious jungle barring us from being able to map every movement we make, the footfalls we take, the caves hiding us, shielding us, protecting us from the ravenous, blood thirsty silencers roaming with a lustful desire to fill their hearts with a thrilling and exhilarating fest of murder on the lives those that prey on the idea of escaping. No one leaves when they enter. Theodore knows where my thoughts have been concentrating, following the guidance left behind by those that used to live here. Ever since childhood, both Liam and I shared a bond unlike any other, before I was bullied for being different. Liam the only true friend I had to support me through thick and through thin, whereas those around me sought after taunting. Keeping me in suspense for their next attack of a vivacious nature with a likeness to those roaming in the woods, abandoned buildings, emptied store houses and ruins of the old church. Alongside the depleting condition of the watchtowers on either side of the beach stretching further out for miles across the frothy waves, colliding with the golden, mystical grains of glorious sand situated beneath our feet every time they touched the millionaire's pot luck. By now, some would get used to the fact that they are stuck in a place like this, all day every day, no one to turn to apart from those who might come after you, the silence less daunting. Invigorating pulses picking your appeal perfectly for the emotions runs high when you hear the voice of somebody you know, calling for you to come back home. It hurts. The lies. It hurts. You cry. Over and over, again and again, a knife in your back stabbing you, jabbing it repeatedly through your skin just as you would with a pen tapping on your skin second by second, picking its moment to ease your anxiety. The stabbing makes it stop, still creating another kind of pain which causes a trickling sensation, itching away at your skin, dripping, the crimson bump at the end of the winding line, straight, drawn by the unsteady hand of the one yielding the knife. Ever since the death, the death of me, times have been difficult on my own. Knowing that you can heal does not help in the fearful trembling the body causes, feeling the pain, even if it will heal unlike others who might not survive. However, it works, it is what they want to harvest from me to save so many others. Those scientists argue that one life is better for the many that could be saved. How do they know I can save all that many? They don't, it hurts to know they sacrifice the lives of others, without even knowing whether or not their trials will work, possibly giving up the lives of young children, maybe their own for the sake of satisfying their cruel tests and games they are playing with us. The deep desire burning in my heart to discover the secrets I know they are hiding in this place, uncover everything from what I know. Those notes pinned to the bodies, just until I removed them in order to figure out why they left them and what they left to be discovered. Dead for their memories coming to recall, at the forefront of their minds.

"What did you get up to while you were supposedly dead?" William was the first to break the silence, giving them their capes in between the parts where the silencers would not go, refusing to take one step there. "I know that you are after something here, what is it?"

"To be honest, Will, I have no clue what I will find, all I know is… it's dark stories will be uncovered."

"What do you expect to find?"

"Enough to be able to uncover why this marking on me will be desirable to those people who had me chained to a bed."

"They chained you!"

"Yes, did you have anything to do with that?"

"No, not at all!"

William's voice became chirpy, over the top dramatic and an all-round good performance *if* I did not know him so well, this told me he was lying. When his mother died, I still felt disbelief as she lay there, shrivelling up, clutching her stomach, that was not a symptom, she certainly died. Our families have a way with death, it seems as though the world prefers us dead rather than alive. Apart from me. They keep me alive for my blood, when I was given part of my memories back unintentionally, that was my body calling them back being able to withstand the pressure of the inner parts, robotic compression on the brain, taking away the memory capacity of all the past that made me. My mother. My father. The real parts of my past, allowing me a real future. Nothing is as it seems. Is it ever? Well, when you are basing everything on things that you think you know, such as being bullied constantly… you begin to fight back much harder to draw yourself away from being withdrawn.

Ahead of us, a light in the opening at the top where the light of the moon crept through the gap, cascading onto the ground, lighting our way in an unusually mysterious fashion, glistening the grass with the morning dew starting to touch the soft, delicate, thin protrusions of emerald grass, capturing all harmful thoughts from my mind for just a minute.

"Where did Theodore go?"

"Who cares about Theodore?"

Swirling around, getting dizzy from watching blurry particles cloud my vision from finding him. "Where is Theo?"

"I think he went on ahead of us. Needed some space."

"Why did he need space?"

"It probably has something to do with you…"

"Me?"

Frankly, his clear nod of acceptance that it was me which caused Theo to go on ahead of us, my lackadaisical mind letting him slip through the net. Two men. Two people I was torn between loving both of them just as much as the other, collapsing my world. Edward… my little boy back home. Wherever that was, it was away from me, I only ever brought danger upon my child.

"Lily…" Lowering my faltering determined gaze to the ground, eyes in solemn praise to the ground being there to keep my body standing, having a cushion to fall. I let everyone else fall but me in this sordid, nefarious affair, cruel and sinister with every inch of detail describable.

"Pardon?"

"Nothing, nothing at all."

"You said *something*."

Staring into his eyes, glaring with a dirty stare emancipating my emotions welling down further than feeling could go, trying to chase the number of times where showing how I feel turns to misery. Snapping back in disgust with wanting to tell him what I spoke in a hush under my voice as a mumble.

"I said nothing! Just leave it!"

"Okay. As you wish."

"It *is* as *I* wish."

Biting the lower lip less injured from the bullet, feeling the back of my head with the hand clean from blood, seeing if the hole was entirely healed. Not fully. After so long of being allowed to heal, the suffering from the pain has been lessened dramatically, the scarring of where the bullet pierced through becoming far more invisible than when I was bleeding. This pair of morons managing to figure it during their moments of murderous intent for one another. Theodore was a lot less vigorous in violence, William was a brash type when he wanted to be, quite predominantly when filling himself with anger and enragement.

"Guys, come here!"

"Was that Theo?"

"I think it was. Come on."

Perilous cold winds blew past our faces, running at high speeds, William's hand tightly crippling mine with a terrible, strong grip, crushing the delicate thin fingers, shrivelling and shaking with the cold, skin cracking on the edges from the icy blasting howls.

"Quickly!"

Urgency. Not knowing if this was going to be a good thing or a bad thing. "Coming!"

"Hurry up! I think we need to move faster."

"Why?"

This time his urgency began stitching up the open wounds of steady paced, easy walking speed as if we were not in any imminent danger. When would there be a time when danger was not hunting me down in a pack of wolves? Just leave me alone. Why me all the time? Halting as one, William pushing me behind him to protect me from whatever was keeping me from seeing what had been found, needing to be seen urgently.

"Oh, come on! Since when did you two huddle together, like besties?"

"Since this, Lucy." Theodore held a piece of paper out for me, glancing at his index and middle finger for me to take it carefully. "Read it. It's a letter addressed to you."

"Okay...

Dear Miss Lucy Berrel,

You don't know who I am just yet, you will not until the day I stand over you to listen to your beautiful screams. They tell me I'm a psychopath. I would agree. Nice name with a pleasant ring to it. My point being I am a psychopath from your past.

Who? You might ask.

Little Lily. Remember me? No? Of course not, that's why I'm here to tell you who I am and why I am going to make sure I haunt you for the rest of your miserable life that I plan on dictating!

"Do you know who that is, Lucy?"

"I intend to read on and find out, see, I know next to nothing about my past."

"Go on then."

"Where was I? Ah…"

Of course, Liam was always yours wasn't he, always with you through thick and thin. No matter how much I tried, the hatred for you stealing him set in thick and fast. I. Was. Alone. Do you know how that feels? Well, you will know how it feels by the time I am done with you, this is not the end of all your issues, Lucy.

I am pure with passionate indignation to see you get hurt more and more, again and again, over and over for my satisfaction and joy to watch.

There is never an end. You owe me a show.

And I owe you the means to do so.

Please feel free to scream as and when you want to, I will see you get hurt. BURN. BURN. BURN.

Lily xx

"Who is this Lily?"

"Our supposed daughter, maybe?"

"No, maybe she was given to me for a reason. A reason."

"What reason could a young girl like that have a need for revenge on you, and why does she want to hear you scream so badly?"

"None of those questions have answers. Where did you find it, Theo?"

Pointing to an area of the tree where he found the note, a carving in the tree, followed by a knife jabbed inside of a heart. "Just here. She obviously wants to kill you."

"Such a childish drawing of a heart as well."

"What are we dealing with?"

"If I'm honest to you both, a child."

"A child!" William's gasps of horror, mixing with the frozen posture of Theo calling my mind to full attention, letting Theo speak properly amid his perplexed eyes. "How old?"

"I don't know exactly. All I know is this. This is the start, and the end."

Chapter 20
Notes by children. Voices of the dead

Orchestrating a harmonious piece of music, gliding across the glorious shining floor majestically swaying, turning and twisting wonderfully to the music as the piano hits the keys, hands moving faster on the white piano keys. To the music the feet follow, one after the other all in the feeling, feeding, hungry for more of such beautiful music welling the eyes. Skirts being dirtied by the floor, escaping the heavy feet thudding the floor in each step, distant and hollow against the pieces of laminate highlighting the grand orchestral playing.

Feel the music. Lily, she kept orchestrating my whole entire life, every note playing perfectly, every hum capturing, every footstep stamping me down, trying to put out my flames. Without success. Since finding that note, we all took shelter in the cave finding us more comfort and ease that being out in the open.

"How long till the morning?"

"I would say about seven hours, Lucy, get some sleep."

"I don't need sleep, my body can cope without it, I don't have that need. Both of you need shut eye, for these days are going to be rough."

"Will you be okay?"

"Of course I will be okay, I survived death, Will."

"Ah."

Smiling in the corner of my mouth, shaking my head lightly, creasing the corners of my eyes gently, folding them a bit. Being lost in thought for a moment I saw the two people wanting to stay awake with me, or wanting me to sleep as well, now lay there soundly asleep without a care in the world. Peaceful. Undisturbed. In silence. The rising and falling of their chests so slightly, growing less and less as their own bodies began to unwind, the tensions releasing, soft snores emanating from both of them, eyelids fluttering as they began dreaming, escaping this life seemingly a dream. This cave we chose to seek refuge in only stretched for a small amount down the back, nothing to harm us, unless the bats sucked us to death which was seeming impossible considering they looked fairly ordinary. Outside of the cave, barely any trees were apparent to my left. On the right, a massive expanse of jungle, shrubs, towering trees larger than all of us on top of one another, vines, flowers, leaves carpeting the ground, drying mud dampening with the dew coming about by the morning. In the sky, I found release from the boredom infesting my mind over and over, wanting at least something to keep me occupied. Being terrified by who this *Lily* was, would certainly not get us anywhere, I need more of it to make me feel a lot worse. From one of the trees over to my right, a miniature bird was perching on a branch, resembling an arm with five longer protruding branches out of the end, holding a piece of paper within its beak, gliding so carefully down towards me, edging his way towards me so I could take the piece of parchment from his mouth. Tugging it away bit by bit, it began slipping away, making him take flight for fear of me hurting him in any way, a natural instinct for anyone, any living thing for that matter. In between the folded pieces of paper, the bird's saliva nowhere to be seen wetting the delicate pieces all in one square. Five pieces. Each of them quite lengthy and detailed, thick when folding them all in one.

"Guys, wake up!"

"Ugh. Going back to sleep."

William tossed over on his side. Theodore perking up sensing the underlying disturbance in my swelling throat at the back, getting more predominant.

"What's wrong?"

"Five notes this time, each of them being numbered at the bottom right corner."

"What do they consist of?"

"Clues we have to follow, like a puzzle that we have to follow precisely to the detail."

"Who from?"

"Lily."

"Oh my… okay. Get up!" Screeching down Will's ear, shaking from the shock, still falling asleep by covering his ears. Theo took his hands, sliding them away to firmly allow him to embrace the current problem occuring. "Five more notes from Lily, five different clues. So. Get up!"

"Huh?"

"Lily! You dimwit. Lily!"

"Here!" Steadily rising from his slumber, rubbing his eyes with his fists, removing the sleep from his eyes. A growing grossness.

"What does the first one say?"

"Merely instructions with a note stuck on the bottom."

Yawning greatly, echoing distinctly down my ear with his sleepy voice. "You best read it."

"Okay, go through the steps as I go."

"Sure."

"Here we go…"

For the first part of the test, you will have to follow my instructions very carefully Lucy, you can either trust what I say or the first person you love will die.

Step One — Stand up and walk towards the opening, fix your gaze on the moon tightly

"I am getting up and walking." Standing there, in the opening, following her instructions precisely as written down on paper.

"Okay next steps…

Step Two — Theodore needs to get up and stand by you, holding the canteen of water in his one hand, in the other, one of the grain bars to sustain life. Both of these things will come in handy as you complete my tasks

"Come on, Theodore."

"I cannot find the bars, where have they gone."

"Hurry up! I think I see someone in the distance." Holding my hand flat, pressing the edge against my forehead to narrow my focus down, to see exactly who it is. "It's a child! And it's coughing and very thin. Oh goodness."

"Here!" Running by my side, with both of the items required in each of his hands.

"Next step, it might involve the child."

The child kept drawing closer, whispering with his voice, spluttering from a dry mouth, holding his stomach from hunger.

"Next step…"

Step Three — Allow Theodore to go to the child and give him a sip of the water, a small bite of the bar and a little more water, then retreat back again.

"Hurry, Theodore, he doesn't deserve this."

Theodore made his way to the child, holding the canteen for him, allowing a little water. Breaking the bar into quarters, he held one of them for him to bite from, repeating the same thing with the water, returning to me once more. The young boy's voice was heightening, crying with tears of panic.

"Finally, one more step and I can read the note she left for me…"

Step Four — Grab all of your things together, everything you have with you, throw the bar to the child but keep the water with you. Move back as far as you can but still have a view of the scene outside. If something happens, stay grounded or I will shoot you, count to five if something happens. Then run.

"Give him the bar. William, pack the bag with the water canteen. Brace yourselves."

Nothing was seeming to happen, the silence with the sound of owls in the distance twit-twooing on their perches, wide yellow eyes gazing upon their territory. Theodore took the bar, lobbing it towards the boy who began picking every last piece from the floor, his crying, his muffles audible. His speech

"I want to go home to mommy, save me. Please."

"What's going to happen to him?"

"I have no clue, Will, it will not be good, so brace yourself."

Trying to breath out my anxiety, his eyes locking with William's eyes, ensuring his gaze made him entranced. Whatever Will was seeing, it was starting to hurt so much in his heart. "That's our son Lucy! That's our son!"

"That is not our son, that is not our son."

Scavenging the ground one more time, his eyes fixating to the left where an animal was thundering towards the boy at swift pace.

"Mommy, Daddy. Remember me."

Coming at the boy, swooping him into his arms, picking him up in the flight of the action. William took his flight, towards the boy, he ran on and on and on. Theodore holding me back, my body lurching towards William in order to grab him, pull him back. All too late. His words final, letters unread, words unsaid, things all too late to do as he took off without looking back.

"I love you!"

"Remember me, Lucy."

Shooting a shot through his head, blood pouring out, this time his death was real. He wasn't coming back... my words known this time. *I love you.* His last words.

Remember me.

Epilogue:
-Outside of the dome

"Did you shoot him?"

"In the head."

"Good. Get back here. It's time for some more games."

Putting my phone back down on the table, the radio buzzing on the intercom for me to answer. Liam calling for me to answer, persisting with the buzzing. Picking up the call, I hear his tone of voice, condescending me. Why should I care? I am taking her on a ride to keep secrets from being revealed. Time to pick up the pace now there's only two of them.

"Why is he dead? We agreed, none of them would die, you promised me!"

"Well promises are made to be broken, Fernsby, remember when you and Lucy were kids?"

"I remember all too well."

"There was a girl in her past who she killed."

"So? What does that have to do with anything?"

"It has everything to do with this and you know it, she's alive, even after Lucy left her for dead."

"And... what do you know?"

"Everything I need to! Give me her name."

"Lily."

"Is that it?"

"She never had parents in her life, hence no last name."

"Revenge is sweet, and so is death."